A NOT-SO-SWEET SURPRISE

A gawker knot had formed around the dark green Cadillac parked a few spaces down the block. The milling crowd parted briefly to reveal Mavis Templeton sitting behind the wheel.

Her hair was perfect and her red lipstick flawless. But her head lay against the seat back at a strange angle, and those snapping hawk's eyes no longer glittered.

It seemed pretty obvious that they never would again.

I raised a trembling hand to cover my mouth. She'd been shaking her finger at us only minutes before, and now she was . . . dead?

"Where's Ben?" The voice startled me, and I spun around to find that Steve Dawes had approached from my other side.

"Um—um—he went out back," I stuttered. "What happened?"

He grimaced, then leaned closer. "Someone broke her neck." The way he said it sounded almost like an apology.

"On purpose?" I asked without thinking.

Dawes nodded. "Most definitely on purpose."

We heard the sirens first, and then saw the flashing lights.

I craned my neck, searching the throng.

"I doubt the murderer is still here," he said.

Murderer. There was the word I'd been avoiding . . .

Brownies *and* Broomsticks

A Magical Bakery Mystery

Bailey Cates

AN OBSIDIAN MYSTERY

OBSIDIAN
Published by New American Library, a division of
Penguin Group (USA) Inc., 375 Hudson Street,
New York, New York 10014, USA
Penguin Group (Canada), 90 Eglinton Avenue East, Suite 700, Toronto,
Ontario M4P 2Y3, Canada (a division of Pearson Penguin Canada Inc.)
Penguin Books Ltd., 80 Strand, London WC2R 0RL, England
Penguin Ireland, 25 St. Stephen's Green, Dublin 2,
Ireland (a division of Penguin Books Ltd.)
Penguin Group (Australia), 250 Camberwell Road, Camberwell, Victoria 3124,
Australia (a division of Pearson Australia Group Pty. Ltd.)
Penguin Books India Pvt. Ltd., 11 Community Centre, Panchsheel Park,
New Delhi - 110 017, India
Penguin Group (NZ), 67 Apollo Drive, Rosedale, Auckland 0632,
New Zealand (a division of Pearson New Zealand Ltd.)
Penguin Books (South Africa) (Pty.) Ltd., 24 Sturdee Avenue,
Rosebank, Johannesburg 2196, South Africa

Penguin Books Ltd., Registered Offices:
80 Strand, London WC2R 0RL, England

First published by Obsidian, an imprint of New American Library,
a division of Penguin Group (USA) Inc.

First Printing, May 2012
10 9 8 7 6 5

PUBLISHER'S NOTE
This is a work of fiction. Names, characters, places, and incidents either are the
product of the author's imagination or are used fictitiously, and any resem-
blance to actual persons, living or dead, business establishments, events, or
locales is entirely coincidental.

The recipes contained in this book are to be followed exactly as written. The
publisher is not responsible for your specific health or allergy needs that may
require medical supervision. The publisher is not responsible for any adverse
reactions to the recipes contained in this book.

The publisher does not have any control over and does not assume any responsibility for author or third-party Web sites or their content.

ALWAYS LEARNING   PEARSON

Acknowledgments

Many thanks to my agent, Kim Lionetti, and to the terrific folks at Penguin/NAL: Jessica Wade, Jesse Feldman, Kathleen Cook, Kayleigh Clark, and all the others whose talent and hard work helped this book come into being. Tarot expert Barbara Moore graciously allowed me to pick her brain and offered advice. Todd Bryan provided excellent information about firefighters and their jobs. The helpful staff at the Savannah Chamber of Commerce and the Planters Inn cheerfully answered my questions, and as always, my writing buddies, Bob and Mark, kept me on my toes.

And a special thanks to Kevin, who has the patience of Job when I'm on deadline.

Brownies *and* Broomsticks

Chapter 1

This was a grand adventure, I told myself. The ideal situation at the ideal time. It was also one of the scariest things I'd ever done.

So when I rounded the corner to find my aunt and uncle's baby blue Thunderbird convertible snugged up to the curb in front of my new home, I was both surprised and relieved.

Aunt Lucy knelt beside the porch steps, trowel in hand, patting the soil around a plant. She looked up and waved a gloved hand when I pulled into the driveway of the compact brick house, which had once been the carriage house of a larger home. I opened the door and stepped into the humid April heat.

"Katie's here—right on time!" Lucy called over her shoulder and hurried across the lawn to throw her arms around me. The aroma of patchouli drifted from her hair as I returned her hug.

"How did you know I'd get in today?" I leaned my tush against the hood of my Volkswagen Beetle, then pushed away when the hot metal seared my skin through my denim shorts. "I wasn't planning to leave Akron until tomorrow."

I'd decided to leave early so I'd have a couple of extra days to acclimate. Savannah, Georgia, was about as different from Ohio as you could get. During my brief visits I'd fallen in love with the elaborate beauty of the city, the excesses of her past—and present—and the food. Everything from high-end cuisine to traditional Low Country dishes.

"Oh, honey, of course you'd start early," Lucy said. "We knew you'd want to get here as soon as possible. Let's get you inside the house and pour something cool into you. We brought supper over, too—crab cakes, barbecued beans with rice, and some nice peppery coleslaw."

I sighed in anticipation. Did I mention the food?

Her luxurious mop of gray-streaked blond hair swung over her shoulder as she turned toward the house. "How was the drive?"

"Long." I inhaled the warm air. "But pleasant enough. The Bug was a real trouper, pulling that little trailer all that way. I had plenty of time to think." Especially as I drove through the miles and miles of South Carolina marshland. That was when the enormity of my decisions during the past two months had really begun to weigh on me.

She whirled around to examine my face. "Well, you don't look any the worse for wear, so you must have been thinking happy thoughts."

"Mostly," I said and left it at that.

My mother's sister exuded good cheer, always on the lookout for a silver lining and the best in others. A bit of a hippie, Lucy had slid seamlessly into the New Age movement twenty years before. Only a few lines augmented the corners of her blue eyes. Her brown hemp skirt and light cotton blouse hung gracefully on her short but very slim frame. She was a laid-back natural beauty rather than a Southern belle. Then again, Aunt Lucy had grown up in Dayton.

"Come on in here, you two," Uncle Ben called from the shadows of the front porch.

A magnolia tree shaded that corner of the house, and copper-colored azaleas marched along the iron railing in a riot of blooms. A dozen iridescent dragonflies glided through air that smelled heavy and green. Lucy smiled when one of them zoomed over and landed on my wrist. I lifted my hand, admiring the shiny blue-green wings, and it launched back into the air to join its friends.

I waved to my uncle. "Let me grab a few things."

Reaching into the backseat, I retrieved my sleeping bag and oversized tote. When I stepped back and pushed the door shut with my foot, I saw a little black dog gazing up at me from the pavement.

"Well, hello," I said. "Where did you come from?"

He grinned a doggy grin and wagged his tail.

"You'd better get on home now."

More grinning. More wagging.

"He looks like some kind of terrier. I don't see a collar," I said to Lucy. "But he seems well cared for. Must live close by."

She looked down at the little dog and cocked her head. "I wonder."

And then, as if he had heard a whistle, he ran off. Lucy shrugged and moved toward the house.

By the steps, I paused to examine the rosemary topiary Lucy had been planting when I arrived. The resinous herb had been trained into the shape of a star. "Very pretty. I might move it around to the herb garden I'm planning in back."

"Oh, no, dear. I'm sure you'll want to leave it right where it is. A rosemary plant by the front door is ... traditional."

I frowned. Maybe it was a Southern thing.

Lucy breezed by me and into the house. On the porch, my uncle's smiling brown eyes lit up behind rimless glasses. He grabbed me for a quick hug. His soft ginger beard, grown since he'd retired from his job as Savannah's fire chief, tickled my neck.

He took the sleeping bag from me and gestured me inside. "Looks like you're planning on a poor night's sleep."

Shrugging, I crossed the threshold. "It'll have to do until I get a bed." Explaining that I typically slept only one hour a night would only make me sound like a freak of nature.

I'd given away everything I owned except for clothes, my favorite cooking gear and a few things of sentimental value. So now I had a beautiful little house with next to no furniture in it—only the two matching armoires I'd scored at an estate sale. But that was part of this grand undertaking. The future felt clean and hopeful. A life waiting to be built again from the ground up.

We followed Lucy through the living room and into the kitchen on the left. The savory aroma of golden crab cakes and spicy beans and rice that rose from the takeout bag on the counter hit me like a cartoon anvil. My aunt and uncle had timed things just right, especially considering they'd only guessed at my arrival. But Lucy had always been good at guessing that kind of thing. So had I, for that matter. Maybe it was a family trait.

Trying to ignore the sound of my stomach growling, I gestured at the small table and two folding chairs. "What's this?" A wee white vase held delicate spires of French lavender, sprigs of borage with its blue star-shaped blooms, yellow calendula and orange-streaked nasturtiums.

Ben laughed. "Not much, obviously. Someplace for you to eat, read the paper—whatever. 'Til you find something else."

Lucy handed me a cold, sweating glass of sweet tea. "We stocked a few basics in the fridge and cupboard, too."

"That's so thoughtful. It feels like I'm coming home."

My aunt and uncle exchanged a conspiratorial look.

"What?" I asked.

Lucy jerked her head. "Come on." She sailed out of the kitchen, and I had no choice but to follow her through the postage-stamp living room and down the short hallway. Our footsteps on the worn wooden floors echoed off soft peach walls that reached all the way up to the small open loft above. Dark brown shutters that fit with the original design of the carriage house folded back from the two front windows. The built-in bookshelves cried out to be filled.

"The vibrations in here are positively lovely," she said. "And how fortunate that someone was clever enough to place the bedroom in the appropriate ba-gua."

"Ba-what?"

She put her hand on the doorframe, and her eyes widened. "Ba-gua. I thought you knew. It's feng shui. Oh, honey, I have a book you need to read."

I laughed. Though incorporating feng shui into my furnishing choices certainly couldn't hurt.

Then I looked over Lucy's shoulder and saw the bed. "Oh." My fingers crept to my mouth. "It's beautiful."

A queen-sized headboard rested against the west wall, the dark iron filigree swooping and curling in outline against the expanse of Williamsburg blue paint on the walls. A swatch of sunshine cut through the window, spotlighting the patchwork coverlet and matching pillow shams. A reading lamp perched on a small table next to it.

"I've always wanted a headboard like that," I breathed. "How did you know?" Never mind the irony of my sleep disorder.

"We're so glad you came down to help us with the bakery," Ben said in a soft voice. "We just wanted to make you feel at home."

As I tried not to sniffle, he put his arm around my shoulders. Lucy slipped hers around my waist.

"Thank you," I managed to say. "It's perfect."

Lucy and Ben helped me unload the small rented trailer, and after they left I unpacked everything and put it away. Clothes were in one of the armoires, a few favorite books leaned together on the bookshelf in the living room, and pots and pans filled the cupboards. Now it was a little after three in the morning, and I lay in my new bed watching the moonlight crawl across the ceiling. The silhouette of a magnolia branch bobbed gently in response to a slight breeze. Fireflies danced outside the window.

Change is inevitable, they say. *Struggle is optional.*

Your life's path deviates from what you intend. Whether you like it or not. Whether you fight it or not. Whether your heart breaks or not.

After pastry school in Cincinnati, I'd snagged a job as assistant manager at a bakery in Akron. It turned out "assistant manager" meant long hours, hard work, no creative input and anemic paychecks for three long years.

But I didn't care. I was in love. I'd thought Andrew was, too—especially after he asked me to marry him.

Change is inevitable . . .

But in a way I was lucky. A month after Andrew called off the wedding, my uncle Ben turned sixty-two and retired. No way was he going to spend his time puttering around the house, so he and Lucy brainstormed and came up with the idea to open the Honeybee Bakery. Thing was, they needed someone with expertise: me.

The timing of Lucy and Ben's new business venture couldn't have been better. I wanted a job where I could actually use my culinary creativity and business knowhow. I needed to get away from my old neighborhood, where I ran into my former fiancé nearly every day. The daily reminders were hard to take.

So when Lucy called, I jumped at the chance. The money I'd scrimped and saved to contribute to the down payment on the new home where Andrew and I were supposed to start our life together instead went toward my house in Savannah. It was my way of committing wholeheartedly to the move south.

See, some people can carry through a plan of action. I was one of them. My former fiancé was not.

Jerk.

Lucy's orange tabby cat had inspired the name of our new venture. Friendly, accessible and promising sweet goodness, the Honeybee Bakery would open in another week. Ben had found a charming space between a knitting shop and a bookstore in historic downtown Savannah, and I'd flown back and forth from Akron to find and buy my house and work with my aunt to develop recipes while Ben oversaw the renovation of the storefront.

I rolled over and plumped the feather pillow. The mattress was just right: not too soft and not too hard. But unlike Goldilocks, I couldn't seem to get comfortable. I flopped onto my back again. Strange dreams began to flutter along the edges of my consciousness as I drifted in and out. Finally, at five o'clock, I rose and dressed in shorts, a T-shirt and my trusty trail runners. I needed to blow the mental cobwebs out.

That meant a run.

Despite sleeping only a fraction of what most people did, I wasn't often tired. For a while I'd wondered whether I was manic. However, that usually came with its opposite, and despite its recent popularity, depression wasn't my thing. It was just that *not* running made me feel a little crazy. Too much energy, too many sparks going off in my brain.

I'd found the former carriage house in Midtown—

not quite downtown but not as far out as Southside suburbia, and still possessing the true flavor of the city. After stretching, I set off to explore the neighborhood. Dogwoods bloomed along the side streets, punctuating the massive live oaks dripping with moss. I spotted two other runners in the dim predawn light. They waved, as did I. The smell of sausage teased from one house, the voices of children from another. Otherwise, all was quiet except for the sounds of birdsong, footfalls, and my own breathing.

Back home, I showered and donned a floral skort, tank top and sandals. After returning the rented trailer, I drove downtown on Abercorn Street, wending my way around the one-way parklike squares in the historic district as I neared my destination. Walkers strode purposefully, some pushing strollers, some arm in arm. A ponytailed man lugged an easel toward the riverfront. Camera-wielding tourists intermixed with suited professionals, everyone getting an early start. The air winging in through my car window already held heat as I turned left onto Broughton just after Oglethorpe Square and looked for a parking spot.

I rubbed cold butter into flour, baking powder and salt, sensing with my fingertips when to add the finely grated sharp cheddar and a bit of cream to the scone dough.

Finally, a commercial kitchen of my own. It was really happening.

Lucy and Honeybee the cat had greeted me at the door with a plate of lavender-laced biscotti.

"Is our mascot going to stick around and charm the

customers once we open?" I'd asked with trepidation, backing away from the orange-striped feline. I adored her, I really did, right down to the bright white tip of her swirly tail. It wasn't my fault I was so allergic to cats. I'd practically lived on antihistamines while staying with Ben and Lucy before I bought the carriage house.

Honeybee did that squinty-eyed thing and started to purr.

Lucy laughed. "Don't worry. She just wanted to check the place out. I'll run her back home after we have a bite."

Well, the place *was* named after her.

Lucy and I'd both chosen vanilla lattes for dunking the biscotti. The combination was heavenly. The flavor of the dried flower buds was light, the aroma enticing. My aunt had excellent instincts when it came to cooking.

My nervousness about the move had evaporated. Not only was I in my element, but it was impossible to be anxious when surrounded by the color scheme we'd selected for the Honeybee. Light amber walls on three sides offset the burnt orange wall behind the counter. A huge blackboard above and behind the register listed the menu items: We would alter them as we learned what our customers liked best. In front of the display case, bright blue tablecloths covered fifteen small tables. The dark blue vinyl chairs on sturdy chrome legs had been chosen for maximum comfort. The array of stainless-steel appliances in the kitchen, visible from the seating area, mirrored their silvery tone. A large bookshelf sat against one wall, waiting for the reading material Lucy wanted to provide for our customers. In front of it, two overstuffed sofas covered in jewel-toned brocade offered more casual seating.

Now, an hour later, the scent of the cheddar tantalized my nose as I worked. "We're going to sell a ton of these," I said to Lucy as she came back into the kitchen, fuzzy feline safely ensconced back at her and Ben's town house.

She peered over my shoulder and breathed deep. "Don't I know it. But let's add a little something to ensure that."

"Maybe some bacon?" I laughed. "Because everything's better with bacon, right?"

"I was thinking more along the lines of this." She retrieved a Mason jar full of dried greenery from a shelf in the overflowing pantry. "Sage. From my garden."

"Sage and cheddar are a great combination," I agreed. "We should try that."

The front door jingled open. Quickly, I wiped my hands on a towel and walked out front. Behind me, Lucy said something. I stopped and turned.

She stood over my scone dough, crumbling dried sage from the Mason jar into it and muttering under her breath.

"What did you say?" I asked.

My aunt didn't look up. "Oh, nothing, hon."

The sound of clicking footsteps caught my attention, and I looked back toward the newcomer. A gray-haired, precisely coiffed woman in her mid-sixties strode into the bakery on three-inch heels.

"I'm sorry," I said. "We're not open for business yet. We'll be opening next week, though, and would love for you to stop back by. There will be daily specials and—"

"I know you're not open for business, missy. I'm not stupid and I can read the sign in the window." Deep frown lines defined her face from forehead to jowl. Her dark eyes snapped like a hawk's.

Startled, I opened my mouth. Closed it again.

Lucy came up behind me.

"Good morning, Mavis," she said. "What can we do for you?"

She pointed a vermilion-tipped finger at me. "Mrs. Templeton to you."

I nodded my understanding in stunned silence.

Her gaze homed in on Lucy. "I want to know what your intentions are."

"Our intentions?" my aunt asked.

"For this place," the older woman said. "The Sassafras Bakery on Lincoln Street closed down six months ago. You would know that, of course, if you have any head for business. I found that bakery quite pleasing, overall. They managed quite a decent brioche."

Lucy spoke carefully. "We are aware the Sassafras closed. The Honeybee will be a bit different, however."

Mrs. Templeton glared, first at my aunt, then at me and then at her surroundings. Her eyes flicked from the richly colored walls to the open kitchen to the empty bookcase. She sniffed when she saw the sofas, made a harrumphing sound as she took in the espresso counter.

"I suppose you'll allow people to bring in those horrible laptop computers and stay all day if they want to."

"Yes, and we'll offer free access to the Internet," Lucy replied.

The red-tipped claw came out again, shaking at us like we were naughty twelve-year-olds. "You'll get all kinds of riffraff in here, ruin the neighborhood."

"We just don't believe that, Mavis." Lucy smiled and put her hand on my shoulder. "Everyone will be welcome here, and after people taste Katie's baking the word will spread like wildfire."

Mrs. Templeton curled her lip and turned those bird eyes on me.

"How old are you?"

"Twenty-eight," I said, slightly terrified.

"Too young. Good business requires experience, not nepotism. You'll be closed in six months."

I felt my face redden as I struggled not to say something we'd all regret later. Who did this woman think she was, anyway?

"Despite that, I'm going to give you an opportunity. This month's brunch meeting of the Downtown Business Association shall be here at the *Honeybee Bakery*." Sarcasm dripped from the last two words.

"When is the meeting?" Lucy asked.

"Wednesday."

"This Wednesday? But we're not open yet," I protested.

"I'm not asking you to be open. The meeting is a private affair, anyway. Can you do it or not?"

I shook my head, but Lucy stepped forward. "Let me talk to Ben, and we'll call you."

Mrs. Templeton peered at the diamond-encrusted

watch on her bony wrist. "I need to know within two hours."

"Why the last-minute rush?" I asked.

She distributed an angry look between us. "The venue I had booked proved to be unsatisfactory at the last moment. Please be assured that if you take on this job the entire future of this establishment will be on the line. There will be thirty to thirty-five attending." And with that she turned on her spiked heel and marched out the door.

I let out a whoosh of air. "Who was *that*?"

"That," Lucy said, "was Mavis Templeton. Savannah mover and shaker extraordinaire and one of the unhappiest women I've ever met."

"She's horrible."

"Her husband is dead." She sighed. "Died about fifteen years ago and left her all alone. She was unable to have children, though I understand she wanted them desperately. She's grown lonely and bitter."

"I'll say."

"In other words, exactly the sort of person who could use a bit of sugar in her life. A cookie here, a brownie there."

Oh, brother. Sometimes Lucy went a little too far with all the sweetness-and-light stuff. "We're not really going to cater that meeting for her, are we? I mean, we never intended to be that kind of business."

A speculative expression settled on my aunt's face. "It would be a terrific way to jump-start awareness about the bakery and a perfect showcase for your cooking talents." Her gaze caught mine, and I found myself unable to look away. "Can you do it?"

Why was my head nodding? *No, no, no.*

And yet, while my head nodded, my mind raced through menu choices, discarding one after another but settling on a few possibilities.

"Whole eggs in brioche, muffins, scones and a baked strata with Italian bread, spinach and sausage as the savory option. Serve a citrus cooler along with their choice of coffee drinks, and plenty of fruit."

Lucy raised her palms to the ceiling and beamed. "See? Easy as pie."

"Very funny," I said.

Chapter 2

A flurry of phone calls later it was official: The Honeybee Bakery would be hosting Savannah's Downtown
Business Association brunch meeting in two days. I began sketching out a shopping list and a schedule. I'd
bake the Italian bread for the strata tomorrow, as well
as mixing the dough for the brioche. Then Lucy and I
could make the muffins and the scones first thing the
next morning, before the egg dishes took up all the
oven space.

A sharp knock on the back door made me jump. "I
bet that's the flour," I muttered under my breath.

"Let the ladies in," Lucy called from out front, where
she was washing windows. Ben had gone to buy vene-
tian blinds at the hardware store.

"Ladies?" Curious, I opened the back door.

"Oh, my stars and garters, will y'all just look at this
darlin' girl! Lucille told us you were pretty, but my
Lord, she didn't tell us the half of it. That red hair is
enough to light up the room all by itself." This from a
short, round woman dressed head to toe in pink. Liter-

ally. A pink bow clung to her smooth white pageboy, and magenta pumps peeked out from under the cuffs of her rosy pantsuit. Twinkling blue eyes didn't miss a detail.

"Um," I said. My fingers ran through my short locks. I'd always thought of them as auburn, not red.

Her gaze shot over my shoulder. "Lucille! We brought the books," she sang out. "Just like we promised."

"Come in, girls," Lucy called from behind me. "We've got fresh scones."

"Yum!" the pink lady said and resumed twinkling at me.

I stepped back from the doorway, and she entered, followed by three other women, all looking me over like I was a horse they were considering placing a bet on. Each carried a fabric shopping bag bulging with books. One by one, they deposited their bags on the counter by the door.

We shuffled into a rough circle in the middle of the kitchen, and my aunt made the introductions.

"As you've no doubt guessed, this is my niece, Katie."

They all nodded.

"Katie, these are the members of my book club, all dear friends." With a languid sweep of her arm, she indicated the effusive woman in pink. "Mimsey Carmichael."

I smiled. "Ms. Carmichael."

She stepped forward and grabbed my hand. "Oh, no, dear. No need to stand on ceremony. We're all going to be great friends. So I'm Mimsey, plain ol' little Mimsey, to you."

I felt my lips twitch. "Mimsey it is, then. It's nice to meet you."

"Well, it is a plumb *delight* to meet you!"

"And this is Bianca Devereaux." Lucy gestured toward the woman who towered over the diminutive Mimsey. Long, straight black hair fell nearly to her waist, and intense emerald eyes gazed at me from her pale face. Her white peasant blouse was cinched with a silver belt over a long, watered-silk skirt in periwinkle blue. Expensive leather sandals revealed blue-painted toenails and a silver ankle bracelet. I placed her in her mid-forties. Between her height and her stark features, she would have been downright intimidating if her gaze hadn't been so calm.

"Hello," I said.

She put her hand on my arm. "Katie." Her voice was low and smooth. "We've heard so much about you. Welcome to Savannah."

"Thank you."

The third woman, a little older than Bianca, stepped forward. She also touched me on the arm. "Oh, there's so much to see here. So much to learn. You're going to love it. I'm Jaida." Her words slid over me like warm butter. In fact, everything about her exuded warmth, from her deep brown eyes and mocha skin to the scent of cinnamon that enveloped her. The scarlet blouse worn under a neat gray suit matched her shoes, giving the impression of a business professional with a bit of a wild side.

"Hi, Jaida. Maybe you can give me some insider suggestions."

Her laugh was rich and sunny. "I'd be glad to. And

if you're interested in restaurants, well, I'm definitely your gal."

My ears perked right up at that.

"And last, but never least, this is Cookie Rios," Lucy said.

Small and delicate, she'd been standing slightly behind Bianca. Now she moved toward me. The light caught a glint of reddish-purple highlights in her shiny black hair. It was a perfect complement to her olive skin. Her sundress, tied at the shoulders, matched jade-colored eyes. No touch on the arm for her; Cookie marched right up and embraced me. "Katie Lightfoot. Finally, we meet."

I couldn't quite identify her subtle accent.

She stepped back and laughed. "What you must think of us, fawning over you like this. It's just that your aunt has been talking about you for months."

"Uh-oh." I smiled at everyone, a bit bowled over by their enthusiasm. "It's nice to meet all of you."

"You must come to our next meeting," Cookie said. "It's next week."

"The book club, you mean?" I asked. "What are you reading right now?"

They looked at each other, and then at Lucy. She said, "I'll fill you in later. For now, let's give that espresso machine a whirl and get to work. Bring those books—I want to see what you ladies chose for our little library here."

The book club ladies hefted their shopping bags and lugged them out to the seating area by the empty shelves.

By the time I made my own latte and went to join

them, the group was surrounded by piles of books. Some looked ancient, others brand-new. I sat down next to Cookie and picked one up at random.

Hypnotize Yourself to Stop Smoking Now.

Really?

I put it down and picked up another: *Self-Defense for Pacifists.*

My eyes raked the titles, flicking from pile to pile. There was plenty of fiction and nonfiction, along with cookbooks, crafts and natural history. Though I considered myself fairly well read, most of these titles I'd never heard of. Almost half the books were how-to and inspirational manuals that ranged from beauty tips to how to parent a difficult child, from installing bathroom tile to exploring the afterlife.

Across from me, Jaida caught my look. Her eyes laughed. "How do you like our choices?"

"I . . . um . . . well, there certainly is a wide selection."

"Honeybee customers'll read these books, darlin'. Don't you worry." The pink bow in Mimsey's hair bobbed up and down as she emphasized her words. "They just don't know they need to yet."

Everyone nodded their agreement, including Lucy. Amazing. Best to stick with the tried-and-true classics, in my opinion. Oh, well. My purview was the kitchen. My aunt's was the library. I'd leave it to her.

"If you ladies will excuse me, I need to finish up my shopping list for an event we're hosting in two days," I said.

"You go right on ahead. Don't mind us."

I took Mimsey at her word, and returned to the tiny

office off the kitchen. If Ben could make a run to the warehouse grocer early in the morning, we'd be all right. I finished my list as another knock came on the back door. This time it really was the flour delivery-man. I signed the receipt and directed him to the store-room.

When I emerged, the ladies were gone, and Lucy and Ben were installing blinds on the windows.

I sniffed the air. "I smell gin. And smoke."

Ben grinned. "You been tippling, Lucy?"

She punched him lightly on the arm. "The ladies dropped by to help us get ready."

Understanding dawned on his face. "Juniper?" he asked.

I was still confused.

"What did you do, burn it?" I joked. "It smells aw-ful."

Ben and Lucy exchanged glances.

My aunt cleared her throat. "Mimsey is putting to-gether some nice flower arrangements for the tables on Wednesday. Little bundles of freesia on each table. She's a florist, you know."

A frown creased my forehead. "No, I didn't know that. Now what on earth—"

Lucy interrupted me. "Ben, we're ahead of schedule. Why don't you pick up what Katie still needs while I get the rest of these windows shined up?"

"Sure thing." He raised his eyebrows at me and smiled. "I bet you have a nice long list for me."

My mind filled with all I still had to do to get ready, and I turned toward the kitchen. "Finished it just be-fore the flour was delivered. Let me get it."

When I brought the list back to Ben, Lucy was scrubbing furiously at a spot on the window all the way at the end of the bakery. He took it, bussed my cheek heartily and left. I watched Lucy for a few moments, but she didn't look up.

I went back into the kitchen and turned on the industrial fan over one of the stoves. In minutes the funny smell was gone.

Chapter 3

Late Wednesday morning local business owners began to trickle into the Honeybee. Ben, looking handsome in his linen jacket, greeted each by name at the door, and Lucy seated them. In the center of every chrome-and-blue table a small vase of yellow and white freesia sat beside a sweating pitcher of citrus cooler. Lucy had told me the freesia would promote peaceful, loving feelings. Seemed a lot to demand from a flower. For me it was enough that it was pretty.

A large glass bowl of chilled melon balls drizzled with balsamic vinegar and sprinkled with cracked black pepper shone like a pastel beacon in the middle of the buffet table we'd erected against the wall opposite the library area. I'd baked like a madwoman the day before and had driven downtown before dawn to start in again. The lemon spice muffins and cheddar-sage scones would be served still warm, the other dishes piping-hot.

Lucy had insisted on adding plenty of cinnamon, cloves and ginger to the muffins, as well as basil to the sausage strata and a sprinkle of parsley over the eggs baked in brioche. All the flavors were welcome additions, but she seemed to do a lot of muttering as she stirred and sprinkled.

I'd spent only short periods of time with Lucy before the Honeybee, though more and more often over the years. When I was a child, she'd visited Mama a few times, but she'd called me every month or so since I'd reached the age of ten. Then when I'd been in pastry school, and later in Akron, she'd made a few trips to see me, but not Mama. I didn't quite know what it was between those two, but it was true that Lucy had an element of what Mama disdainfully referred to as "airy-fairy." Now her herbal embellishments brought to mind how she'd murmured before, when adding the sage from her garden to the cheddar scones.

Mmmm. Cheddar scones. That reminded me: With all the baking I hadn't had time for breakfast. I ducked behind a partition and helped myself to a quick, buttery bite before emerging to help make coffee drinks for the crowd.

I'd debated what to wear, and decided my usual summer uniform of T-shirt over a simple skirt and comfortable shoes would be fine for the DBA or anyone else. Any extra style would come from the extensive collection of aprons I'd gathered from vintage clothing stores, Etsy and wherever else I happened across them. Today I'd chosen a paisley chef's apron that reflected the pink, green and orange of the melon medley.

The door swung open again, and conversations trickled away as Mavis Templeton entered the bakery. She wore a tailored mint green dress that looked like something Doris Day would have worn, complete with matching shoes, handbag and—I could hardly believe it—pillbox hat. Her glittering eyes swept the room.

"Where's Mr. Jenkins?"

"He called to say he can't make the meeting," Ben said.

Her nostrils flared. "And the food? Is it ready?"

"We'll bring it out in five minutes," I said from behind the counter.

"I am especially looking forward to testing your brioche." She sounded more like she was looking forward to having a fur coat made out of puppies. Given her obvious penchant for being difficult, it was hard to believe she'd signed off on my menu so quickly. I hadn't been able to resist including brioche after her diatribe about the Sassafras Bakery.

It just happened to be one of my specialties.

"I'm looking forward to your feedback," I said.

After the drinks were served and the Downtown Business Association members had filled their plates, Ben joined one of the tables. He was, after all, the newest addition to their ranks. Lucy and I retired to the kitchen, but she kept peeking out.

I craned my neck to see around the register. "What's the matter?"

"She's not eating."

"Who?" It looked to me like everyone was tucking in with glee. You could always tell when people enjoyed a meal because they didn't talk until they'd had a few bites of everything, and all I heard was a few murmurs and the clink of silverware on the Honeybee's stoneware plates.

"Mavis." My aunt's fingers twisted in her long batik skirt. "She took one bite of your brioche and hasn't had another bite since. She's not even drinking her coffee."

"No wonder she's so skinny."

"She needs to eat." Urgency threaded through the words.

I looked at her curiously. "Well, why don't you try going on out there and telling her that?"

"Hush."

The group spoke informally over plates piled high with food as if it were some huge family gathering. Mrs. Templeton continued to speak little and eat less, her eyes darting around the room. The main topic of discussion was a new ordinance under consideration by the city council that would eliminate several dozen parking spaces along the riverfront. Many members of the DBA voiced their concern that it would affect the tourist trade, while others argued it would have little impact because so many visitors walked the squares and rode the numerous tour buses and so didn't need to park downtown.

A movement by the bookshelf caught my eye. I turned my head to discover a man sitting in one of the overstuffed chairs, writing in a small spiral notebook. He wore khaki hiking pants, sports sandals and a black T-shirt. A length of leather braid gathered his smooth blond hair into a ponytail at the nape of his neck. Brown eyes sparked with intelligence and a hint of boredom as they flicked among the diners.

"Who's that?" I whispered to Lucy, indicating him with my chin.

Suddenly his eyes met mine, and for some reason it became difficult to breathe.

"That's Steve Dawes," my aunt said. "He's a columnist for the *Savannah Morning News*. Used to be a crime reporter before his column took off. Ben asked him here today, hoping for a mention of the Honeybee in the paper before our grand opening."

I didn't respond, still entangled in his gaze. Finally, I took a deep breath and looked away, but not before his lips had quirked up on one side in a knowing grin.

Shake it off, Katie. I'd sworn to forgo men for at least six months. Nothing good could come of a rebound relationship after being dumped by my fiancé.

Lucy and I began clearing tables. Soon the DBA members rose and began to drift out in ones and twos, the same way they'd arrived. Several stood talking in small clusters, and a few wandered over to the library area to take a look at the books. Once again, Ben took up his station by the door, talking to each person as he or she left. As the former fire chief, he already knew most of them.

"You're going to be a huge success if the food you served today is any indication!" a woman in a smart brown suit said with loud enthusiasm,

And from the woman behind her, "Oh, I agree. That sausage casserole was to die for."

"Thank you, ladies," Ben said, graciousness personified. "Of course the real credit goes to my niece and my wife."

"Well, keep 'em around," said a portly man with muttonchop sideburns. "They sure turn out some tasty eats."

I busied myself in the kitchen, happy for the kudos but mostly waiting for the *Morning News* columnist to leave. No use tempting fate with a closer encounter than we'd already had.

Mrs. Templeton approached the counter where Lucy stood and handed her a check. "The coffee was too strong, and that egg casserole was too rich."

She had to be referring to the strata. The old crab hadn't even sampled it, so how had she managed to develop such a severe opinion? Frowning, I turned toward them.

Her eyes snapped to me. "The brioche would have been quite decent if you hadn't ruined it by baking that egg in it. A bit of strawberry jam would have been far better."

I was silent.

She sniffed and continued. "But overall it was an acceptable meal, and the association was able to successfully conduct its business."

Lucy looked down at the check in her hand. "Uh, Mavis." She leaned forward and spoke in a low voice as she held it out. "This isn't what we agreed upon."

"Nonsense. I'm treasurer of the association, and I'm paying exactly what this job is worth."

"But—"

"And not a penny more."

Ben left his position by the door and joined his wife. "Is there a problem?"

"No," Mrs. Templeton said.

"Yes," Lucy said at the same time. The set of her shoulders, the pinched muscles near her mouth and the look she shot at Ben all shouted her distress. Conflict was not my aunt's forte—nor mine. Tension hung heavy in the air.

And there was Steve Dawes, drinking it all in as if we were finally going to provide some news fit to print.

I was relieved when Ben stepped forward and my aunt leaned back a fraction. He took the check Lucy offered with her fingertips, perused it for a moment and then frowned at Mrs. Templeton. "Mavis, this is less than half of what we agreed upon. You know we can't take that as full payment. It doesn't even cover our expenses."

"You didn't lose any money by having to close the bakery for the meeting," she countered.

"We had to scramble to cater to the DBA at all, given we aren't due to open for three more days."

"So now you're ahead of schedule."

Ben shook his head. "Mavis, either you pay the full amount we agreed upon in writing or I'll have to go to Jack Jenkins."

Her red-tipped talon came out and shook in his face. "You wouldn't dare."

"Oh, but I would. After all, it would be bad business not to bring this up to the president of the association." Throwing her own words back at her.

"On the contrary, Benjamin. It would be very bad business to cross me. Several people have found that out over the years. I can put your little bakery under inside of a month."

She whirled and stalked out.

Slowly, I closed my mouth. Tried to swallow. The dozen or so business owners left in the bakery were dead silent. Lucy's face creased with worry, and Uncle Ben flushed red under his beard. In the corner, the reporter wrote furiously in his notebook. I wanted to run over and yank it away from him.

"Well." Ben cleared his throat and tried again. "Well, thank you all for coming to this, the Honeybee's pre–grand opening."

With that, conversation resumed, though I detected a slight edge to the voices.

Ben came into the kitchen and strode toward the back door. "I need a moment."

Lucy watched him go, threw a look at me and moved out front. Immediately I heard a man compliment her on the food and service, followed by a woman chiming in with her agreement.

At least someone liked my food. I began loading the dishwasher. What if Mavis Templeton—Ms. Nastiness Personified—ruined the Honeybee? Could she do that? I had a sinking feeling the answer was yes, and she'd sleep like a baby afterward, too. Moving to the counter for another pile of plates, I felt Steve Dawes looking at me. Against my will, I raised my eyes and met his.

His smile revealed perfect white teeth. Damn.

The front door flew open, and a tall bald man yelled, "Call 911! We need an ambulance out here!"

Steve ran out the door, followed by everyone left in the Honeybee except Lucy and me. Her eyes were wide as she made the call to emergency services.

A heavy, icky feeling weighed my steps as I moved to the door, opened it, and joined the people on the sidewalk. A gawker knot had formed around the dark green Cadillac parked a few spaces down the block. The milling crowd parted briefly to reveal Mavis Templeton sitting behind the wheel.

Her hair was perfect and her red lipstick flawless.

But her head lay against the seat back at a strange angle, and those snapping hawk's eyes no longer glittered.

It seemed pretty obvious that they never would again.

I raised a trembling hand to cover my mouth. She'd been shaking her finger at us only minutes before, and now she was . . . dead?

"Where's Ben?" The voice startled me, and I spun around to find that Steve Dawes had approached from my other side.

"Um—um—he went out back," I stuttered. "What happened?"

He grimaced, then leaned closer. "Someone broke her neck." The way he said it sounded almost like an apology.

"On purpose?" I asked without thinking.

Dawes nodded. "Most definitely on purpose."

We heard the sirens first, and then saw the flashing lights. Soon the street was crawling with uniforms— police officers, firefighters and paramedics. Two officers quickly cordoned off the area around the Cadillac and asked the crowd to move back. Another two began to question the closest onlookers.

I craned my neck, searching the throng.

"I doubt the murderer is still here," he said.

Murderer. There was the word I'd been avoiding. I turned and hurried back inside the bakery just as Lucy reached the door. "Where's Uncle Ben?"

She looked blank.

Grabbing her shoulders, I gave her a little shake. "Do you know where he went?"

She winced, and I dropped my hands. "Oh, Lucy. I'm sorry," I said.

The sound of the back door opening was followed by Ben's voice. "What on God's green earth is going on out front?" He came through the kitchen to find Lucy and me staring at him.

"What?"

"Someone broke Mrs. Templeton's neck," I said. "At least that's what that reporter told me."

Lucy sucked air in through her teeth. "Oh, that poor woman!"

Bewilderment settled on Ben's face. He opened his mouth, then closed it without saying anything.

I knew exactly what he meant.

The door opened behind me, the bell above it tinkling merrily as two uniformed police officers entered the Honeybee.

"Benjamin Eagel." The shorter one made it a statement, not a question.

My uncle nodded anyway.

"We need you to come down to the precinct."

"Whatever for?" Lucy asked.

"A woman's been murdered." This from the second policeman. His freckled face reddened as he spoke.

"We just heard." She moved closer to Ben. "It's terrible, absolutely terrible. But it doesn't have anything to do with my husband."

Freckles shuffled his feet. "Sorry, Ben. We heard you had an argument with her right before it happened. Detective Quinn wants to talk to you."

The short one looked stoic. No doubt Ben knew them from his tenure in the fire department.

Then the words sank in. An argument right before a murder. The police couldn't help but see it as a possible motive.

The same thought obviously occurred to Lucy, because she vehemently shook her head. "Don't be ridiculous!"

My uncle stepped forward. "It's all right, Luce. I'll go talk to Quinn and find out what's going on." He began to move toward the door.

"Ben," I said, "do you want us to call a lawyer?"

He hesitated. "I suppose that might be a good idea."

"Who—"

"I'll call Jaida." Lucy's voice shook.

Ben nodded, opened the door and left with the two policemen.

I turned to my aunt. "Jaida's a lawyer?"

But she was already speaking into the phone. "We need you. Mavis has been murdered, and the police took Ben down to the station . . . Mavis Templeton . . . Yes, my Ben. Of course I know he didn't do anything . . . No, I don't think he's under arrest. They said they wanted to question him." She sank into a chair, pale with worry. "All right. Thank you, honey. We'll wait for your call."

The hand holding the phone fell slack in her lap, and she looked up at me with wet eyes. "I can't believe Mavis is really dead. We were just talking to her."

I knelt beside her. "Oh, Lucy, it's going to be okay. They'll find who did this awful thing."

The front door tinkled open again. I rose to tell whoever it was to go away and leave us alone. The doorframe filled with a brown-haired, blue-eyed man, and the words died in my throat. His blue T-shirt did little to conceal the muscles beneath, and he topped my five-eight by at least seven inches.

Great. I didn't care how good-looking he was; we didn't need any visitors right then.

He entered and went straight to Lucy. She rose and wrapped her arms around him, leaning against his chest. Giving her a squeeze, he looked at me over her head, eyes full of questions.

"Oh, Deck," my aunt said. "How did you hear?"

"C'mon, Luce. You know we've got a scanner at the firehouse."

Ah. That explained the logo on the sleeve of the T-shirt. A fireman, and one who knew my aunt well enough to call her by Ben's nickname for her. The tension in my shoulders relaxed a fraction.

"I came as soon as I heard someone was killed in this neighborhood. I heard the cops already have a suspect, though, and they expect to make an arrest soon." He held her away from him and looked around the bakery. "Where's Ben?"

"Arrest? Oh, no. They can't really think . . ." Lucy whispered. Tears welled in her eyes.

I stepped forward and held out my hand toward the man. His forehead creased as he reached out and shook it.

"Declan McCarthy," he said.

"Nice to meet you. I'm Katie Lightfoot, Ben and Lucy's niece. And I'm afraid the suspect you heard about might be my uncle."

Chapter 4

"Let me get you a cup of coffee." Lucy hustled to the espresso counter, her multicolored skirt swirling around her ankles.

"You don't have to—," Declan began to protest, but stopped when I squeezed his fingers. He looked down at his hand, still in mine, as if wondering how it got there.

I let go, leaned up and said in a low voice, "It'll give her something to do besides worry."

He hesitated. I sat down. After a few seconds he followed suit. His hands, calloused but clean, rested on the expanse of blue covering the table between us. They looked strong and capable. And bare.

Not that I meant to look for a ring. I just noticed, is all.

"Ben told me you were moving here," he said.

My attention returned to his face. It looked strong and capable, too, with solid planes, a few laugh lines and a jaw that was a bit too square. Good, because we needed all the strong allies we could get.

"I've been looking forward to meeting you," he continued with a small smile. "Too bad it has to be under these circumstances."

"So you and my uncle are friends?"

The smile widened into a grin. "Great friends. He mentored me as a rookie. Helped me through some pretty rough times, too."

"He's a good man," I said.

"That's why I don't understand why the police consider him a suspect. Tell me what happened."

So I did, briefly explaining about the brunch, the argument over money and Mrs. Templeton's threatening to close down the bakery before she walked out.

"Tell him about what you saw outside," Lucy called from the kitchen.

So I did that, too, ending with, "She was sitting there in her car . . . dead."

"Was there blood?"

"Uh-uh. But her head was at a funny angle." I grimaced. "Apparently someone broke her neck."

My aunt returned bearing a tray laden with coffee and leftover scones and muffins. "Have you eaten?"

Declan shook his head. "Don't worry about me."

"Well, here are some of Katie's goodies."

He quirked an eyebrow at me, and suddenly my aunt's offer sounded untoward. I blushed. He reached toward the plate. "Well, in that case."

The door opened yet again, and I cursed myself under my breath for not locking it after Declan's arrival. Two policewomen entered, followed by Steve Dawes.

My stomach was upset enough without the effect he seemed to have on it. I tried to ignore his sudden presence, but couldn't quite. Still, when I did glance over at him he wasn't paying attention to me at all:

All his energy focused on Declan.

And Declan returned the favor.

The air between the two men vibrated with sudden, intense hostility. I could *see* the hatred distort the atmosphere.

No, wait. That couldn't be.

"Mrs. Eagel?" one of the officers asked.

Lucy stood.

"And you're, um"—the other woman consulted a notebook and looked up at me—"Ms. Lightfoot?"

"Yes." I rose, too, still distracted by the interplay of emotion between Declan and Steve.

As soon as I moved, Declan scrambled to his feet and placed himself solidly between Steve and me. Not once did he look at the policewomen, only at the newspaper columnist. Any minute now, they'd bare their teeth and start snarling. Lucy's eyes darted between them, but the police officers didn't seem to notice.

"You're aware of the death that occurred outside earlier?" one asked.

We all nodded.

"We're talking to everyone in the neighborhood and wanted to ask you a few questions. Were you present, sir?" the officer asked Declan.

He tore his gaze from Steve and shook his head. "No."

Promptly ignoring him, she turned back to Lucy and me. "Perhaps over here?" She indicated the reading area.

Lucy and I followed behind the uniforms like zombies. In the back of my mind I wondered whether we should talk to anyone at all without a lawyer. As we settled into the cushy furniture, both policewomen breathed sighs of relief and one absently slipped her foot out of her shoe and rubbed her heel.

Behind us, the door of the bakery slammed. I looked back to see Declan's shoulders slump as he flipped the lock. He looked over at me as Steve stormed past the window outside. I couldn't read his expression.

The policewomen seemed almost bored as they asked their rote questions—*tell us what happened, did you see anything or anyone suspicious, where were you when you learned of the death*. They each insisted on calling it "the death" rather than "the murder," which was what we all knew it was. But I didn't quibble. They hadn't separated Lucy and me, and they didn't seem to be aware that Ben was being questioned by their superior as we spoke.

I didn't enlighten them, either. Just the facts, ma'am.

We'd cleaned up everything and put the extra food away well before Uncle Ben and Jaida returned to the Honeybee, a little before five o'clock. Declan had stuck around, flipping absently through books in the reading area as we tidied the kitchen, and then we'd joined him.

The key turned in the lock, and Aunt Lucy rushed to her husband's side when he came through the door. "Oh, thank heavens! Are you all right?"

"Of course. Detective Quinn was just covering all his bases. No worries." He wrapped his arms around her and buried his face in her hair, but not before his eyes slid past mine. I could tell the situation was far more serious than he was letting on.

Jaida shut the door behind her and threw the dead bolt. She nodded at Declan. "Thanks for coming."

"Glad you're here," he replied.

"What happened at the police station?" I asked.

Jaida placed her brown leather briefcase on a chair and sank into the one next to it. Her lips pressed together as she smoothed her navy suit skirt against her leg, weighing what to say. "Is there any coffee?" she asked. "Just plain old regular coffee?"

"I'll make fresh." Grabbing my apron, I hurried to the counter.

Ben urged Lucy into a chair. Declan continued to lean against the wall. The light began to angle through the slats of the window blinds. It had been a long day. I set up the coffee to drip. The sharp smell of dark roast beginning to brew hinted at invigoration, and suddenly I craved a cup, too.

I returned to the table where Jaida sat, and we all waited for her to speak.

"There was a witness." The tone of her voice made my throat tighten. "A woman," she continued. "She saw a man hurrying away from Mavis Templeton's car moments before Mavis was discovered with a broken neck. The woman's description fits Ben to a T: tall, brownish-red hair, beard, glasses."

Lucy stared at Jaida, then at me, then back at Jaida. "No. No, that can't be."

"Add the fact that several people who attended the DBA brunch this morning saw Ben and Mrs. Templeton have a rather serious altercation, and it doesn't look good. Not good at all. Especially since at least two of the witnesses to that argument cited Mrs. Templeton's threat to put the Honeybee out of business. Both assured Detective Quinn that while a threat like that from someone else might be mere posturing, Mavis Templeton was well known for her ability to ruin the lives of those who crossed her."

Ben leaned forward, grasping Lucy's tiny hand in both of his. "But they had to let me go."

Jaida inclined her head. "True. See, Quinn wanted the witness to see Ben."

Declan pushed away from the wall. "They put you in a lineup?" He seemed almost as upset as Lucy.

My uncle's dry laugh fell short of humor. "Can you believe it?"

"She didn't identify him," Jaida said. "But—"

"Because it wasn't him!" Lucy punctuated her statement with a stamp of her foot under the table.

A smile played around the edge of Ben's mouth. "Well, of course it wasn't me. I was out in the back alley taking deep, calming breaths."

"Detective Quinn let you go because he couldn't get a positive identification from the witness, but that doesn't mean you're off the hook." Jaida's coffee mug banged down on the table. "I was right there. She pointed you out to him, then changed her mind. Said she couldn't be sure enough to put a man in prison."

We were all quiet as that sank in.

Jaida spoke again. "Ben, you're sure no one saw you in the alley after your fight with Mrs. Templeton?"

"It wasn't a fight," Lucy insisted.

"It wasn't a love-in," Jaida countered. "Ben?"

"I don't remember seeing anyone, but someone may have seen me. Not that there are many windows out there. A couple up high, I think. My attention was focused on calming down so I could figure out how to get Mavis to pay the full bill for the brunch without having the whole mess backfire in my face."

"Quinn said they'd check out your story, and that will likely include talking to anyone who might have seen you. But if no one did, then he may try to make a case against you despite the unsure witness."

"I've known Peter Quinn for over twenty years," Ben said. "He's not going to railroad me."

Jaida said, "He's an honest man, but honest men have been known to make honest mistakes. I'm sorry to have to be so blunt, but we have to be realistic."

Tears filled Lucy's eyes. "We have to do something," she choked out.

"We will, honey." Jaida took her other hand. "We will."

Lucy began crying in earnest.

Ben cleared his throat. "Let's go home, Luce. There's nothing else we can do right now. Katie, will you close up? We can reconvene here in the morning after a good night's sleep."

I nodded. "Of course."

Declan put his hand on Ben's shoulder. "I'll drive you."

My uncle opened his mouth to refuse, but then shut it and ushered Lucy toward the door. "Thanks, Deck."

As they went by, Lucy's shoulders hitched in a stifled sob. Ben looked at me with red-rimmed eyes. The lines etched into his forehead had deepened in the course of a few short hours. Even his beard seemed to droop. I felt helpless watching them walk out.

"Don't worry. Declan will get them home and settled in." Jaida flipped the dead bolt again after they'd gone and leaned her back against the door.

"So you know him."

She cocked her head. "Your uncle took Declan under his wing when he first became a firefighter. He's a gentle soul, but there was an incident early in his career that would've made a weaker man quit—or worse. Ben helped him through it. You know, he's good for Ben, too. He always wanted a son."

Lucy had never mentioned that. She and Ben had married later in life, and I'd wondered if she missed having children.

Jaida changed the subject. "It's a shame your big day's been ruined like this."

My shoulders rose in a brief shrug. "It's not about me. Something like this shouldn't happen any day. I'm scared to pieces about Uncle Ben. Is it really as bad as you said?"

She sighed and came back to the table. Sat down. "I'm afraid so."

"I should go over to Ben and Lucy's, too." I got to my feet.

"There's nothing you can do over there, you know." The words were tempered by her gentle tone. "Ben and Lucy have relied on each other for years. It might be best to give them some time. Besides, Lucy will be . . ."

"What?"

Jaida hesitated. "There are some things you don't know about your aunt."

"Like what?"

"Well, she's more resilient than you might think. And she has . . . unusual resources at her disposal."

I stared at her. *Resources?* The word was innocent enough. Even boring. But there was something in the way Jaida said it. Something in the way she was watching me now.

A tingle fluttered down my spine.

I looked away and said, "Yeah, maybe I should wait until tomorrow morning—darn it, I almost forgot." I checked my watch. "I'm supposed to go pick up a box of dishes I found on Craigslist last night. If I hurry, I could still make it."

Jaida stood. "What can I do to help?"

"I just need to lock up and hit the lights." I rose, too. "Thanks for dropping everything for Uncle Ben on such short notice."

"Nonsense. It's what friends do."

In the kitchen, my hand hesitated on the knob of the back door. Rather than locking it, I wrenched it open and took a few steps into the alley. Pipes and cables snaked across the three-story brick walls on each side of the asphalt, punctuated by power meters and locked metal access boxes. Many of the windows high above had been bricked over, but a few remained. Down at the end of the block the driver of a white produce van carried boxes into a restaurant.

Jaida joined me, craning her neck up at the windows as I had. "There might be a witness who saw Ben."

"If someone happened to be looking out at exactly the right time," I said.

Our eyes met. Neither of us thought there was much chance of that.

Inside, we gathered our things, and I unlocked the front door. As Jaida crossed the threshold to the sidewalk outside, I put my hand on her arm.

Her eyes met mine. "You okay?"

"I will be." I wanted to ask about her reference to Lucy's "resources," but I couldn't quite find the words. My hand dropped to my side. "I'll see you tomorrow, right?"

"Of course. Earlier than later, I expect. Good night, Katie."

"Good night."

When I was a teenager I'd heard Mama talking to Daddy one night about Lucy. About how they didn't need to worry about her because she would always land on her feet. Only Mama used a different word than *resources*.

Mama had said Lucy had *powers*.

Chapter 5

That evening when I pulled into my driveway the backseat of the Bug held a mismatched set of funky retro Fiestaware dishes. Now I had something to eat off besides the paper plates Lucy had stashed in the cupboard for me. The multicolored stoneware would look nice with the simple silverware I'd brought from Akron, too.

A plate of cookies sat in the deepening shade of the front porch. So did the black terrier who had surprised me the day I'd arrived.

I stopped in front of him. "Hello again."

Yip.

"You sure are a cutie."

This time the *yip* sounded like *yup.*

I laughed. "And a good dog, too, leaving those cookies alone. Let me get these things inside, and we'll go find where you live. I'll have to know where to return you if you're this determined to visit."

His head tipped to the side. When I opened the door he walked right in as if he'd always lived there.

Oh, dear. I hoped he hadn't. There were all sorts of stories about dogs that had traveled long distances to return to their old homes after their families moved. I put the heavy box of dishes on the counter in the kitchen and returned to the porch for the cookies. They looked like oatmeal chocolate chip, and were arranged on a paper plate covered with cellophane. A note taped to the top read:

Welcome to the neighborhood! Let me know if you need anything at all or have any questions. I'm right next door.

Margie Coopersmith

Back in the kitchen, I put them on the table and scooped up the dog. He settled into my arms and licked my face with a soft pink tongue. "Let's go. You've given me an excuse to meet a friendly neighbor." After such a horrible, exhausting day, friendly was good.

I'd met the man who lived to the west of the carriage house when the Realtor had first shown it to me. He was an accountant who lived alone, and I was pretty sure his name wasn't Margie. So my other next-door neighbor had been the one to leave the sweet treats.

An attractive blond woman with round cheeks and a deep tan answered the door. She wore white shorts, a blue T-shirt, sandals, and a baby on her hip.

"Hello, neighbor!" Her Low Country origins dripped from every syllable.

"Hi," I said. "Margie, right? I believe I have you to thank for the cookies."

The baby murmured, and Margie bounced on the

balls of her feet to quiet him. "My mother-in-law made up a pile of them for the kids this afternoon—I can't cook a lick, makes her crazy—so I cranked up the Welcome Wagon. Thought I might find you home, but no luck. I hope you're not allergic to chocolate."

"Not at *all*."

We both laughed.

"In fact, oatmeal chocolate chip is one of my favorites. I'm Katie Lightfoot, by the way. And I appreciate the welcome."

Her already cheerful face brightened even more. "Nice to meet you, Katie. Come on in, and tell me all about yourself. Bring your pup, too. The kids'll love him to death."

A little girl peeked out from behind one leg. On the other side a little boy jammed his head between her thigh and the doorframe. Both were towheaded blue-eyed wonders. She backed up a few steps so I could see them better.

"These are my twins, Julia and Jonathan. Say hello to Katie."

"Hello," they chimed.

"Hello," I returned. "How old are you two?"

"Four and a half," they said in perfect unison.

"And this here is Bart," Margie said.

I held out my finger, and he grabbed it like a lifeline. "Hello, Bart." But he was a lot more interested in the dog than in me.

"Actually," I said, "this little guy's not mine. But he's showed up at my house two days now. Any idea where he might live?"

Margie put her nose down close to his, and the baby

patted him on the head. When she straightened, she said, "I can't say I've seen him around. He's a Cairn terrier, isn't he? Supposed to be from Scotland. Cute little bugger. I don't think I've run into a black one before."

"Cairn, huh? I don't know, but he is such a sweetie. I was worried that he might belong to the former owners of the carriage house."

"Oh, Lord, no. That woman hated animals. Didn't like my kids much, either. I tried to be nice, but we just didn't have much truck with each other. You're gonna be different, though. I can tell."

"Well, I love animals of all kinds. Don't do very well with cats, though. Allergies."

"Heck, all we've got here is a poky old turtle and two rats. So no problem."

"Rats?"

"The JJs—that's what we call the twins—talked me into them. They turned out to be pretty good pets. Clean, and they don't die all the time like fish. 'Course, I thought it might teach them a little responsibility, too." A grimace flashed across her face. "We're still working on that part."

I smiled and looked down at the dog in my arms. "No idea where he comes from, then?"

"I'm real sorry, Katie, but that little guy just isn't from around here. I know all the families for blocks in either direction, and none of them have a Cairn terrier."

Sighing, I shrugged. "Guess I'll have to take him to the animal shelter."

"N-o-o-o-o!" intoned the JJs.

I looked up at the darkening sky, then leaned down. "It's getting late. I'll take care of him tonight. Okay?"

They nodded vigorously.

Margie looked at her watch. "Oh, Lord, it is getting late. I've got to get these kids to bed. You want to come in?"

I shook my head. "Better get back home and fix something for my overnight guest."

She flipped on the porch light. Her disappointment showed clearly in the yellow glow. "But we'll get together soon, won't we? Have a cup of coffee and get to know each other?"

"You can bet on it," I said. Good neighbors make all the difference in the world, and Margie seemed like a gem.

After she closed the door, I put the dog on the ground to see if he would run off like he had the first time. I could always follow him and see where he went. But he just blinked up at me, waiting, and then trotted at my heels the short distance home. As we crossed the lawn a phalanx of fireflies rose and whirled around him.

I stopped and watched. An image of myself as a child suddenly came to mind, lying on my back in the grass with hundreds of dragonflies zooming and diving above me. The dog sat down as the flurry of lights came closer and closer to his head. Not once did he snap or try to catch one. If a dog could have a dreamy expression, he did. After several minutes, they dispersed in every direction, an explosion of lightning bugs in slow motion. The terrier bounced to his feet and trotted toward the house. I followed slowly behind him.

"What am I going to call you?" In the kitchen, I

stirred up a batch of scrambled eggs. A major trip to the grocery store was in my near future.

He grinned from the position he'd taken up in the corner. His bright eyes watched every move I made.

The smell of bread toasting under the broiler filled the room. I took it out and slathered on the butter. Poured a glass of orange juice. Wished I'd thought to bring home some of the leftover sausage strata from the brunch that morning.

"Something Scottish might be fitting, since Margie said Cairn terriers are supposed to be from Scotland."

Yip!

I divided the eggs between two plates and put one on the floor. He walked over and sat down in front of it.

"What's wrong? You don't like eggs?"

Pulling the chair out, I sat at the table and took a bite. Once he saw me do that, the little dog tucked into his own fare with vigor. As if he'd been waiting for me to start.

What a charmer.

"How about Colin?"

He ignored me.

"Finn?"

Nothing.

"Hmm. How about Mungo the Magnificent?"

I was kidding, but he abandoned his breakfast-for-supper, ran to me and put his front paws on my leg.

Yip!

I was working in the bakery in Akron. Nothing had changed, but I didn't belong there. Under everything rode the keen awareness that back in Savannah, Ben was in jail for a murder he hadn't committed. The Honeybee had failed. My lovely new house belonged to someone who hated animals. Foggy sadness seeped into every corner of the dream, punctuated with sudden stabs of desperate fear.

It wasn't true. I knew it wasn't true. But clawing my way back to consciousness required superhuman effort. Finally, I surfaced to find Mungo whimpering and licking my face, as frantic as if he were performing CPR.

"Thanks, buddy." My voice sounded weak, and my hands trembled as I gathered the dog into my arms. Together we settled back against the pillows and listened to the soothing buzz of cicadas drift in on the scent of roses. My arms relaxed their tight hold on Mungo, but he only snuggled closer.

I hadn't even managed to get my usual hour of sleep, and the short time I had slept was tortured by dreams. At quarter to four, I took a deep breath and rallied my inner resources. The floor was cool on the soles of my feet as I walked into the kitchen to brew coffee. Mungo's toenails clicked lightly on the hardwood.

After getting some caffeine into my system, I decided to buzz over to the twenty-four-hour market while it was still dark and then go for a long run. In the flurry of getting ready for the DBA brunch and then Mavis Templeton's murder, I hadn't bothered with stocking my own kitchen. My makeshift supper the night before impelled me to remedy that situation. Besides, Mungo needed kibble.

I knew it wasn't practical to keep him. The many

hours I'd have to spend at the bakery, especially as we got the business off the ground, meant I wouldn't have time to give the little darling the attention he deserved. But one day spent in the fenced backyard wouldn't hurt him. I could always donate any leftover dog food to the animal shelter. I made a list and headed out.

Grocery shopping before the rest of the world is awake is a mixed bag. On one hand, the market was practically empty, so I zoomed through the aisles, loading up on fresh fruit and vegetables, a nice slab of frozen salmon, and a few packages of chicken. But the deli, meat, and seafood counters wouldn't open for hours. I'd learned to work around that. Finally I added the ingredients for my favorite middle-of-the-night treat: peanut butter swirl brownies.

Back home, I filled a bowl with kibble for Mungo and took off for a run. An hour and a half later I returned sweaty and content. I showered, fluffed my wet hair with my fingers, put on a little mascara and dressed in capris and a tank top.

Mungo hadn't touched his food.

"What's the matter? You too good for dog food?"

He sank to his belly and put his head on his paws.

Hand on hip, I considered him. Truthfully, I didn't blame him. I wouldn't want to eat dog food, either. When I was a child, Daddy had fed our black Labrador what Mama insisted was people food. But he'd said dogs were omnivores just like humans, and members of the family.

"All right. Let's see what we can come up with." I scrambled another egg and mixed it with rice left over from Lucy and Ben's takeout. "Hope you like it a little spicy." I put that and a dish of cool water outside the back door and led him to it. He dug right in.

So much for kibble.

Then he turned and sat, gazing up at me as if awaiting instruction.

All right, then. "I'm sorry to leave you all alone like this, but I have to. There should be plenty of shade out here today, and you have water. I'll be back later. Okay?"

He grinned at me.

"You little lamb. Any creature as adorable as you are will be snapped up and given a good home in no time."

The grin faded. Mungo whined and lay down. His eyes were still glued to mine. He whined again.

My jaw slackened. He didn't . . . he hadn't really . . . nah. He couldn't possibly have understood what I'd said. But as I guided the Bug downtown I couldn't shake the feeling that he knew I planned to get rid of him.

I unlocked the door of the Honeybee and walked in to find Ben and Lucy already ensconced at the table in front of the register. Empty coffee mugs and a few crumbs on their plates indicated they'd been there a while. Ben put down the newspaper section he'd been reading when I entered.

"You don't look like you slept a wink," Lucy said by way of greeting.

"Maybe two or three winks. How about you two?" I tore off a piece of brioche left over from the day before and joined them.

One side of Ben's mouth quirked up. "Not so great." He looked exhausted.

Lucy, on the other hand, appeared far more upbeat than when they'd left the evening before. Now she pushed aside the dirty dishes with a determined gesture.

"I've decided to bring in the ladies to help. They're all coming here this morning."

"The . . . you mean your book club? Whatever for?" I could understand needing Jaida's help; she was a lawyer, after all. But Mimsey was a florist, for heaven's sake, and I didn't even know what Cookie and Bianca did.

"They can help. I'm sure of it. We did what we could to protect the bakery before the brunch. With Mavis Templeton involved, it was the practical thing to do. At first I thought the protection spell hadn't worked, even though it's one of Jaida's specialties." Lucy leaned forward and gripped my arm. "But now I realize we didn't ward the exterior of the building. That's why a murder could occur out on the street like that. It didn't help that Mavis refused to eat the food I made especially for her, either."

I squinted in confusion. "Protection spell?" I turned to my uncle.

He was focusing intently on the sports section and wouldn't look at me.

She flicked a glance at her husband and took a deep breath. "Katie, we need to talk."

Not my favorite words in the English language.

My uncle cleared his throat and stood. "Excuse me." He took his coffee and paper into the office at the back of the kitchen.

I took a bite of brioche to steady myself. *Protection*

spell. What New Age mumbo jumbo was Lucy about to unleash on me?

Bracing, I sipped my coffee and sat back in my chair. "All right. Let's talk."

Her unblinking eyes never wavered. "I don't know any other way to say it except to come right out with it: All the members of the book club are witches." Her statement held an intensity I'd rarely heard from Lucy. "And so are you."

The brioche did a slow flip-flop in my stomach. I spoke each word with care. "Aunt Lucy, that's ridiculous."

She leaned back in her chair. "Good ones, of course."

"Right. You're in a book club with a bunch of witches."

She didn't smile. "It's a spellbook club. We study the spells of others, some very old, in order to develop our own. Like you read old cookbooks to get ideas for recipes."

A couple of beats passed as my mind wrapped around that. My laugh, when it came, was just a tad strained. What she was saying was crazy, absolutely nutso to a degree that went beyond any of her usual tarot-chakra-feng-shui-psychic nonsense.

So why did the very notion wing through me like a familiar wind? Why did I feel more relief than alarm at hearing her words? *Nonsense.*

Clearing my throat, I said, "Oh, now, come on. You can't be serious."

"I can. I am."

Bewildered, I could only blink.

My aunt continued. "You come from a long line of witches."

I snorted. "Tell that to Mama."

"Your mother turned her back on the Craft. And on me, eventually," Lucy said. The deep sadness in her voice gave me pause. "She was frightened that someone would find out what she and your father were. Fillmore is a small town, you know, and not everyone is open-minded. And when we were children in Dayton, there was a problem with a neighbor who happened upon your grandmother casting a spell. It was only a fertility spell for the vegetable garden, but word got around and life was difficult for a while."

I gaped. "Grandmother cast a fertility . . . You've got to be kidding!" My grandmother was a prim and proper lady who always wore an apron in the house and got upset when I used the word *darn*.

Lucy went on. "Mary Jane doesn't embrace her gift, and that's her choice to make. Unfortunately, your mother tried to choose for you, too."

"But—"

"She didn't tell you about your magical heritage, did she?"

Numb, I shook my head once.

"Our family specialty is called hedgewitchery. It's one of the gentler branches of magic."

"Specialty?" I squawked. "Lucy!"

"An affinity for herbal lore, herb craft, and a heck of a green thumb. All of which you possess."

"Well, I can grow most anything, sure. And I do have a particular interest in herbs, but that's only because I like to cook with them!"

"And you're very good at it, too. Pure magic in the kitchen." Her eyes crinkled as she smiled broadly.

"Have you ever had the feeling you were different from the people around you?"

My lips parted to deny such silliness, but no words came out. I'd often felt peculiar, especially as a child. Once I'd even had the temerity to mention it to Mama.

Don't give yourself airs, Katie. You're nothing special, just a normal kid.

I hadn't felt like a normal little girl, though. Not then. But over time I'd convinced myself she was right.

Or was she? The truth was that I still felt different. I'd thought having a husband and a home with a nice rosebush by the door might change that.

"You grew up and decided everyone thinks they're special, even when they're really not. Right?"

I stared at Lucy, then shook myself. "Don't they?"

"Not special like you were. And you had evidence of it, didn't you?"

A telltale shiver ran down my back. I held up my palm in a weak attempt to stop her.

She ignored it. "Think about when you were a child. How you knew things other people didn't know. How you could influence events—not exactly make things happen outright, but nudge them to go the way you wanted. Remember when you and your father went hiking, and you already knew which plants you could eat and which ones were poisonous? No one told you that. It was just part of the knowledge you were born with. And what about how you always knew how Sukie and Barnaby were feeling? Even what they were *thinking*? You may be allergic to cats, but your father always made sure you had dogs around to keep you company. He knew you needed them. That they were truly your friends."

My thoughts shot to little Mungo, waiting for me on the driveway and then later on the porch.

"And don't forget your dragonflies."

I shivered again, despite the heat. "They aren't mine."

"They're your totem, Katie. They manifest whenever there's something you should pay attention to, like a metaphysical tap on the shoulder."

There had always been dragonflies around when I was a child, and I'd been drawn to depictions and representations of them like other little girls loved unicorns. But over time I'd seen them less and less. Until Savannah.

But that was just because of the warm climate. Right?

"When the opportunity for the Honeybee came along, I knew it was kismet," Lucy said. "I would finally have a chance to introduce you to your heritage." Her obvious joy would have made me smile if I hadn't still been so stunned. Then it was replaced by a rueful look. "I hadn't planned on springing it on you quite like this, though. Believe me, I wanted to ease you into it so you'd have a chance to get used to the idea. But then Mavis Templeton was murdered, and Ben's in danger. You needed to know now, even if you're not prepared to use any of your abilities yet. The spellbook club is meeting to see what we can do to help Ben, and I don't want to try to hide that from you."

Spellbook club indeed. I remembered the way they'd all looked at me, waiting to bring me into their . . . Oh, no, did they consider themselves some kind of coven? What would I say to them now? I couldn't get over how *normal* they all seemed, even little pink Mimsey. I shook my head and swallowed. Then I caught Lucy's amused look, and couldn't help but wonder whether she could read my mind.

Stop it.

Lucy rose, then bent slightly to kiss my forehead. "Being a witch is a good thing, sweetie. You'll see."

Ben returned from the office as she picked up our plates. She passed him on her way into the kitchen.

He had to know what she had just been telling me. How did he feel about the whole witch business?

"Ben," I said.

"Gotta go proof the newspaper ad for the grand opening," he said, lurching toward the door.

My eyes narrowed. He ducked his head and escaped.

I put my chin in my palm and listened to the rattle of dishes in the kitchen while I tried to assimilate Lucy's revelation. A witch. Bless her heart, she seemed to really believe it.

Hedgewitchery. I shook my head. *Oh, brother.*

Never mind that the word seemed to wrap around my soul like a cozy blanket.

Chapter 6

I stirred tart cherries into the dark chocolate batter and tasted the concoction. Delish. But it would be even better with a dash of cinnamon and a few more cherries. I measured out another cupful while my mind gnawed on what Lucy had told me about Mama.

My mother, Mary Jane Lightfoot, had thrown a fit when she learned of my plans to go into business with her big sister.

"You'll hate it in Savannah," she'd said on the phone.

"What are you talking about? I love it. The squares, the river, the history. Mama, I'll be able to really use my culinary training in a creative way. And I can have a garden all year-round. Even in the *winter*. How cool is that?" No mention of escaping a romance gone sour. No mention of Andrew at all. My mother had disliked him from the beginning and was not above throwing an I-told-you-so my way.

She'd sniffed. "It's muggy and hot and sticky. The bugs are awful. It smells funny. People are stuck-up. You'll have to get new clothes, do something with that hair of yours, and stop acting like such a tomboy." A pause, then, "Lucy will turn you . . . You'll turn into a whole different person."

Now, Mama was not exactly tactful on her best days, but this diatribe had surprised me. Normally the idea of my updating my wardrobe and fussing with my hair would have sent her over the moon with delight. But on the phone she'd sounded almost frightened at the prospect. I put it down to the decades she'd spent in Fillmore, Ohio, population 563. After all, she'd fought my decision to go to pastry school, and then she'd hated it when I moved to Akron. I was an only child, and Savannah would be the farthest I'd ever lived from my parents. But what did she expect me to do—move back to Fillmore?

Uh-uh. No way.

I'd countered in the gentlest tone I could muster. "Everyone I've met in Savannah is nice as pie. My clothes are fine. My hair is fine. And while I don't intend to turn into a whole new person, I sure hope some things are different. That's kind of the idea."

Well, after my one week in Savannah someone had killed Mavis Templeton, Ben was a murder suspect, and now my aunt had informed me I was a *witch*. Not exactly what I'd had in mind when I'd wished for something different.

Should I ask Mama about what Lucy had told me? As I dolloped batter into the rows of paper cupcake liners, I found myself shaking my head. If Lucy was simply unbalanced, then calling my mother wouldn't help a bit. And if Lucy was telling the truth . . .

Ow. That just made my brain hurt.

*   *   *

"You know, Mavis and I dated for a while back in high school." Ben's words cut through my thoughts.

I looked up from the notebook in front of me. It contained all the recipes Lucy and I had developed, and I was adding the cupcake recipe to a page toward the back. I had a feeling they'd be in high demand once the Honeybee opened. The warm scents of chocolate and cinnamon filled the air. Light classical music played at low volume through speakers mounted high in each corner of the room.

It took a moment for what he'd said to register. "You dated?"

"For almost a year, when we were juniors."

I whistled. "That's hard to believe. How did you stand it?"

He laughed. "She wasn't like she is . . . was . . . Well, anyway, she used to be a lot of fun—happy, lighthearted, almost silly at times. But she hardened over the years. Became bitter." His voice softened. "That bitterness sapped all her joy and left her a shell of the girl I knew, brittle with anger and disappointment."

"She was bitter, yes. But hardly brittle, Uncle Ben. That woman was made of oak, not balsawood."

Silence as I remembered how someone had snapped her neck as if it had been exactly that: balsawood. One glance at Ben and I knew he was thinking the same thing.

I cleared my throat, feeling awkward. "I'm glad she was happy once."

Knuckles rapped on the front window, making me jump. Steve Dawes peered through the slats in the blind, trying to see into the relative darkness.

"Darn him." I launched myself to my feet. "He just wants a story about what happened yesterday."

Ben rose and strode to the door. "Actually, Steve called me this morning. Wants to talk to me about the face of business here in the historic district. He's talking to Croft Barrow in the bookstore and Annette Lander, who owns the knitting shop next door. It's for his column."

His last words accompanied Dawes' entrance into the bakery. The reporter's teeth flashed as he said, "Yes. For a column about the changing and the not-so-changing aspects of this fair city."

He knew I'd suspected his motives.

Wincing inwardly, I said, "Come in, Mr. Dawes."

"Steve, please."

I nodded my agreement and muttered, "Steve it is."

Ben gestured toward a blue-and-chrome chair. "I bet we could talk you into one of the cupcakes Katie just took out of the oven."

The corners of Steve's eyes crinkled, and his lips parted to reveal those teeth again. "Is that what smells so great? Talk about savvy marketing."

My heart went *thumpa*. I scowled.

"Katie," Ben said, the word gentle but insistent.

"I suppose you'd like coffee with that," I grumped.

The smile never faltered. "If you insist. Cappuccino. Dry, please."

"Dry. Right."

As I moved to the espresso machine, he sat down

and pulled out a notebook. "Ben, tell me about your vision for this newfangled bakery in old Savannah. Are you going for tradition or pushing for progress?"

The screech of the espresso machine drowned out the rest of his question and my uncle's answer as well. I topped the cappuccino with dry foam, plopped a warm cupcake on a small plate and took both, along with a napkin, to Steve. Setting them in front of him, I met his eyes. He stopped talking.

We looked at each other for a few years before I tore my gaze away. Ben's expression held mild amusement.

Steve reached toward the notebook of recipes that sat on the table in front of him. Before he could open it, I snatched it out of his hand.

"Proprietary information. I'll let you get back to your interview."

I took the notebook behind the register and bent to search under the counter for the colored chalk we'd use to list menu items on the giant blackboard. The whole time, I was intensely aware of the two-inch strip of skin on the side of my hand where Steve's finger had rested for a nanosecond when I'd taken the notebook away.

There was no reason on earth for it to tingle like that. None.

After a few moments the two men began speaking again, in tones low enough for me to ignore with a little effort. Which I did, studiously concentrating on roughing out the menu design on a blank sheet of paper. Glancing back and forth at the colors of chalk in the box, I tried to imagine what they'd best represent on the board behind the register.

Coffee drinks in white.

Cookies in light blue.

Biscotti in yellow.

Muffins and sweet confections like the cherry-chocolate cupcakes in light pink. Or maybe—

"That was delicious."

I jumped and turned to find the columnist leaning one hip against the counter beside the register.

Thumpa.

"Um, thanks."

"I'm not here to make your uncle look bad."

"Thanks," I said again.

"In fact, I hope the Honeybee will be a big success."

"Th—" I bit my lip.

"Because then you'll be around for a while. And I'd like to get to know you better."

My brain shouted, *Too slick! Don't trust him*! But something considerably south of my brain couldn't have cared less.

"How much do you know about the haunted side of Savannah?" he asked.

"Not much," I managed to get out.

"Want to know more? Not the tourist traps, mind you. The real deal. I could show—"

"Yoo-hoo!" Mimsey Carmichael's distinctive Southern tones echoed from the kitchen, followed immediately by the lady herself. Today's color of choice was turquoise, from the beads around her neck to the surprising blush of blue-green on the toenails peeping out of her sandals. The only incongruity was a tiny blob of white on her shoulder.

"Lord love a duck, what have y'all been getting yourselves involved with? When Jaida told me what happened yesterday you could have knocked me over with a feather! Thank goodness Lucille called." When she saw Steve, her mouth snapped shut. Twinkling eyes moved rapidly between us as if we were batting a tennis ball back and forth. Finally they rested on me—and one closed in a conspiratorial wink.

I was sure he'd seen. Crawling under the counter seemed like a good idea, but there wasn't room. If I'd been a real witch I would have made myself disappear.

"Why, Mrs. Carmichael. What a nice surprise," Steve said.

Sheesh—did everyone here know everyone else?

Mimsey's responding titter was tight with nervousness, which surprised me. The older woman struck me as unflappable.

"Another of your book club meetings?" His eyebrows rose and fell a mere fraction.

Mimsey cut a sidelong look in my direction. "Oh, we're just being supportive friends," she said. "Lucille called and wanted us to stop by, you see."

Steve leaned forward.

"We're going to see what we can do about—"

I put my hand on her shoulder to stop her—and discovered the white blob on her shoulder was slightly sticky.

What the . . . bird poop? Really?

"Do you have any more questions for me?" Ben said.

"What?" Distracted from Mimsey's near revelation, Steve turned. "Oh. No, I don't think so."

My uncle opened the front door. "We sure do appreciate you including us in your column."

Steve took the hint, albeit with reluctance, if the look

on his face was any indication. "I'll check in with you later, okay, Katie?"

I nodded mutely, ignoring the grin on Mimsey's face, and reached for a napkin to wipe my hand.

She noticed and twisted to look down at her jacket. "Oh, dear. Heckle's usually so good when he's on my shoulder. I had no idea he'd gone and made a mess." Shrugging her jacket off, she said, "Heckle's my parrot, you see."

Her parrot. Of course.

Chapter 7

Lucy leaned forward on the poufy brocade sofa and clasped her hands in her lap. "I told Katie this morning."

Four sets of eyes lasered to where I perched on the arm beside her. I met their curious gazes one by one.

"She's still getting used to the idea, though."

"I bet," Jaida said. Her smile was rueful but kind, as if she really did understand how strange it would be to learn out of the blue that you're a witch. Or at least that a dear member of your family believes you possess magical powers.

Bianca said, "Of course you're still a little surprised, Katie. But you'll soon tap back into the heritage deep inside you."

"How do you know that?" I didn't mean to sound so snarky.

Lucy answered. "Because all of us except Bianca were lucky enough to bring our magic into adulthood with us, encouraged by our families."

Unruffled, Bianca nodded. "I became a witch as an adult."

I looked down at Lucy. "You said something before about Grandma."

Slowly, she nodded. "And her mother before her. You're a hereditary witch. It's in your blood—and not only on your mother's side. Your father's as well. He's quite powerful himself."

I remembered she'd mentioned something about him earlier. But now the idea of my father practicing magic shifted my perspective with an almost physical wrench. Dizziness swooped over me, and then I felt a visceral *click*, as if something had finally slid into place.

Mimsey threw up her hands, turquoise and silver flashing from the rings on her fingers. "All that will sort itself out. You can still help us while you come to terms with your magical abilities. We have to help your uncle. Lucille?"

I tamped down my roiling thoughts and the dozens of questions trying to surface, struggling to focus as my aunt jumped to her feet and began pacing back and forth between the sofa and the chair opposite it. The same determination from earlier that morning thrummed in her footsteps. "There has to be a way to use our abilities to help Ben."

Jaida cocked her head. "Another protection spell, specific to him, might be the first step."

Inclining her head slowly, Bianca said, "It wouldn't hurt, I suppose, but isn't that a bit like closing the proverbial barn door after the horse has bolted?"

"A protection spell could turn aside additional mayhem, or at least keep it from affecting him," Lucy said.

A sick feeling crept into my solar plexus. I stood. "I

do so hope you ladies won't take offense at what I'm about to say, but I feel I must."

"Go ahead," Jaida said.

"Ben needs concrete help."

No one said anything. Lucy stopped pacing.

"We need a solid, real-world game plan." I looked around at them. "You realize, of course, that finding out who really killed Mrs. Templeton is the only way we can help Ben. I don't suppose any of you has a working crystal ball. Though even that wouldn't hold up very well in court." I smiled brightly at my lame joke.

They exchanged looks.

For once Mimsey frowned. "Our magic isn't the kind where we wiggle our noses and make something disappear. Our talents are tools we can access in addition to our brainpower, our connections in the community, and a considerable amount of Southern charm to get at the truth about what happened to Mavis Templeton. There is no abracadabra cure-all to crime solving. If there were, believe me, every law enforcement agency in the world would be willing to use our skills."

I sat back down, thoroughly chastened.

Cookie said, "Mimsey's right, of course. So we do need that game plan you mentioned."

Once again all eyes were on me.

I considered. "Well, then, I suppose the first thing is to figure out who had a motive to kill Mrs. Templeton."

My aunt bobbed her head and went behind the register. She emerged with a pad of paper and a pen. "All right. Let's get started."

"Okay," I said. "We know she had the good sense to

date Uncle Ben back in high school. That she married—
just once?"

Mimsey nodded. "Garth Templeton. Made a fortune
in heavy equipment."

"No children."

"But she has a nephew," Bianca said. She put her
elbow on the sofa arm and propped her chin on her
hand. "Albert Hill. Just as charming as his aunt, but not
nearly as bright. I've met him a few times at society
functions. He's an acquaintance of a friend of mine."

So Bianca attended society functions. Interesting.

"He'll likely come into a pile of money from Mrs.
Templeton," Jaida said. "Depending on her will. Though
I suppose she could have left her fortune to a charity or
foundation or something."

"That seems unlikely." Lucy's tone was wry.

"Sounds like ol' Albert had a motive," I said. "I don't
suppose he looks like Uncle Ben, does he?"

Bianca shook her head. "Not so much. I can try to
find out more about him."

"Good idea. What else do we know about her?"

"Ben told me she liquidated most of her assets after
her husband's death rather than pay someone to manage them," Lucy said.

"I can dig around and find out more about that,"
Jaida offered. "Much, if not all, of that information will
be public record, and I know the system."

"Perfect," I said, feeling better now that a hazy plan
began to form.

"Well, I can tell you one thing she still owned,"
Mimsey chimed in. "That commercial property where
Jack Jenkins has his store."

"Where do I know that name from?" I asked.

"He's the president of the DBA," Lucy said. "But he couldn't come to the brunch yesterday. He called Ben this morning, apologized and welcomed him to the association."

"Did he say why he couldn't make it?"

"He has a little store that specializes in Civil War–era memorabilia. Real touristy, though in truth he's a bona fide expert. Takes part in the battle reenactments, all that stuff. He said he had to cover for a sick employee yesterday."

I tapped one finger on the tabletop, considering.

Mimsey got up and withdrew something from the bottom shelf of the bookcase. Unfolding it revealed a large map of Savannah, which she spread out on one of the tables. She stood considering it for a few moments, then looked up at us. "Girls, I'm going to see if I can't use one of those special talents I was telling Katie about to find someone who hated Mavis Templeton enough to kill her."

Cookie laughed, then caught herself. "Sorry, Mims. It just seems to me that a lot of people might fit that bill."

"Can't hurt to try. I'll run home and get my scrying crystal. Be back in about half an hour." She hurried to the kitchen, and we heard the door to the alley open and close.

"That'll give me time to run by the county clerk's office," Jaida said, and she went out the front door to Broughton Street.

"Scrying crystal?" I ventured.

Cookie smiled. "Mimsey's the best of us at divination, though it's always a tricky business, full of hint and innuendo to interpret. I can't do it at all."

Bianca began closing the blinds. "Lucy, do you have candles?"

"Back in the office," she said.

"I'll get them," Cookie said.

I was curious as the proverbial cat, but I reminded myself to be practical. "Where is Jack Jenkins' store?" I asked Lucy.

"Over on Bull Street. It's called Johnny Reb's."

Only a few blocks away. "I need some fresh air. Think I'll run over there and check it out." I fetched my tote bag and slung it over my shoulder.

"Do you think he'll be able to help?" Bianca asked.

I shrugged. "No idea. But since Mrs. Templeton was his landlord, he might know her a little better than some people. Like whatever Mimsey's cooking up"—I nodded my head toward the map—"it can't hurt to try."

In the open doorway, I turned back. "Er . . . don't start without me."

They exchanged glances; then Bianca said, "Don't worry. We won't."

Scrying crystal, indeed. If Lucy was "airy-fairy," what did that make her friends? A bunch of nuts, that's what.

Except . . .

As I strode under the ubiquitous Spanish moss that hung from the live oaks overhead, I couldn't help but think about what Lucy had said about my parents. About how familiar and comfortable her words were even as I scoffed. It would explain so much about my childhood and about the odd things that had happened to me my entire life if my parents truly did possess some kind of magical ability. Ability they had then passed on to me.

In other words, if I were a witch.

A *witch*.

My mind railed against the notion. There was no such thing as magic. Impossible.

Except . . . my heart knew magic *was* real.

It had always known. Now it felt as if Aunt Lucy had simply reminded me of that.

The door of Johnny Reb's was propped open to the warm spring air, and I reminded myself to concentrate on the task at hand. What kind of memorabilia might I find inside, and what kind of man made his living selling it? Lucy had said he was an expert, which coming from her probably meant more in the way of a tweed jacket with elbow patches than a gun-totin' fanatic who flew the Confederate flag from the antenna of his monster truck.

Jack Jenkins, of course, turned out to be neither.

I crossed the threshold and paused to get my bearings. Broad windows in front invited bright light into the small store. Dark wooden counters ran around the perimeter of the single room, with open shelves both above and below. They gleamed from frequent polishing, which explained the strong fragrance of orange oil. Items sprawled in seemingly random fashion, inviting customers to browse. Among worn flags, canteens, musical instruments and books, several display cases housed smaller items—tarnished bullets and cartridges, buttons and currency, coins and faded documents.

A tall man rose from his seat behind the counter near the door. "Welcome to Johnny Reb's." All the edges were worn off his gentle drawl, giving the impression of stately gentility in those few words. He wore jeans and a crisp, white oxford shirt open at the neck. A pale strip of skin around his hairline indicated that his brown hair had recently encountered a very precise barber.

"Thank you. May I look around a little?"

A slow, easy smile lit his sharp blue eyes. "Well, of course, darlin'. Look all you want and then some." His hand swept the air, encompassing the whole interior. "I've tracked down every one of these pieces personally. You won't find a bunch of cheap reproduction gewgaws here, don't you worry."

Mostly for show, I made my way around the periphery of the store. War memorabilia in general didn't appeal to me, though I could see how many of the items in Johnny Reb's brought the past tangibly into the present. But I imagined that many of them also represented grief and tragedy. How could they not?

The daylight didn't quite reach the back of the store, which made it harder to see the contents clearly. Absently, I fingered the worn leather cover of a book, then flipped it open to reveal the scrawled notes of a journal. As I leaned forward to take a look, something in my peripheral vision caught my eye.

Tucked under a shelf was a flat-topped wooden trunk reinforced with dark metal and wrapped with leather straps. Abandoning the journal, I knelt in front of the trunk. No price tag that I could see. That didn't bode well, but I couldn't help it: I had to have that trunk.

Returning to the counter, I asked how much he wanted for it. The response was higher than I liked, but manageable. "You have excellent taste. You should know it's been restored, so the straps are new, but the patina of that old wood is beyond lovely."

"It almost glows," I said in agreement. "Do you deliver?" I dipped into my bag for my wallet. No way would that big trunk fit in the Bug.

"Well, that depends. Are you a visitor to Savannah?" He licked his lips as if in anticipation of my answer.

"Recent transplant." I moved to the counter. "My aunt and uncle and I are opening the Honeybee Bakery."

"You must be Ben Eagel's niece, then! I'm so very pleased to make your acquaintance. My name is Jack Jenkins."

I shook his outstretched hand. "Katie Lightfoot."

"Well, well, well. Of course we can deliver the trunk—for a nominal fee, of course."

"Of course."

"Isn't that something. Ben's family come back to roost."

"Actually, he's my uncle by marriage. I grew up in Ohio."

Unfazed by this information, he went on. "So sorry I wasn't able to come to the extravaganza you threw for the Downtown Business Association." He leaned forward and lowered his voice. "It's so very difficult to get really good help anymore. My latest employee called in ill at the last moment, so naturally I was required to tend to my business and miss the meeting despite my role as president."

I found myself rather taken with Jenkins. "Well, I don't know that I'd call it an extravaganza, but we did feel it was a success. Until, of course, a woman was murdered out front."

His shoulders slumped, and his head swung slowly back and forth. "I could not believe it when I heard someone had done mortal violence to an elderly woman like that. Right downtown, too. Mavis Templeton might not have been the most popular citizen in Savannah, but no one deserves such a horrible end."

"It was pretty awful," I replied. "You knew her, then?"

"Oh, heavens, yes. We were both natives, you see, and despite our age difference it's very difficult not to encounter every soul who was born in this area over a lifetime of living here."

"Plus, she was in the DBA," I pointed out.

"Yes, of course. And she is . . . was my landlady."

I had wondered how I could bring that up, and now I didn't have to.

"Here at the store, of course. This building. I'd no more live in one of her apartments than I'd stab myself in the leg with a dull knife."

I blinked. His voice had remained even and flowed with the same mellifluous tones I'd quickly grown accustomed to, even lulled by, but his choice of words seemed a bit over the top. Then I realized he'd handed me a new piece of information.

"She rented apartments?"

For the first time, he hesitated. "I don't know that I should be talking about the dead like this."

Like what? But I kept my mouth shut and waited for him to fill the silence.

Finally he spoke. "Mrs. Templeton didn't rent out any of the apartments at the Peachtree Arms personally, you understand. She hired a manager to handle all the day-to-day for that"—he took a deep breath—"that place."

I forced a light laugh. "It doesn't sound like a terribly nice address."

"It's a cesspool of neglect." Another pause, then, "It's a shame no one forced her to maintain it properly."

"You couldn't do anything as the president of the DBA?"

Jenkins shrugged. "Our focus is the historic district. Mrs. Templeton's apartment building is in Midtown. Still, I spoke to her about it on two different occasions."

"What did she say?"

"My dear, she just out and out laughed at me."

I believed it.

Jenkins' eyes narrowed slightly, though his manner remained easygoing. "Ms. Lightfoot, you seem inordinately curious about Mrs. Templeton. Are you by any chance a student of the macabre?"

"Gosh, I don't think so. It's just the, um, proximity of her sudden death—" Now he had me talking funny. I cleared my throat. "Sorry if I've been rude."

"Not at all!" He beamed at me. "Death, gruesome occurrences, voodoo—this city has it all, and we do love to talk about it."

My smile in return felt a little weak.

"Now, allow me to show you what I mean." He

came out from behind the counter and went to one of the display cases. Opening it with a key he took from his pocket, he held a handful of yellowing papers out to me. "This is a murder pamphlet from 1860. It details a woman tavern owner who killed three husbands and seventeen of her patrons before she was caught and tried—and promptly put to death."

"Good grief," I said. "Murder pamphlet? So it's just a story?"

"Oh, no, my dear. People have been fascinated by the grisly details of true crimes for centuries. These sensational little pieces professed to contain those details, in addition to trial transcripts and often a confession from the murderer. They were sold on street corners, in taverns and all the other places you'd expect to find newspapers. Quite the moneymakers, I imagine."

Murder as big business. Delightful.

Chapter 8

Mimsey was chattering excitedly to Lucy in the reading area when I walked into the Honeybee. Jaida followed close behind me. Mimsey spied us and called, "Thank goodness you're back. Get that last blind, won't you, Bianca? I can't have any direct sunlight on the work surface. And, Cookie, could you please turn off the lights?"

I blinked as my pupils widened in the sudden dimness.

Reaching into her capacious purse, Mimsey removed a pink quartz sphere and rose to her feet. It was only five inches in diameter but looked heavy. "My shew stone. It's a scrying crystal."

Oh, dear. I'd been kidding earlier about the crystal ball, and this literally was one. No wonder she'd taken umbrage.

She removed a bronze stand studded with green stones and took them both to the table that had the map still spread on it. Then turning to me, she hefted the quartz and put it on the stand. "It would be better to do this after dark, but last night was a full moon, so the stone is fully charged. It should work fine in these circumstances."

Okay.

I began to approach, but Lucy waved me back. When she reached my side, she said, "I don't think you should be inside the circle yet."

Circle? "But you said I'm a witch."

"You don't fully believe it yet."

My lips pressed together.

"Do you?" When I didn't answer, she said, "This is all still so new. I don't blame you. But until you truly believe you are what you are—and that magic is possible—you can't take part in any spell work. Your disbelief would negate what we're trying to do."

"But—"

She held up her hand. "And even if you did believe, I haven't had a chance to give you any instruction or training. Honey, you're just not ready for spell work yet."

I swallowed my disappointment. "Can I at least watch?"

She hesitated, looked over at the expectant faces of the others, then said, "That should be all right." She turned back to me and held up a finger. "Pay attention. And keep an open mind."

I nodded, curious all over again. She led me to a table at the edge of the room. She joined the others, and I heard her explaining what she had told me. Jaida shot me a look of sympathy, and Bianca and Cookie smiled in my direction. Mimsey, on the other hand, looked utterly crestfallen, bless her heart.

I sat down and rested my elbows on the table as Lucy placed four black votive candles at equidistant points on tables surrounding the one with the map on it.

"East, South, West, and North," she called to me as she set each one on a small saucer.

From a tiny brown bottle, she added a drop of oil to each wick. Soon the welcome scent of cloves filled the air. The other women sat around the map, reserving an empty spot for her. Mimsey placed her stone ball in front of her, on top of the word *Savannah* on the map. Lucy went into the kitchen and returned with a bowl.

Looking over at me, she said, "Salt." Beginning at the eastern candle, she walked in a clockwise circle around the tables that held the candles, sprinkling salt on the floor and murmuring under her breath.

I sighed, wondering who'd get to clean up the mess. My guess? Me.

Inside the circle, Lucy lit one candle, then moved around the circle in the same direction lighting the other ones, again murmuring as each one came to life. She ended at the first candle, then joined the others at the table.

The women grasped hands. "We call upon the element of earth," they chanted together.

Mimsey closed her eyes and said. "We call upon the element of earth to reveal mortal hatred for Mavis Templeton."

They repeated this call-and-response four times before they all closed their eyes, except Mimsey, who opened hers. Utterly silent, she stared at the crystal with a slightly unfocused gaze, blinking slowly once or twice. Her shoulders moved with her breath, but everything else was stillness.

I became aware of pedestrians walking by outside, the voice of a trolley tour guide blaring down the block. Those noises faded and the sound of the refrigerator filled the silence, augmented by tiny grumbles from the drip coffeemaker.

But my eyes were glued to the spellbook club at work.

Then Mimsey's eyelids fluttered a few times, and she squeezed Lucy's and Jaida's hands. Her gaze intensified, her eyes widening. The concentration on her face increased until her whole being thrummed with it. A shiver ran down my back.

A loud *pop!* sounded from the map, and everyone's eyes flew open. Mimsey's head jerked back, and then she slumped forward. The women looked around at each other.

Lucy leaned toward Mimsey. "Hon, are you all right?"

The older woman inhaled deeply and nodded. "What the heck *was* that?"

All eyes turned to me.

"What?" I asked.

Jaida looked at the others. "Oh, my gosh. She's a catalyst. Did you know that, Lucy?"

My aunt shook her head, but looked pleased. They released hands, and after several moments Lucy got up again and thanked the element of earth and blew out the first candle. Walking counterclockwise this time, she thanked air and fire and water as she blew out the remaining candles. The smells of burning wax and smoking wicks filled my nose.

Mimsey sighed. With a tired, happy smile, she gestured me over.

"What's a catalyst?" I asked.

Lucy smiled. "It means you add extra . . . punch . . . to magical workings."

"Oh, now, I don't see how that can be. I was just sitting over there."

She patted me on the arm. "Don't worry, dear. Mimsey, why don't you explain the spell to Katie."

"That was a little spell I adapted from water scrying to use with my shew stone," Mimsey said. "Black is an earth color, and always helps me concentrate better, so that's why the votives are black. Besides, even pretty pink crystals are of the earth."

I nodded. Apparently magic adhered to a certain logic.

She continued. "And I think I found something." Grabbing my wrist, she pulled me to the map on the table. "It took a while—I think there are others who despised her, but nothing this strong. The crystal guided my attention to a single block on the map. It's a nexus of hatred," she breathed, emanating delight. "An absolute *nexus*."

With considerably more calm, Jaida met my eyes. "Other than the house her husband left Mavis on East Hull Street, I was able to track down only one other asset belonging to her."

"An apartment building in Midtown?" I non-guessed.

Jaida nodded and pointed to the spot on the map Mimsey had indicated. "In this block."

Wait a minute. That meant the crystal ball thingy had really . . . worked?

"The Peachtree Arms," I said slowly.

Mimsey's face fell. "How do you know that?"

"Mr. Jenkins told me."

Ben and Declan came in then, laden with take-out bags from Mrs. Wilkes' Boardinghouse.

"Provisions." Ben lifted his bag high in the air. "At last."

"Did you find out anything else at Johnny Reb's?" Lucy asked as they unloaded containers of fried chicken, biscuits, corn on the cob, macaroni and cheese, bacon grits and collard greens.

I looked at the spread and barely managed not to groan. Tomorrow. I would eat next to nothing tomorrow.

Gathering flatware and napkins, I said, "Jack Jenkins is Mr. Charm, isn't he? But other than calling the Peachtree Arms 'a cesspool of neglect' and saying he'd rather put a dull knife in his leg than live there, I got nothing. No address, no indication that her tenants hated her." I nodded toward Mimsey and Jaida. "These two did that." No mention of the particulars. Ben must know about their witchy antics, but I didn't know about Declan.

"Sounds like all y'all make a great team," Ben said.

We fell silent and dug into the food. I was ravenous, and only after a few mouthfuls realized I was attacking my food like an animal. Glancing up, I saw Declan watching me with an amused expression on his face.

He winked at me then, and turned his attention back to his plate. For some reason the wink didn't strike me as icky. That was weird. Winking *always* struck me as icky.

"Uncle Ben?"

"Mmmph?"

"Do you know anyone with a pickup? I bought an old trunk from Jack Jenkins, and he said he'd deliver that, but I also found a sofa I like—or I think I like—on Craigslist for a stupidly good price." Which might make up for what I paid for the trunk. "I need help moving it."

"I'll help you," Declan said. "I'm on days off." He cocked his head toward Ben. "If that's okay with you, of course."

I glanced at Uncle Ben, and he nodded his approval. Jaida's words about their near father-son relationship sounded in my mind. Good enough for me.

"Sure. When do you want to go?"

"I'm completely at your disposal," Declan said, a happy grin on his face. You'd have thought he'd won the lottery instead of having volunteered to schlep a sofa across town and into my house.

"How about two thirty?"

"I'll be here." He stood and laid his napkin on the table. "In the meantime I'll go get that floor polisher you wanted, Ben. Be back in a jif."

After he left we cleaned up—including thoroughly sweeping the salt from the floor—and the ladies took their leave. Mimsey was the last to go, and before she did she pulled me aside. Reaching into her ginormous bag, she pulled out three books and handed them to me.

"I picked these up when I ran home for my shew stone," she said.

One claimed to be a beginning spellbook. Another promised to tell me all I needed to know about various kinds of magic, and the third one boasted a familiar yellow and black cover: *Spellwork for Dummies*.

"Well, that's apropos," I said, indicating the last book.

"Now, honey, don't be discouraged. You'll learn very quickly, I'm sure. I'll see you soon." She hastened out.

I turned to my aunt and hefted the books. Ben had managed to disappear while my back was turned. Lucy smiled when she saw what Mimsey had given me.

"I think you'd better tell me a little more about your book club." I needed to know what I was getting into, and with whom. "You've been friends with these ladies for a long time?"

She gestured to the reading area, and we sank onto one of the sofas. I tucked my feet under me and waited.

"We are a coven of five, though we like to stick with calling ourselves a spellbook club. I've known Mimsey the longest. We found each other and began doing spell work together shortly after I moved to Savannah. She's taught me so much."

"She does seem a bit older than you are," I noted. Lucy was fifty-seven.

"Oh, heavens, yes. She'll be seventy-eight this year."

I gaped. "*Seventy-eight?* She doesn't look older than sixty."

Lucy smiled and shrugged.

It took me a moment to cotton on. "You mean she's magically made herself younger?"

"Well, I couldn't really say. There are spells for that, and Mimsey might dabble with them a bit. She's never shared that with me. She's not one to out-and-out glamour, though. She's too proud to try to fool anyone to that extent. Prefers to simply be considered well preserved."

I could feel the skepticism creep onto my face.

"However, practicing magic, at least the way she does it, can make you feel younger," Lucy said.

"Hmm. Okay, tell me more about her and the rest of them." The need to understand these women and what they did grew with every word Lucy spoke, like an itch I needed to scratch.

"Well, Mimsey's the oldest, but she still loves to work. She goes to her florist shop almost every day. As you may have guessed, her special interests are flower and color magic. You've seen the way she dresses?"

I nodded, not trusting myself to speak.

"Well, that's part of her color magic. I'll tell you more about that later. For now it's enough for you to know that there are a lot of different magical things in this world, and what you choose to work with depends on your personal influence, interests and focus."

Another nod.

"Mimsey's family comes from what is now Scotland. She learned about her gifts from her mother, and has passed her knowledge on to her daughter and her granddaughter."

I ignored the twinge of jealousy those words sparked.

"She's a happy person who wants other people to be happy, too. It's hard not to love someone like that."

Speaking of love. "Is she married?"

"To the same man for almost sixty years."

"Is he . . . ?"

Lucy shook her head. "No, he's not a witch. He's a Baptist."

I snorted.

"Then there's Bianca. Her marriage was not so happy. When her husband found out she had become a practicing Wiccan, he left in a big, nasty huff. She has a little girl, Colette, who's about five years old now, I think. Bianca has a small wine shop down on Factors Walk. Doesn't really make a living from it, but she doesn't have to. She is funded—seriously funded—for the rest of her life."

That explained the society functions. Money, old or new, would gain her entrance into those circles.

"From her family?" I asked.

"Stock market. Knows how to get in early on trends, then scoots out before the bubbles burst. Made her first millions during the nineties, investing in all sorts of technology. So she has the luxury a lot of single moms don't: She can still take care of her little girl full-time."

I wanted to ask whether Bianca was teaching magic to Colette.

Lucy took a sip of coffee. "She's a traditional witch, self-taught, and for a long time worked solitary, until she met Jaida in a professional capacity during her divorce. She focuses on straightforward spell work, especially in relation to the moon and sometimes other astrological influences. She's very good at it, too.

"Jaida is next in age. She lives and practices with another witch—and lawyer—who chooses not to be part of our spellbook club. His name is Gregory, and they've been together for more than ten years. She specializes in tarot magic and a bit of divination. Though Mimsey is still the best of us at the latter. Whenever Jaida works spells, either alone or with us, she uses tarot cards to augment her power."

I was confused. "But tarot isn't magic."

"Of course it is. Remember when I did your cards last time I was in Fillmore?"

"Sure. Mama about popped a vein when she walked in on us. You would have thought you were teaching me how to shoot heroin."

My aunt rolled her eyes. "She might have preferred that. Anyway, then there's Cookie. Our Ms. Rios is a young witch—both chronologically and she's somewhat new to the kind of witchcraft the rest of us practice. However, her magical roots go back to childhood. She's from Haiti and grew up with a father who was a voodoo priest. They moved here when she was nine years old. I don't know exactly what happened, but something prompted her to turn her back on the voodoo religion of her childhood and come to us through Bianca—who out of all of us knows her best."

"Is Cookie married?"

"Ha! Hardly. Cookie plays the field. She always has a boyfriend, but never for very long. Every few months she dates someone else, and then she gets out of the relationship. You'd think there would be a string of bitter, broken hearts in her wake, but she seems to stay friends with most of them." She laughed. "That girl has a *lot* of friends. And it's not just boyfriends—she does the same thing with jobs. Right now she's working for the Savannah College of Art and Design, but it's been almost three months, and I bet she'll move on to something else pretty soon."

And here I thought it was a big deal to change my job once.

The back door opened, and moments later Ben came around the corner. He stopped when he saw us.

I crooked a finger at him. "Why don't you join us?"

He looked at Lucy, and so did I. She smiled at her husband, a smile that emanated affection and tenderness in waves. Ben looked back at me and nodded. "Yeah. Okay." He strode over and sat on the sofa opposite us. "You two have certainly had your heads together today."

"And you've been making yourself conveniently scarce."

One side of his mouth quirked up. "Lucy said she was going to tell you about the witchy stuff."

"The witchy stuff. That makes it sound a bit less esoteric." I took a breath, forming the question I wasn't really sure I wanted the answer to. "Are you one?"

Lucy patted me on the knee.

Uncle Ben laughed. "No. I'm not a witch or a sorcerer or whatever you'd call it. I'm just a guy." He licked his lips. "Just a guy who fell head over heels in love with Lucy Sheffield and never found my balance again."

She rose and crossed to the other sofa. He took her hand, and she sat beside him. "Except that's not entirely accurate, because I only really feel grounded when I'm with her. That way you feel when you first fall in love? It's never faded in seventeen years." He looked down at my aunt. "This woman could turn orange or go bald or tell me she's from Mars, and I wouldn't care. So when she told me she was a witch, I figured, why not? I've seen some pretty strange things in my life, and more of them make me think magic is possible than not."

He raised his head. "You're a lot like your aunt, Katie. You glow like she does, from inside."

"Uh. Thanks." The lump in my throat made it hard to talk. Like anyone else, I'd dreamed of loving and being loved like that.

The image of Andrew's face filled my mind. Instead of anger or sadness, all I felt was regret for time lost. Marry him? What had I been thinking?

Chapter 9

Chalk in hand, I climbed the stepladder and began writing the additional menu items Lucy and I had selected for the grand opening on the blackboard behind the counter. We'd developed more than a hundred recipes and planned to add more to our repertoire over time. Each day we'd offer three kinds each of cookies, biscotti, muffins and scones, as well as brioche and loaves of the signature house bread made with the sourdough levain I'd developed in Akron and brought with me to Savannah. In addition, every day there would be a special treat: handmade marshmallows, salted caramels, cinnamon pretzels, truffles and seasonal goodies. Lucy was a whiz at decorating cakes, and she would be responsible for those orders as well as helping me with the regular daily baking.

Ideas for things I wanted to try whirled in my mind as I wrote.

Oatmeal lace cookies. Orange-filled chocolate sandwich cookies. Cranberry macaroons. Molasses biscotti, along with macadamia nut and white chocolate. My favorite peanut butter swirl brownies. Cheddar-sage scones and scones laced with lime zest and pickled sushi ginger.

Wait. That was too long to write. I needed a name for those.

Someone tried the front door, but I ignored the sound. Anyone who had business in here either had a key or knew to come around to the back door. A sharp knock sounded next. I ignored that, too.

Ginger-lime scones? Eh. Didn't quite capture the magic of biting into a mouthful of hot-sweet pickled ginger, all buttery and citrusy and . . . My stomach growled. How could that be after that huge meal from Mrs. Wilkes'?

The pounding on the door was too much. Ben came out of the kitchen, where he'd been installing the convection oven, wiping his hands on a towel. I climbed down and moved to the window. Cracked the blinds. He strode to the door and yanked it open.

"Can I help you?"

A tall but stooped man shouldered my uncle aside to enter the bakery. Ben grabbed his arm before he could get very far. "Excuse me—"

"Take your hands off me, or I'll have you arrested for assault!" Spittle flew from his wormlike lips.

I cringed.

Slowly Ben's hand lowered, and his eyes narrowed. I moved to his side, feeling oddly protective. This guy set off all my alarm bells, and not just because red anger infused his doughy face and made his bald pate glow. He was furious about something, but his anger threw off sparks of danger. I sensed violence roiling just under the surface.

He stomped just far enough past Ben to whirl around and face us. Ben and I didn't take our eyes off him, and neither of us spoke. I was grateful for the open door behind us. I didn't know who this nutcase was, but having an exit handy seemed like a good idea.

"So you're the one who killed my aunt." He spit the words out.

Ben flinched. The color drained from his face.

Enough. I stepped forward. "That's a ridiculous accusation. Who told you that lie?"

He leaned over me. "I know people. Police people. People who know when people are under investigation. And they say this man"—he pointed a shaking finger at Ben—"this man killed my dear aunt Mavis."

Dear aunt Mavis, my hat.

I shuddered as he moved even closer. His lips were shapeless and wet, his brown eyes strangely feminine, his face a map of broken capillaries. "And I'm going to make him pay."

Rank halitosis wafted over me, laced with the strong scent of bourbon.

He pointed at Ben again. "I'm going to make you all pay for this travesty. You. Your wife. Your niece. The DBA. Your business. I'll sue you all. Once my lawyers have finished with you, you'll wish you were in prison."

"Why?" I couldn't help asking. "The police haven't charged Ben with any crime. What can you hope to gain?"

His nostrils flared. "Restitution! You have to *pay*." He moved toward me, and I dodged to my left to avoid him. Without another word, he stalked out to the sidewalk, not bothering to close the door behind him.

I took a deep breath and turned to Ben. "Whew! So that's Albert Hill. I've got to say, that family is just chock-full of charmers."

But my uncle looked worried. "If he goes through with that threat he could ruin us."

"But he can't win—especially if the police don't even charge you."

He shook his head. "It doesn't matter. Fighting a lawsuit like that would decimate our savings, ruin the bakery, and we'd have to default on our loans. And if he hit us on multiple levels like he said, it wouldn't even take very long."

Dear Albert had also threatened to sue me personally.

Why the heck had we decided against doing another protection spell?

Lucy darkened the doorway, at least as much as a five-foot-tall woman can. Her skirt swirled around her ankles as she came in, and then she stopped dead in her tracks.

"What happened?" she cried.

Ben took three steps and opened his arms, but she pushed him away. "Tell me."

"Mavis Templeton's nephew just paid us a visit. Albert Hill. He said he's going to sue us."

"But . . . why?"

"He says he's seeking restitution for his aunt's death."

"It's not like he needs money," Lucy said. "He's going to inherit millions."

"I have a feeling that 'enough money' is not a phrase that's in his lexicon," I said.

Lucy shuddered. "We have to smudge the Honeybee and rid it of this horrid energy. Right now."

Sounded good to me. I, too, could feel Albert's threat hanging in the air like poison.

Declan drove with easy skill, negotiating the heavy afternoon traffic, dodging a tour trolley, and turning left on Whitney. The woman I'd talked to on the phone had given me directions, and now I read them off to him. The paper shook in my hand, which was still trembling slightly after the nasty encounter with Albert Hill.

"Got it," he said.

"So you know the neighborhood?"

"Of course. Savannah isn't all that big, you know. And firemen had better know where we're going without some GPS babe telling us."

"Right." I said, watching him from the passenger seat.

Warm air winged in through the open windows of the king cab, carrying the scent of newly mown grass. It was a huge truck, with big tires, yet he didn't seem like a guy who worried about the size of his . . . truck. Dark curls cut short enough to adhere to fire service regulations softened the edges of his broad, chiseled face. For a brief moment his blue eyes cut my way, and I was startled by how bright they were. The realization that I'd never seen him outside of the bakery slid into my consciousness as his lips turned up an infinitesimal amount. And darn if that didn't show off the dimple in his cheek.

Quickly looking out the window, I said, "Declan's an Irish name, right?"

"Declan McCarthy, displaced Irishman, at your service, lassie." The soft round vowels and the relaxed tempo of his words foiled his game attempt to pull off the lilt of Eire.

"Not first generation, I take it."

He laughed. "Gosh, how could you tell? No, I was born in Pooler, then went away to Florida State University. After college I tried living in Boston, in eastern Illinois, even down in Texas for a summer, but this area is home, even though all my people are gone now. Been back in Savannah for almost ten years."

"Your people are all gone?" Nosy me couldn't help asking.

"Oh, they're not gone gone, just gone from around here. My mother remarried after my dad died, and now she lives in Boston—which is one reason I moved there for a while. My sisters—two married, one divorced, one single—are scattered all over."

"You have four sisters? No brothers?"

"Nope, I'm the only boy, and smack-dab in the middle of them all. But I think I turned out reasonably well despite almost drowning in estrogen growing up. At least I can cook."

He caught my sidelong look and grinned. "You'll have to let me make you dinner sometime. Prove my worth."

I had to admit the idea was pretty appealing. This guy was easy to be around, and practically family. Not that I thought of him as a brother, exactly.

"You said you and Uncle Ben have been friends since you were a rookie."

"We have."

I waited, but he didn't offer any additional information. Declan was still more or less a stranger to me, and even a rube from Ohio like me knew when it was better to shut up.

We pulled into the driveway of a ranch-style home in a neighborhood full of the same. No mansions here. No antebellum anything, but plenty of treeless yards, the bright toys scattered in many of them indicating lots of new families.

A skinny, sharp-featured woman about my age opened the door as we came up the walk and ushered us quickly inside. "No need to cool the outdoors," she said, her voice abrupt and nasal, as she shut the door behind us.

The air-conditioning was going great guns indeed, and I shivered immediately. The sofa was worth the sudden temperature drop, though. It was, in fact, a seven-foot-long fainting couch, the swooping curve of the back sloping from a high arm on one side to a next-to-nothing one at the other end. And best of all? It was a deep, dark purple.

"This weird old thing was still in the house when we bought it. I'll take seventy-five for it if you'll just get it out of here."

It was utterly charming. I loved it. I opened my mouth to speak.

Declan stepped forward. "How about fifty?"

The woman hesitated, then waved her hand. "Whatever. Can you take it right now? Take that lamp, too, if you want it." It was an old-fashioned brass affair with a purple fringed shade that matched the sofa.

"You bet!" I pressed a bill into her hand. Declan took the larger end of the sofa, and together we managed to wrangle it out of the house and into the truck. The woman fretted the whole time the door was open, what with all that frigid air wafting into the humid atmosphere, but I don't know how we could have gotten the sofa outside otherwise. Maybe Lucy had a nice vanishing trick, but Declan and I had to do it the old-fashioned way.

I never did learn the woman's name.

"We're still in Midtown, aren't we?" I asked as we drove away.

"Almost to Southside."

Reaching into my bag, I pulled out a piece of paper with the address Jaida had provided for the Peachtree Arms and recited it to Declan.

"Is that Mrs. Templeton's apartment building?"

"It is. Are we anywhere close? Would it be a bother to swing by and take a look?"

He took a quick right. "No bother at all. It's not far."

In fact it was less than five blocks away. Declan pulled into the cracked asphalt parking lot of a monkey-poop-brown building. I counted eight doors on each of five floors, leading to ratty concrete pads on the ground floor and rickety-looking balconies higher up. The siding was peeling away in places, and at the far end an iron railing dangled from a fifth-floor balcony, directly over the walkway below.

"That looks dangerous," I said, pointing out the truck window.

Declan looked grim. "No kidding." He opened the console between us, extracted a notebook and scribbled something in it.

"Are you going to report it?"

"You bet I am. Want to go inside?"

I most certainly did not. Jack Jenkins' assessment of this place as a cesspool of neglect had been mild in comparison to the reality. The place frankly creeped me out, even though I was safe and sound on the outside. My imagination flinched at the possibilities of what it might be like inside.

"Sure, let's take a look," I said, donning false bravado like a trench coat against the elements.

Declan looked his skepticism at me but didn't protest. Instead he got out and came around to my door, handing me down to the ground from the running board like I was a petticoated lady just arrived on a stagecoach.

Know what? I kind of liked it. Andrew had been a getcher-own-door kind of guy.

Good riddance.

As we neared the building, a big SUV screeched around the corner. I yanked on Declan's arm, pulling us both to the side of the building and out of the path of the speeding Suburban.

The driver didn't even notice us, or if he did he didn't deign to look at us. But I recognized the shiny head, shapeless lips and bitter parentheses carved around his mouth.

"Albert Hill," I breathed. Shaken, I leaned against the brick facade. "Twice in one day. It's a good thing we didn't run into him inside."

"Why?"

"Ben didn't tell you? That's Mrs. Templeton's nephew. He's threatening to sue Ben, the bakery, Lucy, me, the DBA and maybe God himself."

"Pffft. That's ridiculous," he said.

I could only hope he was right.

We walked around the corner and found a door leading into a central hallway in the middle of the end wall. I held both hands up to the glass pane that made up the top half, on either side of my face to try to cut the glare from the sun. But even then the glass was too dirty to see through.

Taking a deep breath, I yanked on the handle and the door swung open with a creak worthy of a horror movie. Declan caught the door and held it, entering right behind me. We squinted in the darkness until our eyes adjusted.

The eight-by-five arrangement seemed to be reflected on both sides of the building. So unless there was a secret penthouse, this ramshackle edifice contained eighty miserable dwellings.

No wonder Mimsey had identified it as a nexus of hatred toward Mrs. Templeton. I would have guessed that after one glance.

Never mind that Mimsey had never seen the place.

Pushing the thought away, I blinked in the low-wattage light and peered down the hallway. Mustard-colored carpet crawled the length of it, stained in the middle and pulling away from the edges in places. I met Declan's eyes, their bright color dimmed in the perpetual twilight of this place, and saw pity in them for the people who lived here.

He took my hand. Warm and dry, his hand completely enveloped mine. I instantly felt better.

"Let's see if we can find the manager," he said.

I nodded my agreement. As we continued down the hallway I had the sense of being in a fun house or a Tim Burton film. Declan paused in front of a door. MANAGER was written in black Magic Marker on a piece of cardboard and taped slightly above my eye level. As if of its own volition, my fist rose and knocked on the hollow wood below the sign.

We waited. No sound came from inside.

"He's not in. Don't know when he'll be back, neither." A stooped black man with a puff of bone white hair stood in the doorway across the hall.

"The manager?"

His confirming nod was elaborate, slightly sarcastic. "Yes, the manager. Who else's gonna put a sign on their door that says *Manager*?"

"What's his name?" Declan asked.

"Ridge is his name. Ethan Ridge. He's probably off seein' his parole officer."

My ears perked up. "Is that so?"

"Oh, he's all right. Just got himself in some trouble back a ways, is all. We got a couple openings here if you're looking for a place, I can tell you that, but I can't show you none of them."

I tried to nonchalantly see into the apartment behind our font of knowledge. Unfortunately, nonchalance was not my strong suit. He noticed.

So I stuck out my hand. "I'm Katie Lightfoot."

He took it. "Well, I'm pleased to meet you, Katie Lightfoot. And is this Mr. Lightfoot?"

I blushed so hard my follicles tingled. What was wrong with me? It was an innocent assumption.

"Oh! Lookie there. She's turning the same color as her hair, almost!" He grinned at Declan. "You two living in sin, then? That it? Well, that's no never mind to me. Can't judge. I let folks be. My name's James Sparr."

"Nice to meet you, James. We'll come back later. Thank you." I turned and strode outside, determined to shake off my embarrassment.

By the time Declan opened the passenger door for me I was thinking about Albert Hill again. Had he stopped by to see Ethan Ridge and left in a huff because the manager wasn't there?

Or had something else deepened Albert's bad mood?

Chapter 10

Declan and I wrangled the sofa through the front door and set it against the wall opposite the entry. The contrast of dark purple against the peach walls translated to a kind of cheerful elegance. And the old trunk would make a perfect coffee table.

He folded his arms and gave one decisive nod. "Looks good." His gaze took in the rest of the living room: plank floors, built-in bookcases, the hall leading down to my bedroom, the stairs to the open loft above, French doors that opened to the backyard. "This is a great little place."

"As soon as I saw it I knew it was right for me." I opened the back door.

Mungo barreled in and right up to Declan. He stooped and picked up the dog. "Who's this?" Mungo wiggled and licked his chin.

"That's Mungo the Magnificent."

Declan laughed. "He is magnificent. Did you bring him from Akron?"

"Nope. He showed up when I arrived. My neighbor says he doesn't belong to anyone around here."

"It's nice that you took him in."

"Oh, I don't know . . ." I trailed off.

Those blue eyes met mine. "No tags? Have you checked the paper for lost dogs? Or taken him to check for a microchip?"

Silent, I shook my head. I should have done all those things, but I realized I didn't really want to discover that the terrier had another owner. No matter what I'd been telling myself, I wanted to keep him.

He handed Mungo to me, and the little guy immediately snuggled up under my chin. I could feel his heart beating against my chest.

"Maybe I'll take him to the vet tomorrow and have him scanned."

Declan grinned. "Sure you will." He peered out the open door. "Mind if I check out your yard?"

"Of course not." I followed him out. "I'm planning a garden along that back fence. See the narrow stream that runs across the corner of the property? In the opposite corner I'd like a little gazebo, maybe with a ceiling fan for hot evenings. In between I want to have a landscape-type bed full of all kinds of herbs, with an eye for beauty as well as utility. Same with the vegetable garden that'll go in after the herb garden is done."

"Like a French potager," Declan said. "Brilliant."

"You're a gardener!"

"I have a little vegetable patch. Tomatoes, melons, cucumbers, that kind of stuff. But my mother's an avid gardener. I learned a lot from her."

Mungo wiggled. I set him down and bent over to say, "I'll be home again in a little bit, okay?"

Yip.

Declan's laugh followed me through the house as we returned to the front door. "You are so not getting rid of that puppy."

"Hush," I said, and locked the door behind us. "Thanks for the help with the sofa. I really do appreciate it."

"No problem." He opened the passenger door and put his hand on my elbow as I hoisted myself in from the running board. "In fact, let me know if you need any help with those gardens you have planned. I happen to be pretty good with a rototiller."

"Oh, you sweet-talker, you." Oddly content, I buckled my seat belt.

The feeling lasted all the way back to the Honeybee but vanished the instant I stepped down from Declan's truck and saw Steve Dawes standing in the doorway. He shot a quick glare at my companion and stalked away down the sidewalk.

A pang of guilt stabbed through me. "Steve," I called.

He either didn't hear or was ignoring me. Well, what did I care? And why should I feel at all defensive just because these two men seemed to have a problem with each other?

I whirled to look at Declan, but he wouldn't meet my eyes. Slamming the truck door, he stepped past me toward the still-open door of the bakery. "Hey. What the heck is the deal with you two?" I demanded.

He paused, but didn't turn around. "It's a long

story." His words were so low I had to strain to hear them.

I softened my tone. "Will you tell me sometime?"

A long pause, then "Maybe." And he went inside.

I followed slowly behind him.

After he'd left I rested my chin on my hand and blinked across the table at my uncle. "Declan seems nice. Did you two work together much?" Leading the witness, trying not to be too obvious.

"We've been through a lot together. Life-and-death stuff."

I sat up and leaned forward in my chair. "Sounds heavy."

"Unfortunately, firefighting is too often about tragedy. Early in his career, we almost lost Declan. We did lose another man."

My fingers crept to my mouth. "Oh, no."

"It was right before I became chief. I was still a commander and Deck was a wet-behind-the-ears rookie. Smart, though. Took his training seriously, did things by the book. That's important because that's how you stay alive in that business. The rules are there to keep you safe."

He stood and shoved his hands in his pockets. Gazing out the window as if the past lay on the other side of the glass, he continued. "A multilevel office complex was on fire. Dispatch sent us out as soon as they got the call, but the flames had already spread to several parts of the building. Deck and another rookie went in with the hose line."

Ben paused, remembering. "One of the most important things they teach at the academy is that you never let go of the hose. It's your lifeline. Between smoke and fire, it's easy to get disoriented. Sometimes the hose is the only way you can find your way back out. Well, the other rookie broke that rule. When the rescue team went in they found Deck right by the hose line. His air bottle was empty, and he was unconscious. The rescue team dragged him outside to the paramedics and went back in for the other rookie. He'd run out of air, too, only he'd removed his mask." He looked down at the floor and gave a slight shake of his head. "Died of smoke inhalation."

My uncle turned away from the window and sat down again. "That other kid was Declan's best friend; they'd gone to college together, went through training at the same time, even shared an apartment."

I closed my eyes, the scenario playing out in vivid detail in my imagination. I saw a younger Declan, frightened and left alone, wanting to help his friend but knowing better than to go after him.

"It must have been devastating," I said.

"He wanted to quit. But Deck's good at his job, and despite what happened that day, he truly loves it. I talked him into staying. It's been nearly a decade, and he's become one of the best men I've ever known in the fire service."

He took a deep breath and stood. "Enough sad talk. I'd better go hook up your fancy convection oven so you can give it a test drive before the big day."

Bianca called as I was getting ready to go home. "I asked around about Albert Hill. The responses I got were wildly inconsistent."

"How so?" I asked.

"Well, people seem to either love him or hate him. According to two society matrons I spoke with, he's the bee's knees. Helpful, generous to a fault with both time and money, an unfortunate, lonely man who needs a good woman to take care of him."

"Oh, brother."

She laughed. "These dears had an almost maternal attitude toward him, as if he were a favored son."

"Albert stopped in to the Honeybee this afternoon. He's just awful, Bianca. Mean, spiteful, and I'm pretty sure he was drunk. It's possible he's grieving the loss of a close family member, but I don't think so. He seemed more angry than sad, accusing Uncle Ben of killing Mrs. Templeton and threatening to sue anyone remotely involved."

"Hmm. Well, that fits more with what I heard from two other friends. Hill loves to take people to court—in fact, one guy called it his hobby. He does not, however, appear to be interested in working at any actual job. His aunt gave him an allowance. They also said he was cheap, greedy and had stepped on the other side of the law a couple of times to make a few extra bucks."

I digested this. "Albert sounds like a sociopath. Someone who can manipulate people when he wants to but who doesn't really care about anyone."

"That," Bianca said, "is exactly what I thought. Do you have any other assignments for me, Chief Investigator Lightfoot?"

"Ha, ha. Not at the moment."

"Seriously, let me know if you think of any way I can help."

"I will. And thank you."

Minutes after I arrived home, a white delivery van pulled into the driveway behind my car. Two teenaged boys jumped out, unloaded my new-to-me trunk and deposited it in front of the purple fainting couch. Though I'd bought it on impulse, it made an attractive coffee table and would serve as much-needed storage in my tiny dwelling.

Speaking of impulse, I didn't even know what it looked like inside. Unbuckling the leather straps, I flipped the catch and lifted the lid. The inside was polished wood and smelled of fresh varnish. I ran my hand over it, relishing the smooth texture before lowering the lid.

Something caught my eye, and I opened it again. Strapped to the inside of the flat trunk lid was a knife.

My first instinct was to slam the trunk shut. Knives of any kind gave me the creeps unless they were whacking food into pieces on a cutting board. This one looked worn and old. I carefully loosened the band that held the weapon snug against the wood and removed it from the tattered brown leather sheath. The dull metal barely reflected the light, and tiny pits dotted the one-sided cutting edge. The blade was a good ten inches long, quite wide, maybe three inches, and separated from the handle by a brass hand guard. The end curved into a wicked point.

I was holding an old bowie knife. I knew this because Daddy had one, only his was newer, with a shiny blade and a polished wooden handle. He used it for . . . What did he use it for? He didn't hunt. He didn't whittle—heck, you wouldn't use a knife like that to whittle, anyway. But I could clearly picture it in his hands. I'd been quite young, no older than seven or eight. No memories of the knife surfaced that were later than that.

This one looked old enough to be from the Civil War. That would make sense, considering how old the trunk was, except the trunk had been refurbished. Baffled, I set the knife on the top shelf of the bookcase, where I didn't have to look at it. It obviously wasn't part of the deal when I'd purchased the trunk that morning. Tomorrow I'd return it to Johnny Reb's.

Still sated from the big meal earlier, I poured a tumbler half full of chilled Chablis and, inspired by Declan's offer to rototill, went out to the backyard. Mungo trotted along as I paced off the edges of each garden bed and imagined how they'd look once planted. Valerian and fuzzy mullein would tower among frothy dill and fennel fronds. Lower, the delicate blue shooting stars of borage flowers would mingle with pink chive blossoms and variegated lemon thyme. Purple varieties of sage and basil would look stunning against the gray-green spikes of lavender and dark green rosemary topiaries.

Which reminded me of the rosemary Lucy had planted by my front steps. She'd insisted that I leave it there, and now I suspected there was some magical reason. Back inside, I flipped through the books Mimsey had given me until I found an entry for rosemary. It had all kinds of magical uses, from improving memory and concentration to purification and protection. Planting rosemary by the front door was supposed to protect the inhabitants from evil, as well as asserting the strength of the woman who lived there.

Well, wouldn't you know.

Perhaps it was irrational, but the knowledge that Lucy had intended the rosemary to protect me actually made me feel safer.

Of course, that didn't stop me from jumping when the doorbell rang. Mungo didn't bark, though; he just looked at me with expectant eyes.

"Some watchdog you are," I said. I could have sworn he grinned at me.

Peering through the single pane of glass high in the door, I saw Margie Coopersmith standing on the front porch, baby on hip.

I swung the door open, and she handed me a potted geranium. "Hi, Katie! Thought maybe you'd like a bit of green on your kitchen windowsill."

"First the cookies and now this? Margie, you're spoiling me."

A smile split her face. "I'm afraid I'm re-gifting. Margie Brown Thumb, that's me. I'd kill it within a week. Figured it would be a good excuse to come over and see your new sofa, though. I saw you and that yummy guy unloading it this afternoon." She lingered over the word *yummy*.

"Well, come on in and try it out." I stepped back.

She entered the living room and made a beeline for the couch. "This is so unique. Elegant, like it came from a palace or a bordello or something." She sat and gently bounced up and down. The baby laughed in her arms. "Comfy, too."

"Bordello?" I cocked my head to the side. "Yeah, I can see that. Can I get you a glass of wine? I'm afraid I don't have any stemware yet." Casually, I gathered Mimsey's spellbooks off the floor and laid them flat on the bookshelf, spines to the wall.

Leaning back against the tall end of the couch, Margie sighed. "I would dearly love some wine, let me tell you. Those kids have been running me ragged all day. But I'd better not."

"The JJs? Where are they now?"

"Playdate, *finally*. At my sister's. She'll bring them back pretty soon, but in the meantime little Bart and I are available for visiting. If you have the time, of course. Or did I catch you in the middle of something?"

I went into the kitchen and opened the fridge, calling over my shoulder, "I was just out back, dreaming of the garden I want to plant. How about some iced tea?"

"Tea would be great. A garden! Well, I'm downright jealous. I swear, I can even kill kudzu."

Back in the living room I handed her the tea and settled myself at the other end of the sofa. "I know you're exaggerating."

"Not a whit! Now tell me, was the man who helped you with the sofa your boyfriend, by any chance?"

"No boyfriends for me, not for a while at least."

She grimaced. "Bad breakup?"

I nodded but didn't explain about Andrew. "Declan is a friend of my aunt and uncle's. He used to work with Ben when he was fire chief."

"Oooh, a fireman. Well, he's a cutie, even if you are on hiatus from the male gender."

I couldn't argue with that. "What does your husband do?"

"He's a long-haul truck driver, so he's gone a lot."

"Does it get lonely?"

"Honey, I'm so busy I don't have time to get lonely. Besides, now you're here. I can't tell you how nice it is to have someone friendly living next door."

Margie told me bits and pieces about the neighborhood and the people who lived in it. She wanted to know more about Lucy and Ben and the bakery, so I filled her in on how everything had come about and how I'd come to live in Savannah. She was funny and smart and seemed genuinely interested in just about everything. She put Bart down on the floor, and he contentedly inched around on the hardwood for a while. Mungo sat at my feet and watched him. As we reached the dregs of wine and tea, I found myself telling Margie about Mrs. Templeton's murder in front of the Honeybee.

"Oh, I heard about that on the news. Had no idea it was so close to you. You actually saw her?"

I grimaced as I remembered. "From several feet away, but yes. It was pretty awful. And now it seems the police are running around in circles." I couldn't bring myself to say my uncle was a murder suspect. As much as I liked Margie, I didn't know her well enough to share that information. "Apparently Mavis Templeton had quite a few enemies."

She nodded. "I've heard stories. She was a bad one to cross."

"Really?"

"Oh, yes. In fact, a friend of my husband's lost his job because of her."

A little shiver ran across my shoulders despite the April heat, but I kept my voice casual. "Good heavens. What happened?"

"Well, let's see here. I don't know Frank very well, but I do know he's a carpenter by trade. Specialty stuff. Craftsman, you know?"

I nodded.

"I've only met his wife once, but she's a sweet little thing, a real Georgia peach, so to speak. They have a little girl who's just cute as the dickens. Anyway, Frank did some job for Mavis Templeton, but something he did made her mad as a wet hen."

"What kind of job?"

"No idea. Redding—that's my husband—told me about it. In fact, I haven't seen Frank since it happened. All I know is Redding said Frank is a real hard worker and very skilled. But whatever happened, Mavis Templeton got him fired from his job."

"That's terrible."

"Oh, that's not the half of it. She also got him blackballed from working for other companies. I guess he's tried to start up his own business, working for himself, you know? But that didn't work out so well, either. He blamed her for that, too. Redding said he's been getting by on odd jobs for the last eight months or so."

Margie's story made me feel a little sick. I couldn't help but remember how Mrs. Templeton had threatened the Honeybee. No wonder Detective Quinn was willing to entertain the idea that his old friend Ben Eagel might actually have killed her.

My neighbor glanced at her watch. "Oh, Lord. I'd better get going. The JJs are due back any minute, and my sister will have a hissy fit if she has to wait. Thanks for the tea." She scooped Bart up off the floor and dangled him high in the air. He shrieked with laughter. Then she settled him back in the familiar curve of her hip.

"You're welcome. Thanks for the company. I've been pretty caught up in getting the bakery open. It was nice to chat for a while."

"Well, we'll do it again real soon, okay?"

"Sounds good." I walked her to the door. "Say, do you know Frank's last name?"

"It's Pullman. Frank Pullman."

"Thanks for the geranium. I'll try not to kill it." Fat chance. I couldn't kill it if I tried.

She laughed. "Better you than me."

I turned back from the closed door to find that Mungo had moved into the kitchen. He sat by the stove, an expectant look on his face.

"Ready for dinner?"

He voted in the affirmative with one sharp bark. I replaced his stale kibble with fresh. He sniffed it, and his brown eyes conveyed deep disappointment. He went back to the stove and sat down.

I was planning on a light salad for supper, and omnivore or not, I didn't think Mungo would get very excited about a bowl full of greens. "I brought home some leftover mac and cheese and a piece of fried chicken. Could I interest you in that?"

Another yip of approval.

I made my salad and dished up his dinner, only half-way paying attention. Frank Pullman sounded like yet another good candidate for murder suspect. But I knew only what Margie told me Redding had told her. Too much like a game of telephone for my comfort.

I needed to talk to Mr. Pullman myself.

Chapter 11

I kept thinking about that knife sitting on the bookshelf. And about Daddy's bowie knife. I should simply call him and ask about it. I mean, it was no big deal, right? But other than giving them a quick safe-arrival call, I hadn't talked with Mama and Daddy since I'd gotten to Savannah. After Lucy's revelation about our family, I was confused and angry. What was I supposed to say to them? Ask them why they didn't tell me I was a witch? Sarcastically thank them for letting me feel like an outsider my whole life?

No, I wasn't ready to start a conversation like that. Not yet.

So I called Lucy instead.

"Do you remember Daddy's bowie knife?"

After a moment she said, "I do."

"What did he use it for? I can't seem to remember."

This time the silence went on a lot longer. Then, "It was his athame. It's a knife used in magic. Sort of a combination wand and sword. We use it in rituals and spell work, to cast circles, and some use it to project power. Usually they're black and sharp on both sides, but your father always liked to be a little different."

His athame.

Of course.

Not that I'd known the name for it then, but I'd seen him use it. I swallowed, not sure what to say. More evidence that I really was a bona fide witch.

"Katie? You okay?"

I cleared my throat. "Tell me more about Mama and Daddy."

"Perhaps they should do that."

"They should have done it already, but they didn't. Now I don't trust them to tell me the truth."

"Your parents love you very much, you know."

"I know," I grumbled. "But still."

My aunt took a deep breath. "Your mother was always a little reluctant to use her abilities after what happened between your grandmother and old Luke Godry. That's who happened upon her casting the fertility spell I told you about. Mary Jane didn't want to be labeled and whispered about in little Fillmore, but she didn't completely turn her back on witchcraft until she and Skylar had you."

"You're saying it was my fault?"

"No. I'm saying that two hereditary witches had one powerful little offspring. Mary Jane was leery about practicing magic in that small town already, but when she realized what could happen to you if people found out what you were, she convinced Skylar to hide the truth from you."

"And he agreed?" A part of me listened to all this with the full knowledge that having a conversation about my magical heritage was ridiculous, if not altogether insane. But a bigger part totally believed and wanted to yell in frustration at what my parents had done to me.

"He was never as afraid as your mother, but he loved her very much, and she was downright terrified for you. He told me once that he knew you would discover your abilities in time. He was happy to see you working with plants and cooking, instinctively interested in herbalism and aromatherapy. And when you wanted to go to pastry school your mother fought against it much harder than you know. I think she might have broken her own taboo on practicing magic to try to get you to stay closer to home, but Skylar put his foot down. Your father has had your back all along. When Andrew and you split, he even cast a spell to protect him."

"To protect Andrew? Good heavens, why? I was the one who got dumped."

"So much of magic comes from intention. You were hurt and angry and it was possible you could have inadvertently done . . . something."

"That's absurd. Something like what?"

"If you'd wanted to, you could have harmed him."

I began to protest again, but the truth was I had been angry, furious even, in addition to feeling betrayed, sad and humiliated.

"Daddy really did that?" I asked in a small voice. "He thought I'd hurt Andrew?"

"Not on purpose. You didn't know what you are."

I needed to digest the conversation about my parents, and figured I might as well digest some comfort food, too. The salad had been healthy to an almost holy degree, and now it was time for sweet goodness. First I stirred up some simple brownies using the old trick of adding boiling water to the batter to make them extra moist. Then came the best part: chunky peanut butter mixed with soft butter, confectioners' sugar and vanilla and dolloped on top of the brownie batter. I drew a knife through the combination to create a chunky marbled effect and popped the pan into a hot oven.

Mungo looked on with great interest.

"No chocolate for you, buddy. Sorry." But I couldn't help giving in to those soft brown eyes. I sat down on the floor beside him and offered the spoon I'd used to scoop peanut butter from the jar. Soon it was sparkling clean, and he was licking the roof of his mouth like crazy.

He frowned at my laughter and trotted over to his water dish.

I spent most of the rest of the night immersed in Mimsey's books on witchcraft, munching on peanut butter brownies and learning about spells and charms, Wiccans, druids and voodoo. About altars and elements and archangels. I even made a rudimentary list of supplies. Other than the candles, I was surprised to learn, I already had many items I might need: dried herbs, essential oils, even the stones I gravitated to in jewelry.

All the information was introductory, but clearly Lucy was right about how magic worked. It was all about intention and the power that came from belief. One book even likened it to quantum physics, in which the expectation of the scientist affects the outcome of her experiment. According to what I read, everyone has magic in them. But there are some people who possess the innate ability to focus their intention more effectively.

More powerfully.

Finally I closed the books and grabbed an hour of sleep before dawn.

As I ran, I listened to the pounding of my feet on the pavement and pushed thoughts of witches and magic aside. We needed to find Mrs. Templeton's murderer, and fast. Now that Albert had entered the picture, there was yet another threat to Ben—and the rest of us. So I wanted more than ever to talk to the manager at Mrs. Templeton's apartment building and see what he could tell me about her tenants. And about her. Everyone seemed to have a story about that woman.

I also had to track down Frank Pullman. I could only hope he'd be willing to talk to me about Mrs. Templeton and what she did to him. Questioning two men I'd never met. One with a murder motive.

My mother would have had a fit if she'd known.

I ran until I was a sweaty mess, but the clean, open feeling that usually accompanied the endorphins eluded me. I couldn't stop worrying about Ben, the Honeybee and my future. Steve Dawes entered my thoughts more than a few times, and so did Declan McCarthy. Then I started feeling guilty about what Declan had said about someone missing Mungo. I should have looked harder for his owner. Taking him to the pound now was out of the question; he'd wiggled his furry little self right into my heart.

Then I turned to obsessing about the details of the Honeybee's opening, running over and over in my mind the things we might not have thought of. But my job at the bakery in Akron, hard and thankless work though it was, had provided me with a wealth of experience, not only in the particulars of baking but also in how to run that kind of business.

The practicalities of getting the Honeybee up and running were really the least of our worries. Maybe another protection spell would help, though. And something to encourage success and abundance. The thought came to me so easily I almost didn't notice how strange it was.

After showering and dressing in my usual skirt and T-shirt, I fed Mungo bacon and eggs and took my coffee out to the back patio. We sat on the grass, and I watched the dragonflies patrolling the yard. Another name for them was mosquito hawks, and given the abundance of the little flying vampires, I was glad to have that particular kind of hawk as my friend.

My sleep disorder was ideal for a baker, because we keep crazy hours. But I didn't have to be at the Honeybee early today, so I forced myself to putter around the little house for a bit, doing dishes and making the bed, wiping down the bathroom and running a dustcloth over the few surfaces. Mungo encouraged my tidying up by following me everywhere. Finally, I scooped him up and carried him out back. The soulful expression in those doggy eyes looking through the glass as I closed the French door almost broke my heart. Sighing, I grabbed the bowie knife off the bookshelf, slung my tote bag over my shoulder and headed out the door.

Steering the Bug around Lafayette Square, I glanced in the rearview mirror and almost swerved into a Bermuda-shorts-clad couple taking pictures.

Mungo sat looking back at me with a happy grin on his face.

"How did you manage that, you little stowaway?"

He licked his nose.

I bent the mirror down and saw he was sitting smack-dab in the middle of my open tote bag. Now what was I supposed to do? Drive all the way back home? I sighed. The Honeybee wasn't officially open, so I could probably sneak him into the office for a few hours without the food police closing us down.

The operative word being *sneak*.

It didn't surprise me when he burrowed into the bottom of my bag, not even poking his twitching nose out as I carried him down the street and into the bakery. He was a very smart puppy, after all. Maybe too smart.

Ben and Lucy were already inside, sitting at a table. When I saw the looks on their faces, inexplicable dread settled into my stomach.

"Is everything okay?" I asked without preamble, sinking onto another chair and putting my tote on the floor. Mungo popped his head out, but they didn't notice.

"Detective Quinn just left. He stopped by to talk to Ben."

The dread intensified.

"Stopped by? So it wasn't official? What did he want?"

"Slow down." Lucy put her hand on my wrist. "It was official, all right. He made Ben go over everything that happened that day, from the minute we got to the bakery. Everything that happened at the DBA meeting, exact times, where he stood in the alley, what people said to each other. They've talked to everyone who attended the brunch, but no one was able to shed any light on what happened. They've got nothing but that woman who saw someone who looks like Ben by Mavis' Cadillac around when she was killed. No one saw Ben in the alley behind the bakery."

I rubbed my hand over my face and stared unseeing at the empty display case. "The police have talked to people who could have looked out and seen him, then?"

"They've talked to everyone in the area. In fact, the detective said he wanted to talk to you. Go over what you told the policewomen who interviewed us that day."

"Well, that's fine, but I won't be able to add anything helpful." Frustration leaked into my voice. "What about you, Ben? Are you okay?"

"I'm fine." But his tone said he wasn't fine at all. "Peter Quinn was just covering all his bases."

I took a deep breath. "You're still a suspect, though. The main suspect. Am I right?"

A pause, then, "It does look that way."

"Oh, Ben." Silence fell between us for a long moment.

Ben roused himself. "I talked to Declan last night. He said you two went to the Peachtree Arms yesterday. I don't like it."

I frowned. "But you knew we were going to try to find the killer. After this latest encounter with Detective Quinn I'd think you'd be doubly on board."

"I knew Lucy's spellbook club included you in their magical workings. I never expected you to go out and play private eye."

"But it's the only way to prove your innocence. Witches or not, we need concrete evidence."

"I don't want you putting yourself in danger."

"I won't. I promise."

"Does that mean you'll stop nosing around?"

I smiled and patted his arm.

Fat chance.

Lucy stood, hands on hips, and gazed down at Mungo. He sat pertly on the office chair, mouth open and tongue lolling as if laughing at us both.

"I don't know how he got into my car. The windows were up. I'd say he crept into my tote bag, and I ended up carrying him out. But I would have noticed, right? Besides, he was in the backyard. How could he have gotten back inside?"

"You are a clever one, aren't you?" She leaned down until they were almost nose to nose. "Don't want to let her out of your sight right now?"

Yip!

I stared.

My aunt turned to me. "You know what he is, don't you?"

"He's a Cairn terrier."

"He's your familiar."

I looked down at him.

Yip! And more of the laughing.

"Oh, for Pete's sake. Aren't you taking this whole magic thing a little too far now?" After all my reading the night before, I was even more convinced that magic was real. Heck, maybe it was science we hadn't discovered yet. But familiars? Come on.

Lucy smiled. "They are a bit old-fashioned. Not everyone has one, but some of us do. Honeybee has been my familiar for almost twenty-five years."

"Cats live that long?" I asked in a weak voice.

"Oh, yes. Mimsey's is a parrot."

"Heckle," I said, remembering the bird poop on her shoulder.

She nodded. "And Jaida's Anubis is a Great Dane."

"Who does not, I take it, hide in her purse."

That elicited a laugh. "No, he lets her have a longer leash, you might say."

I rolled my eyes. Mungo groaned.

"As does Honeybee, I suppose?"

"Cats are independent creatures. Dogs like to stick closer. He can come in to work with you some days as long as he promises to stay in the office." She looked the question at him.

He rolled over, kicked his hind legs in the air, and flipped back onto his stomach.

"Good," she said.

"What about inspections? They'll close us down if they find a dog in a bakery."

"Don't you worry about that," Lucy said. "It'll be fine." She paused in the doorway. "After all, you two need to get to know each other better, don't you?"

After she left, I said, "You're not going to start talking or anything weird, are you?"

Mungo looked at me with pity.

Chapter 12

"Good morning, Katie."

Startled, I smeared bright pink chalk through two lines of white writing on the blackboard. I turned and glared down at Steve Dawes from the stepstool I was standing on.

"Darn it! Look what you made me do. I'll have to erase and rewrite that whole section."

White teeth flashed. "Sorry."

Shaking my head, I stepped down. "No, I'm sorry. I'm in a bad mood, but that's no reason to snap at you."

"You seem kind of jumpy."

"That, too."

"Worried about Ben?"

I sighed. "What do you think?"

"It's rough, I'm sure. But I know Peter Quinn pretty well from when I was on the crime beat. He's one of the good ones."

I cocked my head. "How well?"

"Do I know him? Just professionally. We don't hang out or anything."

"Could you ask him what's going on with his investigation?"

One side of his mouth quirked up. "I doubt that he'd fill me in on the details. I still work for the paper, you know."

"I don't need details. I just want to know if they're planning on charging Ben. Maybe there's someone else in the department that you could ask?"

"Hmm. I'll let you know if I think of anyone."

Right. So much for that.

He changed the subject. "So when are you going to let me show you a few old phantoms of Savannah?"

I remembered his earlier offer, but was still a bit peeved about his reluctance to tap his police contacts to help Ben. Also, if witches were real, then maybe spirits were, too. I wasn't sure I was ready to go down that road.

"Don't tell me you lead ghost tours in your off hours." Kidding, of course, but I'd seen the goofy-looking hearses around the historic district at night, the drivers regaling sightseers with tales of haunting and tragedy.

Steve snorted. "Very funny. I merely thought you'd be interested in a few stories they don't tell the masses. A lot of Savannah natives don't even know about what I want to show you."

"Sounds intriguing, but I can't commit to a time right now. Things are so busy here at the bakery with the upcoming grand opening, and . . . well, I have another project I'm working on."

"With your aunt's 'book club.' "

It wasn't the words that raised the red flag, but the

implied quotes. Steve either knew something about the spellbook club or thought he did. Either way, I wasn't biting.

I smiled. "Maybe we could do it in a few weeks."

His smile disappeared. "I had something a little sooner in mind. Along with dinner out?"

The idea of getting to know this guy was enticing. But what about my promise to myself after Andrew dumped me? I still had two months to go before I met my "no rebound" deadline. My completely arbitrarily imposed deadline born of hurt and anger. Funny thing was, during my morning run I'd mentally gnawed at pretty much everything under the sun, and Andrew hadn't even made the list.

"Mmm. I don't know when I'll be available."

"You have to eat."

"Eating and going out to dinner are different things."

"How about if I bring dinner to you? At your house, maybe. Totally casual. We could grill some steaks, maybe drink a beer. What do you say?"

I laughed. "I don't have a grill."

The brown eyes crinkled at the corners. "All right. I get it. It's enough for now that you like the idea. We'll work something out."

After a quick hesitation, I nodded once. Hardly much of a commitment, but at least I'd have a chance to think about the effect this guy had on me.

His phone rang, and he pulled it from his pocket. "Yes? . . . Right . . . Okay. I'll be there in a few minutes." Returning the phone, he said, "I've got to go. But I'll see you again soon, Katie-girl."

Katie-girl? Really?

He didn't look back as he exited the bakery.

"There is something about that one, no?"

I turned to find Cookie leaning one shoulder against the kitchen doorway. Her eyes flashed a smile.

I shrugged. "I guess he's nice enough."

"Nice enough and yet not too nice. He has a streak of something in him. I would be surprised if he is not one of us."

My fingers tightened on the piece of pink chalk still in my hand. "One of . . . a warlock?"

"We don't use that term very much. Not politically correct, if you know what I mean. But he exudes an aura, an energy. Can you not sense it? That man is a witch."

I sank down on the top step of the stool. It was bad enough to seriously think that I myself had been born with a gift like that. But to entertain the idea that Steve Dawes could share that gift as well? It was frightening.

And thrilling.

I looked up at Cookie. "A witch."

She smiled. "Oh, yes. And a very sexy one, too."

The menu was set, the kitchen gleamed, supplies were laid in, even the cash drawer was ready and waiting in the office safe. Mimsey brought in two hanging ivy plants for the reading area. She and Lucy were arranging these last details while Ben worked on the accounting program on the computer in the office, Mungo keeping him company.

No one seemed to mind when I said I had to run out for a while. Not even my dog.

Cookie had been flipping through one of the books

spilling out of the stuffed bookshelf. When I mentioned an errand, she looked up and quickly returned the book. "Would you like some company?"

In fact, I very much wanted company. "How did you know?" The words were out before I realized that she probably just Knew.

The slow upturn of her lips confirmed my suspicions.

"The manager of the Peachtree Arms wasn't there yesterday when Declan and I stopped by to check it out."

Ben must have heard me from the other room, because he came around the corner with concern etched into his face. "You're going back there?"

"We've been over this, Ben. Someone has to. From what Detective Quinn was asking you this morning it sounds like the police are only concentrating on the area around the Honeybee. We can't be sure they're looking into the pile of enemies Mavis Templeton seems to have had. And we can't let the system railroad you into a murder charge."

My uncle shook his finger at me just like Mrs. Templeton had when we first met. "We have a good police force in this town. Let them do their jobs."

I felt my eyes go wide. "Maybe so. But if you think I don't intend to do what I can to find who really killed that woman, you're very wrong. I love you, darn it." I blinked at the tears that stung my eyelids and lowered my voice. "I'm a grown woman. I can take care of myself."

"Especially with a little help from her friends," Cookie chimed in.

Ben still looked unhappy.

Cookie put her hand on my arm. "Let's go, Katie."

"Let me go with you," Ben said.

"You're a murder suspect. Don't you think it might be a problem if you go around questioning witnesses?"

Lucy and Mimsey had been watching us in silence from the far end of the room where they'd been loading small vases with the tulips and violets Mimsey had brought from her florist shop.

Now Lucy stepped forward and held out her hand. "Katie, I want you to wear this amulet until this is all over." She handed me a silver chain with an O-shaped medallion hanging from it. The middle was open, and six etched dragonflies chased each other around the circle. "It's for luck and protection."

It felt warm, almost hot, in my hand.

"Thank you." I put the chain over my head and turned to Cookie. "Ready?"

"Of course."

Frowning, my uncle stalked back to the office.

We went outside and walked down the block toward my VW. The heat reflected into the muggy air from the pavement, but our gait was slow.

"I wish Ben realized I'm only trying to help. That he didn't feel guilty about it. He was just in the wrong place at the wrong time."

"There are no coincidences," Cookie said.

That stopped me in my tracks. "You don't think he's to blame, do you?"

Cookie paused and met my gaze. "I never said anything about blame. But things, they always happen for a reason. The more you learn about how magic works within the web of reality, the more you will realize that what I say is true."

We continued walking toward my car. "You're talking about fate, then? Inescapable destiny?"

"On the contrary." She waited while I unlocked the passenger door. "Everything is related. Everything and everyone are on a path at any given time. But we influence our world in everything we do, and that path can change in an instant. And I don't mean only those who practice magic. Every single thought and action has consequences."

That more or less jibed with what I'd read the night before. Suddenly just being human felt like a huge responsibility.

I removed the shade from the front windshield, and Cookie slid into the blazing-hot interior. Looking up at me, she said, "Our—witches'—intentions have more effect because we understand the fabric of reality."

I went around to the other side of the car, got in, started the engine and turned on the air-conditioning full blast. Two days ago Cookie's words would have made me roll my eyes, but I'd believed for a very long time that personal intention and goals shape our lives. Then my job in Akron turned out to be awful after all my hard work at pastry school, and my engagement to Andrew fell apart to a spectacular degree. After that, I came to wonder whether it wasn't fate after all. Fate and bad luck.

Except it wasn't bad luck: I'd gone to pastry school and because of that I was now in Savannah with my own bakery. I couldn't have done what I needed to at the Honeybee without the experience of working long hours and getting a taste of every aspect of the bakery in Akron. I had to do that in order to get to where I was now.

And Andrew? For the first time, I admitted we'd never been a good fit. I just wanted us to be so badly that I ignored the fact that we weren't. I wanted a husband and kids and, yes, a white picket fence, dog and garden. But I didn't want them for the right reason. I wanted them because I thought that was what normal people had, and I desperately wanted to be normal, too.

But I wasn't normal. I was a witch.

I was a witch, I had always been a witch, and now I knew other people like me.

I could belong and still be myself.

The realization tightened my throat, making it hard to swallow away the sob of relief that threatened to surface.

"See?" Cookie said from beside me. "You're beginning to understand."

We rode in silence for a few minutes before Cookie spoke again. "I will tell you this: Ben should not have so much faith in the police. Where I come from, the system is never to be trusted. Sometimes it works, but that is not something to count on."

"Lucy said you're from Haiti?" I prompted.

"Mm-hmm. My parents brought my brother and me to the United States when we were only ten and nine, but they have told us many stories of our home country."

"And what about your . . . powers?"

"My people practice voodoo."

"I don't really know anything about voodoo." There hadn't been much information in Mimsey's books, either. "Not that I know much about witchcraft, for that matter, but some of what Lucy's told me feels familiar."

"Voodoo is the national religion of my first country. As with any religion, people practice it in different ways and to different effects. My father was a voodoo priest before we left, and he is the one who taught me as a child."

My curiosity raging, I asked, "But isn't that much different than the kind of magic the others in the spellbook club practice?"

"I do not practice voodoo anymore. I have seen the dark side of that kind of magic. My father died because of it."

"I'm so sorry." I resisted the urge to ask what had happened. Perhaps when I knew her better she would want to tell me.

"Thank you. I turned away from voodoo but could not turn away from the power I possess. Your aunt and the others have been a coven for over a decade. Others have come and gone, from what I understand. But those women have helped shape my new magical practices. Not that all of them are happy with my background."

"Like who?"

A pause, then she gave a short laugh. "Jaida does not believe I always practice white magic. Or gray, for that matter. Most magic falls into the gray category, you know."

I didn't know that. I didn't know a lot of things.

Turning the Bug into the parking lot of the Peachtree Arms, I asked, "Is Jaida right?"

Cookie smiled, and her jade eyes flickered in the sunlight pouring through the window. "Yes. She's right."

I didn't know what to say to that, so I didn't say anything.

"What a dump." Cookie opened the car door to the afternoon heat after I'd pulled into a space. She got out and waited while I exited the car.

I joined her, and we headed toward the door Declan and I had entered the day before. Cookie stepped inside, and I was right behind her.

She stopped and sniffed the air. "This is a bad place."

"I thought that, too. But I didn't know why. Can you tell?"

"There is pain here. Desperation."

She was right, but it didn't take any special abilities to figure that out. The people who lived here were down and out, or they wouldn't be here.

"Death," she added.

"Probably." I led the way to the manager's apartment.

The door across the hall opened and James Sparr stepped into the hall. "Got yourself a girlfriend to check out the place, eh? A second opinion. Well, you're in luck. Ethan's in there. Just bang on the door and he'll come out and show you around."

"Thank you, James. We'll do that."

Cookie shot me a glance as he went back into his apartment and closed the door.

"We met yesterday."

The hand-lettered MANAGER sign quivered as loud music suddenly vibrated through the cheap wooden door. I glanced at Cookie and raised my fist to pound on it. The volume lowered, and Ethan Ridge opened the door.

His greasy brown hair hung to bare shoulders. Long, prehensile toes protruded below his faded blue jeans. His skin glowed golden brown over the wiry muscles of his arms, chest and abdomen. Small brown eyes, red-rimmed and set too close together, peered at us above a sharp nose and thin lips. His face faded away at the bottom without benefit of a chin to define where it ended.

He blinked at us. "Yeah?"

"Are you the manager?"

"Yeah."

"My name is Katie Lightfoot and this is Cookie Rios. Can we ask you a few questions about the place?"

"We're full."

"That's not what one of your tenants said."

"There was a death. It's a bad time." He started to shut the door.

From the corner of my eye I saw Cookie's hands moving. But when I turned she was still.

"Let us in," she said. Her voice had taken on a new dimension.

Chapter 13

Ethan frowned for a long moment, then stepped back. We walked into his cluttered living room. The air held the skunky pungency of marijuana smoke. From the pizza boxes and beer cans that littered every surface it appeared that was all he ate. I wondered how he stayed so skinny.

"What do you want?"

"An apartment ," I began.

Cookie stepped forward. "We want to know about Mavis Templeton."

Okay. That was one way to play it.

Ethan cleared one end of the sofa with a sweep of his arm. He waved at it. "You and everyone else. Sit."

Gingerly, I sat. "We're not the first?" Cookie perched on the arm of the sofa.

He snorted. "*Hardly*. Cops been here twice so far. Blah, blah, blah. And then there's her family."

I leaned forward. "By family you mean Albert Hill?"

Ethan's eyes narrowed. "You a friend of his?"

"*Hardly*," I said.

His head bobbed forward. "Good. You want a beer?"

"No, thanks. So he's not the new owner of this building now that his aunt is gone?"

"Oh, you bet he is. Wanted to throw it in my face, too. Thinks things are going to be just like they've always been. You sure you don't want a beer?"

"I'm sure."

"Suit yourself."

He disappeared through a doorway. A refrigerator opened and closed, and the metallic sound of a pop top drifted back to us. A few moments later he reentered the living room.

"So things are not going to be just like they've always been," I prompted.

"No, ma'am. They are not." Ethan shook his head in emphasis. "Ol' Albert is gonna have to find himself another manager."

"You don't care for how Mrs. Templeton ran this property?"

"Mrs. Templeton didn't run this property. I ran this property, and no thanks to her. Tightfisted old bitch wouldn't pay for any repairs. I did what I could, but I wasn't going to put my own money into this place. She barely paid me enough to live on, and that was counting this crappy apartment."

"Surely, as a landlord, she must have authorized some repairs," Cookie said. "There are laws." But the look she directed down at me belied her belief in such laws.

Ethan snorted again. "Laws don't make no never mind when the people who're supposed to enforce them are willing to look the other way for a few Benjamins."

"She bribed officials?" I asked.

"Paid off the safety inspectors. Or threatened them. Maybe both. She was good at both."

I tipped my head to one side. "Why didn't you leave?"

"Like I said, she was good at making threats." He paused. Blinked. Shook his head.

"Go on," Cookie said.

My head whipped around at her odd tone. One corner of her mouth turned up.

Ethan's face cleared. "Ah, well. Told the cops already, anyway. I'm an ex-con, and she swore she'd make it impossible for me to find any kind of job in Savannah if I quit working for her. Or anywhere else, for that matter. She had that kind of power, but Albert doesn't—he only likes to think so. People have had to put up with some rotten things here, and I'm not going to be part of it anymore."

"Rotten how?" I asked.

But Ethan was looking at me now as if he was just seeing me for the first time.

"Who are you again? And why are you asking all these questions?"

"Katie Lightfoot," I began.

Cookie stood. "I think we're done. Thanks for talking with us."

He pointed at her. "Cookie? Is that right? What kind of a name is that?"

Her fingers closed around my arm, and she pulled me to my feet. "We're just going."

"But—," I protested.

"*Now*, Katie."

The loquacious, beer-offering Ethan had vanished, replaced by a glowering, hunched doppelgänger with darting eyes and a twitchy upper lip.

"Yeah, okay." We backed quickly to the door, the apartment manager pacing us like a predator. I heard it open behind me, and then we were in the hallway.

"Thanks!" I said brightly and pulled the door shut in his face.

"Come on!" Cookie pulled me to a door marked STAIRS. We ducked through just as Ethan Ridge came out of his apartment and turned toward the exterior door.

"What happened in there?" I whispered to Cookie. In the dim light I saw her look away. "You cast a spell on him? To make him talk to us?"

She shrugged and darted down the stairway. I followed. The stairs ended in a dingy laundry room.

"Cookie!"

Defiance flared across her face as she turned back to me. "I used my Voice."

I realized the charge behind her words, once in the hallway and again in Ethan's apartment, felt familiar. And not necessarily in a good way. I shivered as another memory surfaced from my childhood.

"Is that ethical?" I asked.

"It depends on who you ask. Didn't you want him to answer your questions? Wasn't it for the greater good that he did?"

Well, yes. "I guess you're right."

"You're welcome." She didn't smile when she said it. Despite her argument in favor of the greater good, she exuded defensiveness.

An eight-foot-long fluorescent bulb flickered and hummed above. The harsh light revealed cinder-block walls painted an undefinable light color. Streaks of dark gray marred the mottled surface, and rust stains dribbled down from a tangle of metal pipes in one corner. A large drain enhanced the center of the grimy concrete floor. The taint of mold rode behind the chemical flavors of laundry detergent and fabric softener in the air. Three cheap washers and two dryers backed up against the walls, and at the far end a framed opening exited into darkness.

"Only one of those washers works." The voice came from behind us.

As one, we turned to discover a white-haired lady who barely came up to my shoulder. She leaned on an aluminum walker and blinked at us behind thick lenses. A pillowcase with laundry spilling out of it was tied to one handle.

"You two must be new here," she said.

"We don't live here," I said. "We're just checking the place out."

"Well, honey, if you have another alternative, I'd take it. No one lives here if they can help it." She pushed the walker to one of the washing machines and opened the lid.

Cookie and I exchanged a look.

"Why is that?" Cookie asked.

"Because the place is a dump. But you don't need me to tell you that if you've been looking around. You talk to the manager yet?"

We nodded.

She sniffed. "Not the brightest bulb, but the boy

does what he can, I suppose." She leaned against the washer and struggled to open the pillowcase.

"May I help you?" I gently reached for the pillow-case, afraid I'd offend her, but the older woman seemed relieved to hand it to me. Cookie lifted the box of deter-gent from the walker's basket and began measuring powder.

"How long have you lived here?" I asked.

"About four years. My husband passed. He wasn't too good with money, you see. A lot of us here are older. My name is Eugenia Perkins."

We murmured introductions in response.

So the rent was cheap. Of course. I had to wonder whether it wouldn't have been better for Mrs. Temple-ton to have fixed the place up and charged more. By the look of things it would have been a pretty major under-taking, though. Like companies that profit by laying off employees and increasing the workloads of those who remain, Mrs. Templeton had profited from her low rents by eliminating practically all the overhead.

"The main problem is that I can't get up and down stairs very well," Mrs. Perkins continued, thumping the walker in front of her. "My apartment's on the main floor, but every once in a while I need to come down here when I can't get to the Laundromat. Have to drag this thing out to the back entrance, which goes straight into the basement here."

"I thought I saw an elevator," I said.

"Wouldn't be caught dead on that elevator." Her laugh was bitter. "Or maybe I would be caught dead."

Cookie said, "The elevator doesn't work, either?"

"Oh, it does now. Supposedly. It's one of the few

things the owner took care of, but not until someone almost died."

My hand flew to my mouth. "Oh, my gosh. What happened?"

"Girl was here visiting her folks about a year or so ago. Sweet little thing, name of Gwendolyn Landis. Came every Sunday for supper. Her people, they live on the fifth floor, or at least they did up until then." Her mouth turned down at the corners, and rheumy eyes searched the corner of the room for memories. "When she left that evening, she got in the elevator like she always did. You had to chivvy it along now and again, but it had always gotten the job done. That time it didn't. Started out, but when it got to the fourth floor a cable snapped or something. The whole shebang plummeted down to this level. Made the loudest sound I ever heard."

I tossed the pillowcase into the washer after its contents. "Was Gwendolyn all right?"

"No, ma'am. She most certainly was not. Poor thing broke her neck. Now she's in some state-run nursing home. She's only your age, maybe a few years older. Still so young. Can you imagine? She's a quadriplegic now."

"That's horrible," I said, shaken by her story. The more I learned about Mrs. Templeton, the more I realized what an evil woman she was.

"It sure is. That girl's life is ruined, along with the lives of her entire family. They got out of here, but now they're living with relatives so they can pay for a little extra care for their crippled daughter. The family wanted to sue, but no one would take their case against the owner of this place. Old-family Savannah royalty. Should have been shot." Vitriol threaded through her voice.

"Too late," I said without thinking. Then I backpedaled. "The owner of this building . . . was recently killed." No need to share the gory details if she didn't already know.

Mrs. Perkins stared at me. "No kidding. What happened?"

"Someone broke her neck," Cookie answered.

I looked at her in surprise.

"Someone did the world a favor, then." Then Mrs. Perkins looked worried. "I wonder what will happen around here now, though."

Better the devil you knew? I had to admit Albert wasn't likely to be much of an improvement over his aunt.

"Will you be okay down here?" I asked. "Do you want us to stay?"

She waved me away. "Heavens, no. I'll just take it slow like I always do. And I have my magazines to keep me company. Nobody needs to worry about me."

I wavered, hating to leave her. She was obviously lonely, but also proud.

"How do we get to the back entrance from here?" Cookie asked, ever practical. We needed to avoid Ethan if we could.

"Just go out there and turn right." Mrs. Perkins indicated the gaping doorway at the end of the laundry room. "You'll find the back door down at the very end. It's not locked during the day."

Cookie started for the dark hallway. I hesitated, putting my hand on the older woman's shoulder. For a brief moment, she leaned into my touch, then straightened and smiled. "It was nice talking with you, honey."

"Thank you." I patted her arm one more time and hurried to catch up to Cookie.

"Wait up," I said, blinking in the dimness that was relieved only by a low-wattage lightbulb near the back door.

Cookie slowed.

"It sounds to me like this whole place needs a great big protection spell," I said.

She nodded. "For a start."

"How long would it take?"

"More time than we have."

"What about Mrs. Perkins?"

"Do you think she's in danger?"

"I think her life is pretty miserable."

Cookie directed a sympathetic look my way. "You can't help everyone, Katie."

"I don't want to help everyone. I just want to help Mrs. Perkins."

As we neared the end of the hallway, the walls gave way to a series of storage spaces enclosed by chain-link gates fastened with padlocks. The yellow light from two bare bulbs above revealed the detritus of an apartment dweller's life jammed into the partitioned areas: an exercise bike, a small rubber raft and fishing gear, old tires, a few boxes. The space right by the back door was full of empty moving boxes, some of them flattened, ready to be employed in an eventual escape.

Most of the boxes read NEW START MOVING and showed a logo of an old truck piled high with belongings. The only thing missing was Granny from the *Beverly Hillbillies* in her rocking chair on top.

A new start, indeed. Not knowing what else to do, I whispered *Blessed be* and imagined the wish winging into every nook, cranny and life at the Peachtree Arms.

Chapter 14

Cookie asked me to stop at the 7-Eleven down the street so she could get some water. She sounded hoarse. Apparently using her Voice was hard on her throat. She hurried back out, and we continued on our way to the bakery.

As the air-conditioning kicked in I asked her if she was seeing anyone.

"A building contractor for the last few months. He's nice. We're almost through, but I've enjoyed spending time with him."

I remembered what Lucy had told me about Cookie's dating habits. "So why would you break up with him?"

She shrugged. "I can tell it will be time to move on soon."

Well, that was cryptic. Maybe she stuck with short-term relationships because she didn't want anyone to find out she was a witch. I could understand that. On the other hand, maybe she was commitment-phobic.

Cookie seemed to know everything about me already, thanks to Aunt Lucy. Probably more than I knew myself if everything Lucy had told me about my family background was really true.

We got back a little after two o'clock. Mimsey popped her head out of the kitchen as soon as the door opened.

"Lucille!" she called. "They're back."

Lucy, Jaida and Bianca joined us in the library area, passing around glasses of sweet tea. I welcomed the cool, syrupy liquid sliding down my throat.

"Okay, spill." Mimsey practically shook with anticipation.

I settled into the sofa. "We talked with the apartment manager, Ethan Ridge. He said Albert Hill will own the Peachtree Arms now. He didn't want to keep working there now that Mrs. Templeton is dead. She threatened him with his past if he didn't stay and now he's free. He also said Mrs. Templeton had bribed inspectors so she wouldn't have to fix anything in the building."

Jaida raised her eyebrows. "I'm surprised he told you all that."

My eyes cut to Cookie, but I moved on to what we'd learned from Mrs. Perkins. When I finished we were all quiet for a few minutes as everyone thought about the woman injured by the elevator fall.

Finally, Jaida broke the silence. "I did some more checking and can confirm that Mavis Templeton liquidated all her other assets after her husband died. She invested heavily in gold and foreign currency. Rumor is she's done well, despite the bad economy. The only real estate she owned besides the commercial property on Bull Street and the apartment building was her home, off of Chippewa Square."

I imagined her house. It would be big, fancy . . . and cold even on the hottest summer day. I was tempted to go see where she had lived.

Really tempted. I had to return the bowie knife to Johnny Reb's anyway. "Lucy, has Uncle Ben talked to Jack Jenkins about getting full payment for the DBA brunch yet?"

She shook her head. "With everything else going on it must have slipped his mind."

"I need to run by there anyway. If you have a copy of the agreement he and Mrs. Templeton signed I'll take it with me. And you still have the check she gave you?"

I followed Lucy into the office. Mungo jumped off the chair he'd taken over and ran to me. Once in my arms, he snuggled under my chin. "You want to come with me?"

"Of course he does," Lucy said.

"I don't have a leash for him."

She laughed. "He seems to like that big tote bag of yours just fine."

Yip!

Mungo sat up in my tote, peering over the top. His head bobbed along with my footsteps. Never in my life would I have dreamed I'd end up being that lady who carried a dog around in her purse.

Mrs. Templeton's address was farther away than Johnny Reb's, so I'd walk there first and then circle around. Following Broughton to Abercorn, I turned right and walked to Oglethorpe Square. You'd have thought General Oglethorpe, the founder of Savannah, would be venerated in the square that bore his name, but no. His statue dominated Chippewa Square, more famous these days for the bench where Forrest Gump talked about a box of chocolates.

Tour guide voices blared from loudspeakers as buses passed by. Tourism was a big industry in Savannah, and plenty of the residents made their living from visitors to the city. But how many times could you repeat the same stories? I wondered as yet another bus went by. Even in a place as historical and unique as this one, how jaded to its beauties would you become the more you had to sell them to the masses?

Colonial Park Cemetery on my left, I turned onto East Hull and found Mrs. Templeton's address. The house wasn't as large as I'd anticipated. Only two stories high, and extending deeply onto the lot behind, it was obviously very old. Like, antebellum old. It would bring a pretty penny if Albert decided to sell. The rare Savannah gray-brick facade would be enough to see to that.

"Should I go ring the bell?" I murmured to my companion, thinking there might be a caretaker or a housekeeper that would talk to me.

Mungo whined.

Moments later I saw why. Recognizing the dark Suburban heading our way, I ducked my head and continued walking toward Bull Street. Albert Hill screeched to a stop in front of his aunt's house, slammed out of his vehicle and ran up the walk.

Was he living there? Already? Mrs. Templeton was barely cold.

"Has anyone seen the movie *Forrest Gump*?" an enthusiastic voice yelled from a trolley tour bus. "And do you recognize that bench?" I shook my head and turned right onto Bull Street before she got to the rest of the spiel.

Looking worried, Jack Jenkins stood immediately when I walked in. Today he wore a pink shirt with his jeans, and a pair of silver-framed glasses. "Miss Lightfoot! I presume you received your trunk yesterday?"

"I did. Thank you. It's perfect."

Relief replaced the worry. "Excellent news. When I saw you in the shop so soon again I thought perhaps there was a problem."

"No problem, but I did find something inside it that I don't believe you intended as part of the deal." I reached into my bag and extracted the knife rolled in fabric. Mungo hunkered down, out of sight. I unwrapped the parcel and put the weapon on the counter.

Jenkins picked it up and unsheathed it. Tested the blade with his thumb. "This was in the trunk? I'm sure I glanced inside before the boys loaded it into the van."

"It was strapped to the inside of the lid," I said. "Can you think of any reason why?"

Jenkins looked thoughtful. "The gentleman from whom I purchase many of these restored trunks does his very best to maintain the integrity of the inherent history of each piece. It would not surprise me to learn that this knife was originally strapped to the interior lid, and he replaced it after his work was complete."

"I guess that makes sense."

"Thank you for returning it. Technically, though, it was a part of your purchase. You may have it, if you like."

"No, thanks. I don't care much for knives. But I wouldn't mind if you knocked a little off the price of the trunk."

His smile was charming as ever, but didn't quite reach his eyes. "But I didn't know it was in there when I set the price, Miss Lightfoot."

"Hmm. Fair point. Anyway, I stopped by for another reason." I put my hand into my bag to fish out the agreement Mrs. Templeton had made for the DBA brunch and was surprised to find Mungo positively vibrating. I felt terrible. He probably didn't like knives, either, and here I'd made him ride around right beside one. I rested my hand along his back for a moment, and he quieted.

Jenkins watched me expectantly. I put the paper on the counter, and he leaned forward to take a look.

"I don't know whether Mrs. Templeton has been replaced as treasurer of the DBA yet, but we never received full payment for the brunch. This is the contract she and my Uncle Ben drew up. And this is what she tried to pay us."

"Oh, my. Isn't this what they were fighting about directly before her life was cut short?"

I pressed my lips together. "There was a small disagreement after she tried to break the contract, yes."

"I see. Well, thank you for bringing this to my attention. I will attend to it and get a check to your uncle as soon as possible."

"Thank you." I looked at my watch. "I need to be getting back to the bakery. Still a lot to do before the grand opening tomorrow. I hope you'll stop by."

He waved his hand through the air. "I assure you, I wouldn't miss it for the world."

"Here. I made these up while you were gone." Lucy held out a plastic container. "Eat one tonight as a bedtime snack. It'll help you sleep."

"What are they?" I asked.

"Seven-layer bars."

I gave her a look. "You mean the kind that are sometimes called magic bars?"

Lucy grinned. "Trust me."

I opened the lid and peered in. A multitude of scents curled up from the container, and I almost swooned on the spot. "They smell delicious. What's in them?" I recognized the chocolate chips, coconut, graham crackers and walnuts from the traditional recipe Mama used to make, but there weren't any butterscotch or white chocolate chips, and their smell was different from that of the seven-layer bars I'd eaten as a child.

"All sorts of good things," she said with a smile. "And a pinch of agrimony. I know you haven't been sleeping well lately, and you need your rest if you'll be hitting the kitchen at five every morning."

For a moment I considered telling her about my sleep disorder, but I just said, "True enough," and sniffed the contents once more before snapping the lid back on. "Thanks, Lucy."

She grinned. "Plus, you're not nearly as grumpy when you get a good night's sleep."

I rolled my eyes. If she only knew.

*   *   *

We'd renovated and designed and arranged the space. We'd developed the recipes. And tomorrow we would throw open the door of Honeybee Bakery to the public. In addition to hitting the kitchen at five a.m. to start the day's baking, I would be baking on and off until each afternoon, with Lucy's help. And besides the trios of cookies, biscotti, muffins and scones, each day there'd be a special. The grand opening special would be individual peach-and-pecan pies.

I added flour, water and salt to the giant glop of sourdough starter in the big mixer and set it to churning on low. After the mixture had grown and burbled for a few hours, I would put the wet sponge into baking pans and those into the refrigerator to slow-rise overnight. In the morning the loaves would be ready to bake, with no kneading and without my having to start work at three o'clock in the morning.

Yes, that crappy job in Akron had taught me a few things.

The back door opened and Steve Dawes walked in without even bothering to knock. I folded my arms and raised my eyebrows at his entrance. Was he simply confident or downright arrogant? At least I didn't get the girlie shivers this time. This time my blood surged like a tide responding to the proximity of the moon.

Great.

"Hey there. All ready for the big day?" he asked.

"We're set to go. Now we just need the customers to show up." I flipped the switch on the mixer, lifted the beater, and draped a towel over the bowl.

"Oh, you'll get those. There's a buzz about this place, you know."

A smile crept onto my face. So word had already spread. Excellent.

"People will want to see where Mavis Templeton was killed."

My smile slid away. "Terrific."

He laughed. "There's no such thing as bad publicity, right?"

"Hmm. I guess." It would be nice if people came to the Honeybee because of the fabulous baked goods, though. I reminded myself we had to give it time.

"So, I barged in for a reason," Steve said.

"Really? Do tell."

"I'm looking for Ben. Got a couple follow-up questions for my column. You know, the one about the changing face of business."

"Right. Sorry, but he's not here right now." He'd looked so ragged Lucy and I had insisted that he try to get a little rest. Lucy had sent some seven-layer bars home with him to encourage a nice nap.

"When will he be back?"

I shrugged. "I know he'll be here tomorrow, manning the counter and charming customers."

"I'd sure like to get the column in. I'll give him a call."

"I'm sure he'll get back to you as soon as he can."

"Hmm." Steve peered at my face. "You haven't been sleeping well, have you?"

I frowned. "I look that bad, huh?" What was with all the concern about my sleeping habits?

"Not at all. I can just . . . tell. Okay, I'll let you get back to work. But don't forget dinner. I'm going to keep at it until you give in."

And now I was nodding, just like I did when Lucy had asked me if we could do the DBA brunch for Mrs. Templeton: against my will.

"Good. And soon." He turned to go. "See you."

"Wait a second."

He looked back at me. "Change your mind?" The hope on his face was disconcerting and charming at the same time.

"I was wondering if you'd had a chance to talk to any of your pals on the police force about the murder."

The hope turned into a wry smile. "Of course you were."

I refused to feel sheepish. A girl's got to keep her priorities straight.

"And?"

"And nothing. Yet. Give me your number, and I'll call if I find out anything."

"Oh. Um, okay."

"Now, come on. I won't bite." His grin was awfully toothy, though.

I recited my phone number, and he tapped it into his cell phone, then looked up. "There. You're officially on my list." Surprise registered on his face. "Don't look like that! You act like I'm some stalker. Here." He took out a business card and gave it to me. "That's my number. Now we're even, right?"

Hardly.

Donning my best poker face, I asked, "How would you go about finding out what someone went to jail for?"

"Someone who?"

"Ethan Ridge."

"You're kidding."

"You know him?"

"Of him. When I worked the crime beat for the *Morning News*, it was common knowledge that eighty percent of the people law enforcement deals with are folks they've run into before. Ridge was one of those repeat customers. Then he went away for a while, and it was common knowledge when he came back."

"He's the manager of the Peachtree Arms."

Steve's response was a blank look.

"That's Mrs. Templeton's apartment complex. Now her nephew's, I guess."

He took out a pen and his ever handy notebook. "Ethan Ridge. Like I said, I know he was in prison, but I don't know what landed him there. I'll see what I can come up with, okay?"

"That'd be great," I said with a big smile.

" 'Bye, Katie-girl." He walked out without looking back.

The door latch clicked behind him. " 'Bye," I said to empty air.

Chapter 15

Ethan Ridge wasn't the only one who'd had problems with dear Mavis. Now that Steve was looking into his nefarious past I wanted to find out what had happened to Redding Coopersmith's friend before we got too busy at the bakery. I'd related Margie's story to Lucy and Bianca, who came in soon after Steve left,

"I'd sure like to track down Frank Pullman before the grand opening tomorrow," I said now. "We've heard Mrs. Templeton made a lot of threats, and we even witnessed some right here in the Honeybee, but it seems she actually destroyed Pullman's life."

Bianca slid into the chair across from me. "He lives a few miles away. We could go see him right now." She recited an address.

"You know him?" I asked. A sense of urgency settled on my shoulders.

She shrugged. "Never heard of the gentleman before you told us about him."

"Then how did . . . Is there an address location spell or something?"

Her lips quirked. "Yes. It's called a telephone book. Very old school."

Lucy laughed. I ducked my head, feeling my face redden. I had to stop thinking everything these ladies did involved witchcraft.

"I have some time right now. Can you leave?" Bianca asked.

I glanced at Lucy. "I think we should. What else is there to do to get ready for the opening? Other than the baking I'll do in the morning." The bakery was scheduled to open at seven o'clock the next morning. Because we wanted everything to be perfect, I'd be at the Honeybee bright and early at four a.m. I'd already prepped everything I could.

My aunt waved her hand. "We're all set, hon. You go ahead with Bianca and see what Mr. Pullman has to say. I'll take care of anything that comes up."

Standing, I said, "We shouldn't be long."

Bianca offered to drive. When I saw the red Jaguar convertible I was sorry we had to go only a few miles.

In no time we pulled up behind a battered pickup parked at the curb in front of a white bungalow centered on a small lot. The porch sported an elaborate wooden railing, and the low cedar pickets surrounding the yard stood out in contrast to the neighbors' wrought-iron fences. The gate was open, as was the front door. Several cardboard boxes emblazoned with the NEW START MOVING logo filled the back of the truck, along with a Naugahyde recliner and two large suitcases.

As we approached the gate, a tall bearded man wearing black-framed glasses carried another suitcase out of the house and shut the door behind him. He jingled the keys in his hand and regarded us from the shade of the porch. Exchanging glances, Bianca and I entered the yard and walked up the sidewalk.

"You from the bank?" Anger flared in his eyes as we came nearer.

"Um, no, sir," I said.

"Don't tell me those bastards put the house on the market already."

"I'm afraid I don't know anything about that. Are you Frank Pullman?"

The heat in his glare diminished a fraction. "Who wants to know?"

I climbed the stairs and stepped onto the porch. "Katie Lightfoot." I gestured at Bianca, who stopped halfway up the steps and leaned against the scrolled railing. "And this is Bianca Devereaux."

"Pleased to make your acquaintance," she drawled. "Assuming you are indeed Mr. Pullman?"

A couple of beats passed and then his shoulders slumped. He looked down at the painted floorboards and muttered, "Yeah. That's me."

On the brief drive over I'd racked my brain for the best way to ask him about Mrs. Templeton. Nothing terribly clever had occurred to me. Now I blurted, "My next-door neighbor is Margie Coopersmith. She told me about your trouble with Mavis Templeton, but that you're a good carpenter. I just moved here and I need a little work done on my house, so my friend and I thought we'd stop by and introduce ourselves." It was partly true. I did need someone to build my dream gazebo in the backyard.

Bianca stared at me. I couldn't blame her. I'd more or

less invited a possible murderer to come work on my house. Even told him right where I lived.

Dumb move, Katie.

Pullman shuffled his feet. "That was nice of Margie. Redding's a good buddy of mine, one of the few who didn't pay any attention to that whole hullabaloo."

"You mean losing your job?"

He froze. Then his eyes flicked up to meet mine. "What did Margie tell you?"

"Not much."

"Good."

"I'd like to know what happened, though. If I'm going to hire you, I mean."

"I thought you believed Margie."

"Well, I do, of course. As far as that goes, but she didn't know any details. I'd at least like to understand who I might be working with."

Bianca stirred behind me.

Frank's head swung back and forth in an exaggerated negative. "Sorry, lady. That old bat ruined my entire life, and I'm not inclined to revisit the details. I'm planning to move in with my sister over in Pooler, anyway. My brother-in-law may have a line on some work for me there."

Margie had mentioned a wife and daughter. Where were they?

Bianca stepped up next to me. "Mr. Pullman, painful as the entire situation must have been, surely you don't mind telling Katie a few details in exchange for paid work. After all, Mavis Templeton is dead now."

He froze, searching her face. His attention returned to me. "Dead? How?"

Watching his reaction carefully, I said, "She was murdered."

Pullman blinked. He seemed more stunned than anything else.

"I'm surprised you haven't heard," Bianca said. "It's been all over the news."

"I've had too much on my mind to read the paper. And my wife took the television when she left with Ellie."

"Oh, I'm so sorry," I said.

Distracted, he ran his hand over the smooth wood of the railing. "After I lost my job, I couldn't get regular work anywhere in town. Someone—either Templeton herself or someone doing it for her—contacted all the companies who hire specialty carpenters like me and told them not to. Hire me, I mean. I found a few projects here and there, but most people wouldn't even talk to me. All in all, it wasn't enough to make the house payments. And when we were served with the foreclosure notice, my wife had had enough. She took my little girl and went to live with her parents in Atlanta."

"Mrs. Templeton really had that kind of power?" I asked.

He ran a shaky hand over his face. "She did. Oh, my, yes, she did."

"Why on earth was she so angry with you?" Bianca asked. Blunt, but effective.

"She said I left too much of a mess when I was done fixing a big fancy stair railing in that old house of hers."

"A mess," I repeated in a flat tone.

"Well, there might have been some sawdust, but

that's all. She refused to pay for the work, even though it had taken me two days to refit and fix that banister. When it was finished, you couldn't even tell it had been restored. But that wasn't good enough for her. I think she was just too cheap to pay for my skill."

"Sawdust on the floor," I said. "Surely that's not enough to ruin someone's life over."

"I sure didn't think so."

"Why would anyone listen to her?"

He shook his head. "I don't know. Everyone did, though." Slowly, his expression brightened. "But you say she's dead now. Really gone?"

Bianca and I nodded.

A huge grin of relief split his face. "That's great!"

Bianca's eyebrows knitted.

Suddenly, Frank Pullman let loose a big *whoop!* and leaped over the railing. We watched slack-jawed as he raced to the truck and climbed inside. The engine roared to life and he sped away.

I wondered how long it would take him to realize he'd left his suitcase on the porch.

Bianca let out a whoosh of air. "Well, he certainly seemed surprised by the news."

Still somewhat stunned by his reaction, I said, "Yes. And, uh, gleeful."

"Do you think he could have been faking it?" she asked.

"That seemed like a heartfelt, if utterly inappropriate, reaction."

Our eyes met, and we struggled not to laugh.

"Come on. Let's go back and let the others know Frank Pullman, though he might have liked to murder

Mrs. Templeton, doesn't appear to have done so," she said.

"Well, let's not count him out entirely," I said.

"Why?"

"Wouldn't you say he and Uncle Ben look awfully similar, what with the beards and the glasses?"

Her eyes widened. "Now that you mention it, they look very much alike if those things are all you're paying attention to."

"Beards and glasses stick out. A witness might not notice much else."

And perhaps Mr. Pullman was a very good actor indeed.

On the way back to the Honeybee I asked Bianca if she had used any magic to get Pullman to talk to us.

"Of course not!" She looked scandalized. My confusion must have shown on my face, because she continued. "Good witches never use magic to infringe on the rights of other people. We don't make people do anything."

"But Cookie—" I stopped myself.

Bianca blew a very unladylike raspberry. "Cookie Rios does not take the Rule of Three seriously. Did she do something to make Ethan Ridge talk?"

"Um. Yeah. She used her Voice."

"Katie, I want you to know right now that you should question any instruction you receive from Cookie. She's a member of our coven, but her magical background is, frankly, a little sketchy. And she sees the line between white and black as being a little more flexible than you or I might."

Be careful what you wish for. That was what Daddy had said after I'd inadvertently used what must have been my own nine-year-old Voice on the playground during fourth-grade recess. We were climbing the monkey bars, and Monty Night had asked if Daddy was an Indian chief. The question hadn't been mean, and it hadn't been inaccurate, either. Daddy was part Shawnee, after all, and there actually were a few chiefs among his ancestors.

But another kid had heard Monty and yelled, "Katie Lightfoot thinks she's an Indian princess!"

I'd bristled. "Do not!"

But I found myself standing in the middle of the playground with a dozen kids circling me, dancing and whooping that Hollywood Indian "Woo woo woo woo," fingers returning to their pursed lips over and over. I'd laughed at first, thinking it silly fun.

But then it felt scary, and not so fun at all.

"Stop it," I said. But no one listened, not even Monty, who joined the others. His eyes held laughter and affection. He'd have loved it if I'd really been an Indian princess.

"Please. Stop," I begged, searching the playground for the teacher. She leaned against the school's brick facade, smoking a cigarette and watching us. I waved her over.

She waved back and took another drag.

Woo woo woo woo. Woo woo woo woo.

"Leave me alone!" I'd yelled. Only it had been more than a yell.

It had been a Command. And the other children responded immediately. They left me alone. From then on. None of them spoke to me again unless it was absolutely necessary. They avoided me completely, throughout my entire school career. No hostility. No nothing. It was as if, for those people, I had ceased to exist.

Even Monty, who had been my best friend until then.

My parents had never told me about the Voice, or what it could do. And now that I thought about it, that incident may have confirmed Mama's decision to discourage and hide any hint of my magic.

Well, now I was going to learn everything I could. "Tell me about the Rule of Three."

"It's a Wiccan thing," Bianca said. "But most light witches believe in the truth of it. It's simply the belief that whatever you do, whether for good or ill, will come back to you threefold."

"Talk about a carrot and a stick."

Her eyes widened behind her oversized designer sunglasses. "Ha! I guess it is. Do good to attract good, don't do evil and avoid it in your own life."

"What other rules are there?"

"Well, not rules so much as . . . tenets. The Rule of Three is more or less the same as the Golden Rule found all over the world: Treat others as you would want to be treated."

"Only on steroids, with that whole threefold return thing."

"Right. It's part of the Wiccan Rede. That's a kind of poem that outlines all the basic Wiccan beliefs. Another part of it that guides my magic—and my whole life, for that matter—is the last line: And harm you none, do what you will."

"Cookie isn't Wiccan, though?"

"Cookie picks and chooses what's convenient for her, including some of the old voodoo ways—more than she tells us, perhaps. A lot of voodoo is white magic, though, and Cookie is good—good at heart and good for the spellbook club. She keeps us on our toes and enriches our workings. Please don't think I have any serious problem with her. I just want you to learn about your magic from a positive and joyful perspective."

"I'm still amazed at the things I'm willing to believe since Lucy told me about my family only a few days ago. But it makes so much sense when I think back on things that have happened to me."

"You'll get used to it. And to us. When Lucy told us she wanted to bring you into the spellbook club without our ever meeting you, I had my doubts. That kind of thing isn't usually done. And the murder hastened her revelation considerably. But in one brief week I already know she was right to invite you. You belong here with us, Katie."

Belong. It was a word I'd never known the true meaning of before.

Now I did.

Chapter 16

"Looks like the gang's all here," I said upon entering the Honeybee.

Lucy and Ben sat with their arms around each other on one of the brocade sofas. He looked more rested, so I assumed he'd managed a nap. Jaida sat on the sofa opposite them, and next to her Cookie flipped through a magazine. Teetering on a stepstool, Mimsey fussed with one of five ivy plants hanging above. I still couldn't believe she was seventy-eight. Today she was dressed in sherbet yellow.

Light classical music played softly from a hidden speaker, and the ivies added a final touch of atmosphere. Add the good baking smells and the chatter of happy customers, and it would be the perfect place to draw people back again and again.

Lucky me, to be able to spend my days there.

As long as Albert Hill didn't mess things up.

"What did you find out?" Jaida asked.

I grabbed a couple of coffees while Bianca pulled a table over. I joined her, and we took turns relating

Frank Pullman's revelations. Lucy frowned when she heard his joyous reaction to Mrs. Templeton's death.

"He never asked for details about her murder. Perhaps he wouldn't have been so cavalier if he'd known," I said. "His story was pretty strange, too. If all he did was leave a bit of sawdust behind after restoring some woodwork in her home, why would she set out to systematically ruin him? I mean, she had to convince his boss to fire him, and a lot of other people not to hire him. There had to be more to it than some fictional mess."

"Not necessarily," Cookie chimed in, tossing her magazine on the low table between the sofas. "The condition of her apartment building makes it obvious that she was a woman who pinched her pennies until they squealed."

"Hmm. Maybe," I said. "But why would everyone else go along with it?"

"They were frightened of her," Lucy said. "You saw how she threatened Ben. Threatened us all."

"But a threat isn't the same as having actual power. Yet she was able to ruin Frank Pullman's life, and she kept Ethan Ridge working at a job he hated and paid him next to nothing. He used the word *power* to describe her influence in Savannah as well."

Jaida's eyes narrowed, and she looked around at the others. "Katie's right. Do you think perhaps Mrs. Templeton possessed real power?"

My jaw slackened. "You mean that old witch was a . . . witch?" The last word came out as a squeak. Someone that mean and bitter with real magical power scared the bejesus out of me—even after she was dead. But it certainly would explain a lot.

Lucy wrinkled her nose and dusted off her hands as if she'd been handling something distasteful. "Well, it doesn't matter now. We still have to find out what happened to her so the police will leave Ben alone."

Finished fussing with the plants, Mimsey climbed down from her stepstool. As she joined Bianca and me, she grimaced. "It might matter, Lucille. What if she cast spells to protect herself? Or to keep her secrets?"

"If she cast a spell to protect herself, it sure didn't work very well," I pointed out.

"All I'm saying is that if she had real power, we might run into vestiges of it in the course of trying to find out what happened to her. She wasn't close to any-one, as far as we know, not even Albert. So some of her wards may never have been breached."

"But if she's dead . . ." Lucy trailed off.

Cookie's chin jerked up. "It may not matter, espe-cially if she was strong in black magic. In fact, her own magic may be why the police are having such difficulty finding the real murderer."

We looked around at each other.

My uncle stood. "That's enough. You need to stop this . . . this . . . whatever it is you're doing. I won't put any of you in danger. This problem is mine and mine alone."

"That's not entirely true, Ben." I regretted the words as soon as they left my mouth.

"She's right," Lucy said. "Anything that happens to

you affects us. Katie, the Honeybee, and most especially me. You are not going to prison for a crime you didn't commit, and that's that."

My aunt and uncle glared at each other for a long moment.

Appalled at the rift between them, I said, "Please, don't fight. Please. We'll figure it all out, and no one will get hurt. Uncle Ben, you just have to trust us."

"Of course I trust you. But I most certainly don't trust the people you've been talking to."

It was almost seven when Mungo and I got home. His dish was still full of kibble, but after a quick sniff he turned his back on it.

"Fine. If you want some of the chicken salad I'm planning for supper, you're welcome to it."

But first: a quick run to get the endorphins going. I went into the bedroom, took running clothes out of the armoire, and stripped down.

Of course that would be when the doorbell rang.

Hurriedly, I yanked on shorts and a T-shirt, ran my fingers through my hair and went to see who it was.

Mungo barked and bounced around the living room like a furry maniac. He hadn't reacted that way when Margie had come by the day before, but I didn't know who else it could be. A quick peek around the corner of the window shutter provided the answer.

What the heck was Steve Dawes doing on my front step?

I threw open the door. He wore jeans and a T-shirt, and he'd let his hair down—literally. It was the color of honey and fell nearly to his shoulders. I hate it when a guy has prettier hair than I do, but Steve Dawes had prettier hair than most women. I resisted the urge to touch it, instead waiting in silence for him to speak.

His smile faltered when he saw my expression. "Now don't get mad, okay?" He waved a white paper bag at me like a flag of surrender. His other hand held a bunch of yellow roses. "I know you wanted to wait to go out, but you have to eat. So I brought supper to you. No fuss, no muss, no bother, and no need for a grill."

"How did you know where I live?" I demanded.

"Oh, I have my ways," he said. "Are you going to let me in? This bag contains she-crab soup, bourbon-pulled pork, and a nice big salad to round things out if you're one of those girlie eaters."

My eyes narrowed.

"Plus . . ." He lingered over the word. "I have information about Ethan Ridge."

Behind me, Mungo growled.

Surprised, I whirled to look down at him. "What's the matter?"

Completely still, he stared at Steve. Baffled, I turned back—and saw that three dragonflies had landed on his right shoulder. He looked down at them, then back up at me. Flashed those pearly whites. "Looks like I need to make friends with your canine companion there. But don't worry. I'll bring him around."

Strange though I found it, Mungo's reaction to Steve was the least of my worries. Was Cookie right? Was this guy a witch? Was he capable of using magic on me? Why else would I get that flutter in my stomach every time I saw him?

I hesitated, but the smell emanating from the bag made my decision for me. "Okay. Come in. But you're really pushing it, you know?"

"Oh, trust me. I know."

I tend not to trust anyone who tells me to trust them. Mr. Dawes was no exception.

The dragonflies zoomed off, and Mungo backed slowly away from the door as our visitor entered. Steve knelt in front of my familiar and held his hand out. "I brought enough for you, too, buddy. We're going to be friends. You'll see."

"Mungo," I said, "it's okay."

The little dog threw me a look of disgruntled disagreement. How did he do that?

"He's just protective. That's good. A woman living alone can't be too careful." He stood and walked the few steps to the kitchen door.

"I'm afraid we'll have to eat in there. The patio in back is shaded, but I don't have anyplace to sit out there yet."

"I bet the mosquitoes are terrible, too."

I shrugged. "They're not so bad."

Steve held my gaze for a few beats, then inclined his head in acknowledgment. "You've already solved that problem, then. Good."

"It's just that there seem to be a lot of mosquito hawks around here."

"Uh-huh," he said.

He went into the kitchen, and before I could stop him he picked up Mimsey's *Spellwork for Dummies*, which I had planned to review again while I ate my chicken salad. His eyebrows climbed his forehead, and he held up the book. "You've got to be kidding me."

"It's nothing," I said, trying hard for casual. Maybe a little too hard. "Just one of the books from the Honeybee shelves. It looked amusing."

"Amusing, huh." He flipped through the pages. Frowned. Blinked. "Well, there is some good basic information here." He put the book on the counter and moved back to where I stood in the doorway.

I realized I'd never been this close to him before. The space between us thrummed with energy. Nervous, I licked my lips.

"Are you really just learning?" he asked.

"What?" I managed.

He moved even closer. "Oh, yes. You have power indeed. But am I wrong in thinking you've only recently become aware of it?"

I opened my mouth to speak, but managed only a small croaking sound.

"Oh, my. Oh, Katie-girl. That's delightful."

"Don't call me Katie-girl." There: actual words.

"But you are a girl. A maiden, still wet behind the ears. I have a feeling you'll mature quickly, though."

Bewilderment vied with irritation, all flavored with a significant dollop of physical attraction that belied any notion of girlhood.

"How do you know . . . Are you . . . ?" How could I come right out and ask without sounding like an idiot?

"How could I not know? Didn't you realize we were the same the first time we saw each other?"

I found myself nodding.

"That sense of familiarity, of having met before. But we hadn't, had we? No, but in a sense, we are kin. Of the same family. Though I must admit I've never had quite this reaction to another witch."

"You are a witch." Stating it, I knew it was true. And I knew I'd known all along, just as I'd known I had special abilities.

Steve was like me.

He was very close now, our bodies almost touching. Deliberately, I breathed him in. He smelled like cloves and leather. For a moment, I closed my eyes, savoring his presence like a sip of fine wine.

A small shift in his position, and my eyelids flew open. I ducked to the side, almost escaping the kiss. Our lips barely brushed, but it felt like fire shot out of my toes.

Trying not to gasp, I stumbled to the counter and opened the bag. "She-crab soup, you say."

He laughed. "Okay. We'll do it your way."

Taking a few deep breaths, I unloaded the food and put plates and flatware on the card table. I put the roses in a glass of water and placed them on the trunk in the living room, since there wasn't room for them on the kitchen table. We sat, staring across the table at each other.

"May I serve?" Steve asked.

At first awkwardness threatened to overcome my appetite, but that faded. After sampling the soup— laced with plenty of cream and dry sherry—we piled the bourbon-pulled pork on asiago-and-basil buns. Steve gave Mungo a bit of everything, and the terrier dove right in. Apparently gourmet Southern cooking did a lot to earn favor with us both.

"Do you have any siblings?" Steve asked.

"Talk to me about Ethan Ridge," I responded.

"God, you're prickly." He took a bite and regarded me while he chewed and swallowed. "Okay. I talked to a friend of mine who's a parole officer. Not Ridge's, mind you, but he did me a favor and checked some records. The guy was in for fraud and assault."

I cocked my head. "Really." So Ethan officially had a violent background. "What kind of assault?"

"The kind involving fists and boots."

"Hands-on, then." I grimaced. Breaking someone's neck was pretty much a hands-on situation, too. "Let me guess—bar fight?"

"Oh, no. Much better." Steve grinned.

I raised my eyebrows.

"The reason he went after his victim was because the man threatened to turn him in for the fraud. See, Ridge sold a lot of people funeral plots that didn't technically exist. The same ones, over and over, at Greenwich Cemetery. "

"So he's a con man who tried to solve a problem by attacking someone. And from what he told me, he had a heck of a problem with his employer, too. An unsolvable problem, at least to his way of thinking. Maybe he fell back into old habits."

"Could be. Are you the only one poking your nose into the murder, or is the coven helping?"

"Er . . ."

"I mean, the 'book club,' " he said. "I'm pretty fair at

sniffing out other practitioners of magic and, darlin', those ladies definitely fit the bill."

"Do they know you know?" I didn't think so. Cookie had only been guessing when she suggested Steve might be a witch.

"Mrs. Carmichael does. We've had . . . dealings . . . in the past."

Come to think of it, Mimsey had acted kind of funny around Steve. "What sort of dealings?"

"I'll tell you when you stop pushing me away."

"Guess I'll have to wait, then."

He looked plaintively at the ceiling, as if pleading with the gods. I ignored his theatrics.

We ate in silence for a few more minutes. My thoughts darted from Steve-as-witch to Ethan the con man. The manager of the Peachtree Arms didn't look anything like Uncle Ben, though. But the witness hadn't actually seen the murder, only someone hanging around Mrs. Templeton's Cadillac. I wondered whether Quinn was pursuing Ethan Ridge as a possible suspect.

Finally, I sat back in my chair and dabbed at the corner of my mouth with a napkin. "This is insanely good, you know. So much for going for a run."

"You're a runner?" Steve asked. "Of course you are. I should have guessed from your lean and lithe physique."

I gave him a look.

"I'm serious. Listen, I run, too. There's a great trail through the wildlife refuge. We should go sometime."

Mungo yipped and ran into the living room, saving me from having to answer. Seconds later, the doorbell

rang again. Half glad for an excuse to delay more ca-
loric intake, I rose to answer it. But when I saw who it
was, my stomach fluttered all over again—this time
from apprehension.

Declan greeted me with a big grin. "Hey, there. I
brought you a present." He gestured to his truck, now
parked behind the Bug in my driveway. Black iron
scrollwork poked up from the bed.

"A present? That's so nice. What is it?"

But Declan didn't answer. He was looking over my
shoulder, into the living room. He looked less than
pleased.

I winced.

"What's he doing here?" Declan asked.

I stepped back to let him in. Steve stood in the
middle of the living room, arms held slightly out
from his sides. And there I was, caught in a crossfire
of glares.

"All right, that's enough, you two," I said. "I don't
know what your problem is, but I wish you'd try to get
along while you're in my home."

A moment of silence stretched out long and thin,
then snapped. "Don't worry, Katie-*girl*," Steve said. "I
have no intention of remaining in your house as long
as this guy is here." He pushed past me.

I stumbled.

Declan's hand shot out and grabbed Steve's shoulder. "Don't touch her."

I watched red fury pass through Steve. He shrugged
Declan's hand off. "I'm not the dangerous one, McCarthy. I'm not the one who lets people die."

My jaw dropped. Steve stalked down the front walkway without another word, climbed into a black Land Rover parked across the street, started the engine and roared off.

Shocked, I raised my palms toward Declan. "What the heck is he talking about?"

Chapter 17

"It's kind of a long story." Declan took a sip of wine and settled back in one of the chairs he'd brought over. Mungo lay down and rested his chin on Declan's foot.

Funny that I'd been talking about not having any patio furniture, because that was exactly what Declan had in the back of his truck. His neighbor wanted to get rid of the bistro set, and my new fireman friend offered to take it off his hands—and put it into mine. He also brought a two-burner hibachi, a bottle of lovely Cabernet Sauvignon and two stemmed wineglasses.

"Then I guess you'd better get started telling it," I said. A bit blunt, perhaps, but I was determined to get to the bottom of the enmity between Mr. Dawes and Mr. McCarthy. I wasn't above plying my guest with some of his own wine to get the story, either.

"It's nice out here." His gaze took in the expanse of green lawn, the tidy wooden fence around it all. Somewhere nearby, honeysuckle had started to bloom, the fragrance barely teasing through the air. We could hear the water in the little stream, and crickets chirped in the bushes.

"You're lucky."

I nodded my thanks to the iridescent dragonflies patrolling the edges of the property, grazing on their prey while creating a zone free of biting insects for yours truly.

"Yes, very lucky," I said. "You know, I thought you two might actually mix it up in there."

Declan sighed. "Yeah. Sorry about that. We usually manage to avoid each other, but since your arrival that's been kind of difficult." He stopped and licked his lips. "Is he . . . Are you, um, interested in him?"

"Honestly? I recently had a bad breakup, and it doesn't seem like a good idea to date anyone right now." My answer was automatic, though I wasn't convinced it was true anymore.

"What, exactly, do you call having supper with Steve Dawes, then?"

"An accident—at least on my part. He asked me out, I said I couldn't, so he showed up with takeout."

"That's pretty pushy."

I nodded. "Sure was." Never mind how sexy his confidence was, or my own purely physical reaction. "But it wasn't a date."

Relief played across the planes of Declan's face. "Well, that's good news, at least. I'd hate to see you get mixed up with him."

I poked the bear. "Still, he seems nice enough. You know, after my dating hiatus is up and all."

"He's a player, Katie. If your heart is still bruised from your last boyfriend—or if you simply don't want to be hurt—you should stay away from him. Please. I'm telling you that from the perspective of someone who knows him pretty well, not because of any problem we have with each other."

"You were friends once, then?"

"Not really, but his brother, Arnie, and I were best friends. We trained to be firefighters together, were roommates for a while even. We went through our first year as rookies pretty much joined at the hip."

Alarm bells sounded in the far recesses of my brain.

"What happened to him?" I forced myself to ask. But I knew the answer from Uncle Ben already.

Declan's head dropped, and he pinched the bridge of his nose. "He died."

"I'm so sorry."

He raised his head. Unshed tears blurred the intense blue of his eyes. "I didn't kill him. But I couldn't help him. I miss him, and yet I still get so darn angry when I think about what he did!"

I let him talk.

"It was a bad fire, the building fully engaged by the time we got there." He was still looking out at the yard, but I could tell he was seeing the flames. "See, you have to know firefighters live by the two-in-two-out rule," he said. "You go in with your partner, you stick together *no matter what*, and you come out together. No exceptions. Ever. You can keep each other alive that way. But at that fire, Arnie didn't follow the rule. He left me and the hose line to search a room on his own. I tried to stop him, but he wouldn't listen." He spoke the last words through gritted teeth.

"It got bad fast. The smoke increased and visibility

deteriorated. Arnie got turned around and couldn't find the hose line or me. So he called a mayday to let Ben know he didn't know his exact location. They sent in help immediately, but they couldn't get to him fast enough."

My hand covered his, and I squeezed his fingers. "I know it wasn't your fault. Ben told me a little about it."

"But Steve blames me for his brother's death. Always has. And frankly, I'm getting tired of it."

Oh. Wow.

"Declan—," I began.

"Arnie screwed up! I couldn't stop him."

"I know," I repeated. "Ben knows." I pushed his wineglass across the table toward him.

He grabbed it and took a big slug.

"Why does Steve blame you? He has to know about Arnie's mistake."

"Doesn't believe it. Thinks his little brother could do no wrong. So it must have been my fault, right? See, he not only accuses me of getting his brother killed, but of shifting the blame for the whole incident to Arnie. It's been years, and his hatred is still white-hot. It took me a long time, but I finally realized that I'll never be able to do anything to change that." He moved his free hand to sandwich mine against his fingers. "But it's important to me that you know what really happened."

I reached for my wine with my unencumbered hand, curiously content to leave my other one right where it was. I kept my eyes on his face, only now realizing how much daylight had faded from the sky as we'd talked.

Mungo lifted his head, barked and ran out into the

middle of the lawn. We both turned to watch him trotting and whirling among hundreds of tiny lights. The fireflies moved around him, first clockwise and then counterclockwise. Deosil and widdershins, as my coven—*my coven*—would say. As I watched my familiar dance joyfully within the glowing circle, I wondered whether their movement was purposeful.

Well, of course it was. Everything was purposeful, whether we understood the purpose or not. That had resonated as deeply as any of the things the spellbook club had told me.

"I've never seen anything like that," Declan breathed, still holding my hand in his.

Gently, I extricated it. "Maybe they're attracted to doggy smell." Lame, but I couldn't tell him the truth, however much I wanted to. How wonderful it would be if this sweet man could share my secret, though.

Shaking his head, he stood. "Amazing." He drained his wine. "But I know you have a big day tomorrow, so I'll get going."

"Let's just hope it goes off without a hitch. We've had enough excitement from the DBA brunch to last a lifetime." I stood, too, and we walked around the edge of the small house to the driveway.

"Then let's hope for plain, boring success." There was still a note of sadness in his voice, but I had the feeling it had been there for a long time and would be for a while longer before it was gone altogether. I could only hope that it had helped for him to talk about his friend.

Though I hadn't given him much choice.

"I'll check in when I get a chance." He opened the door of his truck and turned back to me. "I really am sorry about running into Dawes. I never would have stopped by if I'd known he was here."

"No worries. It was harder on you than on me."

He stroked my cheek with his thumb. Before I knew it, his lips were on mine. His kiss was quick, casual and undemanding. Warm and comforting. Nice. My body pressed against his for a moment before I gathered my wits and stepped back.

"Um," I said.

He grinned. "Don't worry. That was just an accident. Like having supper with someone."

My lips parted in surprise, and he climbed into his truck. Rolled down the window. "See you, Katie. Break a leg—or whatever bakers do."

I stood in the driveway for a full minute after he drove away.

"Just a friend?"

I turned to see Margie standing on her front steps, a smile playing on her face in the yellow porch light. "I need me a friend like that. Only Redding would pop a vein."

"It was . . . Oh, never mind, Margie!"

Her laughter erupted. "Don't mind me. You have fun, darlin'. Just save some details for your old married neighbor, if you will. Not the best ones, of course—just a few goodies to get me through Bart teething. Speak of the devil . . ." The sound of a crying baby drifted out onto the night, and she raised her hand. "Good night, Katie."

I waved at her and went back inside, Mungo at my heels as always. I turned the floor lamp on and plopped down on my purple sofa.

"Well, mini-me, what am I supposed to do now?"

His head tipped to one side.

It had been a busy night, indeed, but now everyone was gone and the rest of the night stretched out ahead. My nerves were on edge, and energy thrummed under my skin. Images flashed like strobes through my mind: Steve, then Declan, then Ethan Ridge and finally Mrs. Templeton sitting in her car, her head at that funny angle. I rubbed my eyes, but they kept coming.

Yip.

Mungo ran into the kitchen. I followed to find him standing on his hind legs pawing at the cupboard. On the counter above was the container of Lucy's seven-layer bars.

"Okay, okay. I suppose you want some, too."

Yip.

"But no chocolate for you."

Pant. Grin.

I ate the cookie bar, surprised to find it less cloying than some I'd sampled in the past. Coconut and chocolate chips combined pleasingly with the graham crackers and slightly bitter walnuts, all glued together with condensed milk. As I chewed I realized Lucy had substituted peanut butter chips for the usual butterscotch chips. But that was only six layers. What was the seventh?

Holding the bar up to the light, I picked at it with my fingernail. Flecks of green were sandwiched between the coconut and the chocolate chips and walnuts. Of course: an herb. What had Lucy said she'd added? Agri-something.

A quick search of the Internet reminded me that her

not-so-secret ingredient was agrimony, a member of the rose family with a reputation as a sleep aid. It wouldn't work for me, of course, but I'd have to remember to ask her about it.

After making sure it didn't contain chocolate chips, I gave Mungo a small bite. He practically inhaled it, and we headed off to get ready for bed. At least I felt like I could concentrate enough to read now.

Head on the pillow, I thought about how Declan's lips had felt on mine. About how they might feel again. How would he react to the word *hedgewitch*?

On the other hand, Steve already knew what I was. Not from any independent knowledge—I couldn't imagine anyone had told him. He just *knew*, the same way I knew things. Was that why my skin almost burned when he was in the same room? Why my teeth ached?

The signaling shiver ran down my back.

I wondered what Mama would say about all this. What Daddy would say, for that matter. After everything Lucy had told me, I kept imagining the conversation I would eventually have with him. As she put it, he'd had my back.

Well, sort of.

The problem was, I absolutely could *not* imagine the conversation I'd have with Mama, and so far that had prevented me from doing anything more than making that quick call to check in and let them know I was all right.

Mungo started snoring next to me. Next thing I knew, Lucy's seven-layer bar hit me like a sack of bricks. My last thought before sinking into blessed oblivion was how much I adored the scents of clove and leather.

I slept for *five whole hours*. Not since the age of twelve had I slept that long at one time.

The problem was, I hadn't set an alarm clock since back then, either, so I was over half an hour late getting to the Honeybee. I burst through the door, shedding my tote in the office and donning a white chef's apron in seconds flat.

"You look refreshed," Lucy said, calm as could be.

"Well, I feel frazzled as all get-out. I overslept, on this morning of all mornings." The more I thought about it, the more upset I became.

She smiled. "You ate a seven-layer bar, didn't you?"

"Yes. Thanks a lot." Couldn't quite keep the sarcasm out of my voice.

Lucy ignored it. "You're welcome. Where's Mungo?"

"I asked him very nicely if he minded staying home today since it's the grand opening and I can't afford to be distracted. He graciously agreed."

Luckily, we'd prepared well, and the aromas of hot baked goods soon wafted into every corner. As the sun rose, Lucy and I moved from oven to counter, counter to display case in a synchronized dance of efficiency. Her tie-dyed cotton skirt swished and twirled, and in the end I switched out my smeared apron for a frilly bright red one. By the time Ben showed up we were calmly sipping lattes and crunching on sesame biscotti.

He grabbed a biscotti to eat while he got the cash drawer ready and checked the supplies behind the espresso counter. Lucy got up and turned on the music, light jazz for first thing in the morning. At seven o'clock the three of us went to the front of the Honeybee together. Ben kissed Lucy on the cheek and gave me a squeeze. "Here we go!" He flung the door open.

I almost hooted with joy: A dozen people were waiting on the sidewalk.

Ben ushered them in and slipped behind the counter. The owner of the knitting store next door stepped up to the register first. She peered at the display case through a pair of rhinestone-rimmed glasses and ran her tongue over her lips.

Ben adjusted the chef's apron he wore over a yellow short-sleeved shirt and khakis. "What can I get for you, Annette?"

"Oh, dear. There are far too many enticing choices." Then she laughed. "I guess I'll just have to work my way through everything. Today let's make it one of those." She pointed to a pumpkin–cream cheese scone. "And a cup of coffee. Dark roast."

"Excellent choice." He rang up her order while Lucy poured her coffee, then moved on to the next customer.

"Oh, my," Annette mumbled around a bite of scone. "That's too good." She swallowed. "I'm going to be in serious trouble, having you right next door."

I caught her eye and grinned. She could talk with her mouth full all she wanted if she was going to say things like that.

The way Ben filled orders, took money and joked with customers, it seemed as though he'd done it forever. Meanwhile, I continued to mix and whip and sprinkle and bake in the kitchen while Lucy played barista.

Only it wasn't play anymore. The Honeybee was really open!

After the initial rush, a slight lull caused me concern, but soon the pace picked up again. People going to work and early-bird tourists made up most of the clientele until close to ten o'clock, when the laptop-bearing crowd arrived. They settled in at tables and on the sofas, and most stayed for much longer than the previous group had, sipping and munching and typing away.

We gave away a ton of peach-and-pecan mini-pies, a kind of loss leader for our first day only. The peaches were spiced with cinnamon and plenty of Lucy's muttering with the intention to increase good luck and money. Sure enough, once customers tasted the sweet concoctions, they ended up purchasing other goodies to take home to their families.

Wearing a pale orange twinset, Mimsey breezed in about noon and took up a station by the bookshelf. Instantly, she began chatting with customers. She seemed to be having a ball, and so did they. Many left with books in their hands.

"Wait a minute," I said to Lucy. "Now we're a lending library?"

"We are whatever people need us to be. Those books are there to be found by those who need them. If they want to take them home, so be it. You have to trust that books—whether those or others—will come back to us."

"Threefold?" I muttered.

She laughed.

Mimsey wasn't the only person steering people toward what they needed. My aunt did her share of guiding customers to this cookie or that scone, which I now knew were not only delicious but also contained magic. Besides adding cinnamon to the mini-pies, she told me allspice was good for money, luck and healing; basil was protective and facilitated change; and caraway and rosemary both promoted fidelity. The last two she'd mixed into the savory Parmesan muffins—a brilliant combination.

There was so darn much to learn.

As I refilled the display case, I mused on Steve's assertion that there was no such thing as bad publicity. Perhaps that was doubly true given Jack Jenkins' comment that the folks in Savannah had a particular interest in the macabre. But no one had asked any questions about the murder or said a word about Mrs. Templeton.

Until, that is, a tall man with a shock of gray hair and searching eyes approached the register.

"Ben."

"Peter."

Uh-oh.

"I'd like to talk with your niece. Is she here?"

I came out of the kitchen, wiping my hands on a towel. "I'm Katie Lightfoot. Detective Quinn, I presume?"

He nodded.

"Let's go back to the office, if you will. I'd rather not talk in front of customers." A couple nearby watched us with great interest.

"Of course," he said.

The detective followed me through the kitchen, and

I shut the office door behind us. As he settled into the office chair that Mungo had claimed as his own, I could only hope his dark blue slacks wouldn't show any of my terrier's black hair when he got up. The last thing we needed right now was a visit from a suspicious health department.

"Thank you for taking the time to talk with me. I know y'all opened to the public today," he said.

I pulled the chair out from behind the desk and sank into it, grateful to be off my feet. "No problem. Though I can't imagine there's anything new I can tell you about Mavis Templeton's murder. That is why you're here, isn't it?"

"Yes. I understand you witnessed the argument between Templeton and your uncle."

"It wasn't an argument."

He started to speak, then stopped, reconsidering. "All right, then. Tell me what happened."

"Well, she wouldn't pay the amount we contracted for when we agreed to provide brunch for the Downtown Business Association. Naturally, Ben told her that was unacceptable." I spoke slowly, choosing my words with care. "She continued to refuse, so Ben told her if she didn't pay us the full amount he would contact the president of the DBA. Mrs. Templeton went off the deep end, not Ben. She threatened and harangued and stomped out." I took a deep breath and continued, my tone low but intense. "But you can't possibly think that's a motive for murder. For heaven's sake, you know Ben, don't you?"

"We've worked together, yes."

"Then you know he's not one to fly off the handle.

He was the *fire chief*—how many times has he had to deal with difficult situations? Besides, we only had to talk to Mr. Jenkins to get the money."

Quinn cocked his head to one side. "What about her threats?"

"Bah. What of them?" Words far bolder than I felt, but I didn't want Quinn to sense any weakness. "Why aren't you investigating all the people who hated Mrs. Templeton? The ones who truly despised her? Because of a witness who happened to see someone who looked vaguely like my uncle in the vicinity of the murder?"

"Not in the vicinity. On the sidewalk. Right by her Cadillac."

I waved that away. "So you're not looking at the apartment manager of the Peachtree Arms? Or any of the tenants who had to put up with how Mrs. Templeton ran the place, as if it were some kind of slum? There's a girl who's a quadriplegic now because of an elevator accident there. What about Mrs. Templeton's own nephew, Albert Hill? Doesn't he inherit? Oh! If you're looking for someone with a beard and glasses like Ben, someone who utterly *loathed* that old woman, try talking to Frank Pullman." Now my words spilled out, heavily flavored with indignation.

His eyes narrowed. "I thought you were a recent transplant to Savannah. How would you know all those people?"

Too late, I realized I'd overstepped.

I rubbed my face. "Sorry. Really. Of course you're looking at everyone. Ben keeps telling me how good you are at your job. I'm just frustrated."

"So am I," he said.

My head jerked up. "Really?"

"What do you think? Someone was murdered in full daylight, right on Broughton Street, and I don't have any viable suspects except a man I happen to personally like very much."

My shoulders slumped.

"You mentioned the name Frank Pullman."

"Yes! You know about him, then."

"I'll follow up. But I still think you know an awful lot about a woman you barely met."

"I've heard some things," I began.

He gave me a look.

"And asked a few questions."

"That's what I thought. Ms. Lightfoot, you need to leave homicide investigations to the professionals."

"But—"

"You don't know what you're doing."

"If you don't know about Frank Pullman, neither do you."

Oops.

Detective Quinn stood abruptly. "I'll be in touch if I have any more questions." His voice held barely contained anger.

"You didn't ask me very many."

"Yeah, I noticed that, too. Kind of hard to get a word in edgewise with you." He opened the office door and strode into the kitchen. The back door opened and closed.

Had I just made things worse for Ben?

Chapter 18

When I emerged alone from the back, Ben shot a worried glance my way. The two women buying a dozen ginger-molasses muffins came first, though. It was almost two, and I expected a lull before another influx of customers in the late afternoon seeking a caffeine-and-sugar fix to get them through to the evening hours.

When he was finally free, I sidled up beside my uncle and murmured, "I don't think I made a very good impression on your Detective Quinn."

"Why?"

"Hmm. He didn't like it that I've been asking questions about Mrs. Templeton. And I might have been a little, well, snarkier than I should have been."

He sighed.

Injecting a hopeful note into my voice, I said, "But I was able to give him a bit of information he didn't have."

My uncle adopted a stoic expression. "That's good."

I gave him a quick hug and ducked away as another customer approached. But guilt followed me as I poured a cup of coffee and snagged a muffin. I was supposed to be helping Ben, not making things worse.

Biting into the soft, molasses-laden crumb stuffed with golden-pink candied ginger, I made my way to the reading area. Mimsey perched on one of the sofas, chatting with a young woman who struck me as extraordinarily dowdy for someone so close to my own age. Compared to the orange of Mimsey's twinset, the woman's pale skin, peanut-butter-colored hair, beige slacks and blouse were sedate at best. But the stretched-out brown cotton cardigan, out of place in the spring heat anyway, distinctly dragged the whole ensemble right down to drab.

Mimsey patted her on the arm and handed her a book. I almost choked on my muffin when I saw the title: *Sex Secrets of the Stars*.

"You go ahead and take this home, sweetie. Believe me, your hubby will start staying home in the evenings again. And don't forget to give him some of those Parmesan muffins. After all, the other way to a man's heart is through his stomach."

"I don't know how to thank you." The woman stood. "For that matter, I don't know how I ended up telling a perfect stranger so many details about my life. You were so kind to listen. And to offer such practical advice. I feel much better now." As she walked by me she smiled, and her entire face was transformed. I found myself thinking of her as beautiful mere moments after thinking exactly the opposite.

"What did you do to her?" I asked.

Mimsey blinked her innocence. "I don't know what you mean."

"Did you glamour her?" I'd read about glamouring in *Spellwork for Dummies*. And given the older woman's youthful appearance, I could only imagine how good she was at such things.

"Don't be ridiculous. She was always a gorgeous woman. Over time life got heavier, and her husband started looking around. The more he did that, the uglier she saw herself, because she was judging herself through his eyes and not her own. It's a scenario that plays out over and over, all around us. Hardly rocket science, dear. She only had to be made aware."

"What about sending her home with those muffins that Lucy magically primed? Isn't a spell for fidelity interfering with her husband's will? I thought that was verboten."

"Oh, Katie. Giving a love boost to two people who are already in love but have managed to forget it isn't introducing anything new to their relationship. It's a reminder more than interference."

I harrumphed.

"Besides," she said, "Lucy has a fine touch. Her hedgewitchery never forces. It only . . . encourages."

Shrugging, I chewed my last bite of muffin while pondering what magical effect it might have on me. Knowing my gentle aunt, I probably didn't need to worry. Much.

Absently, I reached over to realign a book on the shelf next to me. It was one of the ones the spellbook club had brought to the bakery the first time I met them: *Self-Defense for Pacifists*. Curious, I pulled the heavy tome out and flipped the pages. Huh. The suggestions to kick out your attacker's knee, poke your fingers in his eyes, jam your heel into his instep and hit him in the throat with your fist seemed a bit violent for most pacifists. The emphasis seemed to be on doing anything you could do to protect yourself without outright killing the other person.

As I slipped the book back on the shelf, a brash voice drifted over from where a large woman stood talking to Ben at the register. "I declare, Mr. Eagel. That woman got what was coming to her. I don't condone that kind of violence, mind you, but everyone knew Mavis Templeton was difficult at best and truly dangerous if you crossed her. I never had any real truck with her, thank the good Lord, but I know her nephew. Heavens, the things he had to put up with! Fetching and carrying, driving her around, running errands—always at her beck and call."

My tired feet forgotten, I launched upright and then toned down my approach to look a bit more casual than I felt. Albert Hill was high on my list of suspects, and not just because I disliked him so much. Still, how handy would it be for him to be the murderer? It would be hard for him to sue anyone from prison.

"You know Albert, then," I said over my shoulder as I removed the grounds from the big drip coffeemaker behind Ben and dumped them in the compost bucket.

Her horsy face swung toward me. "Oh, my, yes. Such a nice young man."

Ben and I exchanged poker-faced looks.

"He and that friend of his helped me with the arrangements after my husband died. We never had children, you know."

I tried smiling my sympathy at her.

"Well," she continued, "if it weren't for dear Albert and that friend— What was his name?" She peered at me as if I might really have an answer.

I held my palms up to the ceiling. "I'm afraid I don't know."

She looked down at the floor and tapped her foot. "The name is on the tip of my tongue. Right there. I can almost taste it. Edward . . . Evan . . . Ethan! His name was Ethan, just like Ethan Frome!"

My brain wrenched at the juxtaposition of Ethan Frome and the only Ethan I'd met since coming to Savannah. "Ethan Ridge? Was that his name?"

She pointed a victorious finger at me. "Yes! You know him, too, then? What a sweet boy. He has some kind of pull in the mortuary business. He and Albert handled all the details of Harry's cremation last year, and all I had to do was show up at the service."

"May I ask a question, Mrs. . . . ?" I offered my hand.

"This is Mrs. Standish," Ben said. "Mrs. Standish, this is my niece, Katie Lightfoot."

"Oh, I am so very pleased to meet you." Her hand enveloped mine in a crushing grip.

"Likewise," I said through gritted teeth.

"You had a question, dear?"

Extricating my bruised digits from her grasp, I nodded. "I was just wondering whether you paid the funeral home directly, or if you gave the full amount to Albert and Ethan."

"Only to Albert," she said. "He paid all the bills for me. It was such a relief to have all that worry off my hands."

Ben and I exchanged another look.

"I imagine it was," I said. "Here, let me give you a few little pies to take with you."

"Oh! How generous of you! They look absolutely scrumptious." Half of one went immediately into her mouth.

"We want our customers to be happy," Ben said with a grin. "And, of course, for them to tell their friends if they enjoy our baked goods."

She swallowed. "Yummy! I'll be sure to tell everyone I know, Mr. Eagel. We'll get the whole town in here! Toodle-loo!"

We watched her considerable backside sway out the door, two bags of goodies in one large hand while the other guided the remaining half of the mini-pie to her lips. When the door had closed behind her, Ben glanced around at the half-populated tables to see if anyone could hear, then leaned close to me.

"What was that all about?" he whispered.

In a low voice, I said, "It turns out Ethan Ridge used to dabble a bit in fraud. Steve told me he went to prison after being convicted of assault. He'd conned a man into buying nonexistent cemetery plots, and when the man found out about it he challenged Ethan. Ethan's solution was to beat him up."

Ben shook his head. "Cemetery plots, and now contacts with a mortuary. Makes me wonder whether Harry Standish was actually cremated at all."

I grimaced. "Preying on the grief-stricken is the worst. And if Ethan is back to his old ways, it sounds like he has a partner in Albert Hill. Who, it's rumored, is willing to cross to the other side of the law if there's money in it."

Two men with motives to murder a cranky old woman. Ethan hadn't seemed too fond of Albert. Though in truth he'd only said it was good that I wasn't his friend. That didn't mean *he* wasn't Albert's friend. According to Mrs. Standish, the two men were friends, but the look on Albert's face when he'd screeched out of the Peachtree Arms and almost hit Declan and me had been anything but friendly.

Could they have done it together? Or had one chivvied the other into killing Mrs. Templeton? It was a stretch to imagine Ethan convincing Albert to kill his own aunt, but it was possible. Albert struck me as a potentially violent and definitely immoral man. But it was easier to imagine him convincing Ethan to commit murder. After all, the apartment manager had an official history of hands-on brutality and felt Mrs. Templeton had forced him into a life he didn't want to lead.

Plus, there would be plenty of inheritance money that Albert could use to pay for services rendered.

Detective Quinn made me wait on hold for almost fifteen minutes before he took my call, but I pushed away the idea that he would do something like that out of spite. When he finally came on the line, I changed my mind about that.

"There's a new connection between Albert Hill and Ethan Ridge—"

He interrupted me. "I told you to stop asking questions, Ms. Lightfoot. Do I have to force you to comply?"

"Hey, wait a minute. First off, I found this out from a simple conversation with a Honeybee customer. And second, what do you mean, 'force me to comply'?"

"I can arrest you for obstructing justice." He didn't sound like he was kidding.

"That's ridiculous." I tried to imbue my words with amused verve. It didn't work.

"Is it?"

"You wouldn't."

He sighed. "Probably not. But I could. Don't you see? *Someone out there broke a woman's neck. On the street. In the middle of the day.* The idea of you poking that bear gives me the willies."

"But you think my own uncle did it! Good heavens, doesn't *that* give you the willies?"

His voice hardened. "And you're trying to protect him. I understand that, at least in theory. But I'm good at my job, and you need to trust me."

Did I mention I rarely trust people who tell me to trust them?

"Albert Hill and Ethan Ridge are not people you want to mess with. You have to trust me on that, too." His condescending tone made me want to kick something.

"What, are you afraid Albert's going to sue you?" I couldn't quite keep the sarcasm out of my voice.

The silence on the other end of the line dragged on for a painfully long time. Finally Detective Quinn said, "Now that is exactly the kind of thing I don't want you to go around doing."

"What?"

"Pissing people off." And he hung up on me.

Chapter 19

Stunned, I slowly replaced the office phone in its cradle. I didn't go around making people angry at me. Not Katie Lightfoot. Uh-uh.

Except . . . I had. Detective Quinn had made me mad first, of course, with his patronizing attitude and his insistence on viewing Ben as a suspect. Still, it wasn't like me to be so defiant in the face of authority. I'd always followed the rules, careful to dot my i's and cross my t's.

Maybe Mama was right. Maybe Lucy was turning me into a whole different person.

Or maybe it was simply the confidence that resulted from knowing who—and what—I was.

I stood and began pacing back and forth in the small space.

At any rate, it was obvious Quinn didn't care about what I'd learned, and he wouldn't follow up with Albert or Ethan. Frankly, I wasn't much for confronting Albert, either. For one thing, his vitriolic attitude made it unlikely he'd give me the time of day.

Not to mention he smelled bad.

However, I was up for another visit to Ethan. Perhaps Cookie would be available to help again, to use her Voice to impel him to give some answers. It had worked pretty well before.

At least at first. The effect of her Voice had seemed relatively short-lived.

I had my Voice, though.

Nah. That would be stupid, right? No matter my heredity or the innate ability Lucy was so convinced about, I was a newbie witch. Going around and using what must be a pretty rusty Voice to get people to talk made no sense. Not to mention how badly it had backfired the one time I remembered using it.

Besides, I was haunted by the whole Rule of Three thing Bianca had told me about. My gut—and almost three decades of life experience—told me she was right. I paused in my pacing and leaned against the desk. Despite a murder and the police suspecting Uncle Ben, life was better than it had been for a very long time. No way was I going to start messing with karma now.

So I needed someone other than Cookie to go with me. My thoughts flew to Steve Dawes. After all, he was a witch and a man. Double your protection, double your fun. But I didn't know him well enough to trust what he'd do if confronted. In other words, I'd only just discovered he was a witch, and I didn't know what kind of witch.

Though I could at least infer he wasn't the type to take magical revenge on the man he blamed for his brother's death.

A man I realized I didn't know much better than I

knew Steve, but whom I did trust. Part of that feeling I could rationalize from Declan's relationship with Ben, and part came from the short amount of time we'd spent together.

Plus, he was a very nice kisser.

I was pretty sure Steve would be, too, given the chance. Not so much *nice* as *hot*. But for all I knew, Steve wasn't even talking to me after the encounter with Declan at my house the evening before.

Focus, Katie.

Okay, Declan it was. If he wasn't working.

I went out front. "Ben?"

"Hmm?" He looked up from the register receipt tape he was changing.

"What is Declan's work schedule like?"

My uncle smiled broadly. "Firefighters typically work two twenty-four-hour shifts a week. The rest of the time they're free. He should be free now, in fact."

Excellent. I asked for Declan's phone number then, which elicited yet another big grin. I ignored it. The less Ben knew about what I wanted to do, the better.

"Katie!" Declan's surprise at my call was evident. "How's the grand opening going?"

"It is indeed grand," I said. "I'm actually surprised at how many customers we've had the first day." I suspected Lucy et al. had cast a prosperity spell that went beyond cinnamon-laced peaches. If they had, it had sure kicked in quickly. However, Ben had also worked hard on the advertising, and word had certainly spread after the DBA brunch. And perhaps Steve was right about people wanting to check out the bakery where Mrs. Templeton had been just before someone killed her.

We chatted for a few minutes before I sprang my request. I was surprised when Declan showed so little enthusiasm about accompanying me.

"But, Deck," I said, trying out Ben's nickname, "I found out today that Ethan Ridge and Albert Hill knew each other long before Mrs. Templeton was killed. In fact, they've likely had some illegal dealings already."

"So tell the cops," he said.

"Um, yeah. I tried. They aren't exactly open to my suggestions," I said. "Detective Quinn doesn't think I should be involving myself in the investigation."

"He's not exactly wrong about that."

"Oh, please. Not you, too!" Irritation flared. How was I supposed to find Mavis Templeton's killer like this? "I'm getting darn sick of people trying to protect me when I'm only trying to help Uncle Ben. And by people, I mean men. The women who know I'm looking into her murder are all very encouraging."

"Katie . . ."

"Don't you 'Katie' me. Ben is your friend, your mentor even. How you could walk away from a possible clue is beyond me. But don't you worry. I'll take care of talking to Mrs. Templeton's apartment manager without any help from you."

His soft sigh drifted through the earpiece. "Oh, for Pete's sake. All right, I'll go with you. But I'm busy until six o'clock."

"That's fine. Can you pick me up?"

"Your place at six thirty. See you then."

"Declan?"

"Yeah." Defeat in his tone.

"Thank you."

A pause, and then he laughed. "You're incredibly stubborn. And you're welcome."

Nobody seemed to mind Mungo riding around in my tote bag in the hardware store. In fact, while I was selecting a shovel, the guy in the garden department made goo-goo eyes at the terrier as if he were the cutest baby in the world.

Which, come to think of it, maybe he was.

At home, with an hour and a half to kill before Declan came to get me, I changed into grubby clothes. Then I quickly fixed Mungo a snack and grabbed my shiny new shovel. We went out to the backyard, where I stretched my arms wide and inhaled spring deep into my lungs. A heron flapped lazily in the blue above, heading for water.

Walking along the fence line in the backyard, I dropped stakes in a rough outline of the garden area while Mungo delicately ate his poached chicken from a plate on the patio and watched me. I was vaguely aware of the sound of children's laughter as I rearranged the stakes a few times. Once satisfied, I pounded them all in. Finally, I began cutting the outline of my herb garden from the sod. Mungo, his belly full, trotted over to supervise.

"Whatcha doin'?" Margie called.

I turned, and realized my neighbors could see my garden area from their patio. She and two men were sitting under a ginormous umbrella, sipping from green bottles. Unwilling to bellow back at her, I waved, then dropped my hand as I saw that one of the men was Frank Pullman.

He really did look like Uncle Ben from this far away, especially in the few seconds it took to register his beard and glasses. Was there a killer sitting on my neighbor's lawn chair, drinking and laughing? What would Pullman have to say to me now? Or had Quinn even talked to him?

"Come on over!" Margie called. "I want you to meet Redding."

I sighed and looked at Mungo. He licked his lips in concern.

"I'll come around front, okay?" I said in a loud voice, then murmured to the dog at my feet, "It'll be okay. You stay here, though."

Margie launched to her feet and hurried inside.

She was waiting when I came around the corner of her porch, still removing my work gloves. She led me through a living room littered with so many toys you could hardly see the beige wall-to-wall carpet. It looked clean, though, and I could only imagine how hard it was to keep up with the JJs as well as a baby.

Outside, both men stood. I gestured them back into their seats. The JJs waved from their bright plastic play structure, and I waved back. Bart lay sleeping in a playpen on the shaded patio.

"This is my husband, Redding Coopersmith. Say hey to our new neighbor, Katie."

Tan and blond like his wife, Redding's crooked smile was wide and friendly. "Hey, neighbor. Margie's talked a lot about you. Glad to have you here, especially since I'm gone so much these days."

I leaned forward and shook his hand. "I'll keep an eye on her, don't you worry."

Margie rolled her eyes and turned to Redding's companion.

But before she could say anything, he said, "Ms. Lightfoot," with a nod.

I couldn't read his expression. Of course, the last time I'd seen him, he'd been so giddy about Mrs. Templeton's being dead that he'd hooted out loud.

"Call me Katie, Mr. Pullman."

"Oh! You've already met Frank?" Margie asked.

"I, uh, sought him out after you told me about his attention to craftsmanship."

She looked puzzled. "Are you planning to make changes over in that adorable little carriage house?"

"Actually, I was thinking more along the lines of a small gazebo in the backyard."

"I could probably help you with that," he said.

Uh-oh.

My smile felt like it might split my face. "That's wonderful! But it might be a while. I'm still getting my feet under me at the bakery, and finances are a little up in the air."

"You let me know, all right? Looks like I might be able to start working here in Savannah again, now that . . . well, you know. Margie here will know how to find me."

"Okay." All brightness and sunshine.

"Frank here was telling us the cops came to talk to him about that old witch who was murdered," Redding said.

Old witch, indeed. "Really?" I prompted.

"Wanted to know where he was and who he was with and what he was doing. Can you imagine? Someone treats you like that, then gets herself killed, and the cops have to go bother poor Frank here."

I kept the smile pasted on my face.

"Oh, it wasn't such a big deal, Red," Pullman said. "You know, they have to do their job. I'm just glad she's gone." He saw the expression on Margie's face and quickly looked between us. "I am sorry, ladies. And, Katie, you in particular must think I'm a horrible person after my reaction to the news that Mavis Templeton had forcibly met her Maker. I'm afraid intense relief is my only excuse."

"I think I understand."

"How about a beer, Katie?" Margie said, gamely trying to change the subject.

"Sure."

She jumped up and went inside.

"I might not have time to finish it, though," I called.

She reappeared in the doorway. "I'm afraid you won't even be able to start it. Your fireman just pulled into your driveway."

I looked down at my frayed cutoffs and dirty sneakers. "Darn it. He's early." I stood. "It was nice to meet you, Redding. I'll see you around. Frank. Good luck, and I'll call if I decide on that gazebo."

As I hurried across the front lawn to where Declan stood on my front porch, I reflected that Detective Quinn must not have told Frank Pullman I was the one who suggested he might have a motive for killing Mrs. Templeton. At least Frank didn't seem to blame me.

Chapter 20

I changed clothes in a jiffy and told Mungo I'd be home soon. Declan held the truck door open for me, and I could see it was habit and not something he'd been doing to impress me before. Come to think of it, that I was impressed in the first place said a lot more about my previous taste in men than about his good manners.

"What exactly are you planning to ask this Ridge guy?" He buckled his seat belt and backed the truck out of the driveway. The engine rumbled as we took off for the Peachtree Arms.

"I've been thinking about that. It would probably be a good idea to come at him sideways, you know? I think we'll have to play it by ear. Did I did mention he wasn't very happy when Cookie and I talked to him the other day?"

"No, you didn't say anything about that. I'm afraid we only discussed me last night. Sorry."

"Don't be silly. I'm glad you feel comfortable talking to me."

He signaled a left turn, a small smile tugging at his

lips. "So Ridge didn't tell you anything when you finally tracked him down?"

"Oh, he talked all right. He just didn't like us being there," I fudged.

Declan's eyes cut my way. "What makes you think he'll say anything else now?"

He was more right than I liked to admit. A part of me wondered whether Ethan would even remember what he'd told us after Cookie had used her Voice. But that was probably just wishful thinking.

Cookie's Command had worn thin in a matter of minutes. Mine had lasted for years. Heck, for all I knew those kids were still obeying my Voice. I wasn't in contact with any of them. Could Cookie have used a diluted version? Were there variations in Voice strength? Could I have somehow reversed my Command to the other children to leave me alone way back then?

Darn it. If Mama and Daddy had given me the proper instruction about what I'd done, I might have been a lot less lonely in school.

Stop it. Feeling sorry for yourself won't do any good now.

"Tell me about Ridge's association with Hill," Declan said.

So I did, relating most of what Mrs. Standish had said verbatim. I finished with, "We can't know for sure that those two didn't help with her husband's cremation like she said. They could have been as sweet and generous and selfless as she seems to think. But having met both of them, I highly doubt it. We could always tell Ethan that Albert blurted out something he shouldn't have when he came into the bakery and threatened us. See if he takes the bait."

I had a few other ideas, too, including coming right out and asking the apartment manager about Mrs. Standish. After all, he'd been susceptible to Mrs. Templeton's blackmail and threats. Maybe he'd respond to mine.

Of course, he might have killed Mrs. Templeton as a result of her machinations. Besides the fact that the Peachtree Arms creeped me out, Ethan Ridge emanated trouble. I was very glad Declan had agreed to come along on this investigative foray, even if I'd had to guilt him into it.

We pulled into the lot and parked close to the building. The late sun cast long blue shadows. Declan pushed the door open, and we paused in the sudden dimness to blink our pupils wide. I started down the hallway as my eyes adjusted, wrinkling my nose at the pungent smell of cooked cabbage. Nearing the manager's apartment, I saw that the hand-lettered sign on his door had lost a piece of tape on one side and now hung askew.

Then I noticed the door was open a crack.

I stopped across from it and looked up at Declan. He put his hand on my shoulder, a strangely comforting gesture under the circumstances. I rapped on the hollow wood with my knuckles. The report echoed in the silence.

The pressure pushed the door open another six inches.

"Mr. Ridge?" I called. "Ethan?"

No answer. My gaze flicked up to Declan's as I turned around and knocked on the door across the hall. "Mr. Sparr?"

But James Sparr was apparently out.

"Maybe Ethan is down in the laundry room," I said. "Maybe he left his door open because he'll be right back after putting fabric softener in or something."

Declan gave me a look. Okay, maybe Ethan wasn't a fabric-softener kind of guy, but how was Declan to know that? He'd never even met the guy.

With one finger he pushed the door open farther. And farther. I clutched the O-shaped amulet around my neck. Now we could see into the apartment, brightly lit by the dying sun. The yellow light angled across liquid spattered on the floor and reflected off shards of glass.

The smears were mostly dry. And red. Very dark red. Wine?

A hint of copper-and-coffee smell hit me then. I whirled to escape it, covering my nose with one hand.

Not wine.

Blood.

Declan pulled me into his side, shielding my face.

Why? What else was in there? Had I missed a dead body or something? I pushed away and stood fully in the doorway, looking over everything. Two overturned chairs. Pizza boxes and beer cans strewn across the floor. A broken liquor bottle. A dozen half-packed cardboard boxes with the ubiquitous blue truck logo on them.

And blood. Not as much as I'd first thought, but enough.

But no Ethan. I took a deep breath of relief and instantly regretted it. Pungent whiskey fumes had joined the stench. As I recalled, this apartment hadn't smelled so great when Cookie and I had been there before, but now it was definitely worse.

Declan palmed my shoulder, pulling me back from the doorway. "I'd like to report an accident," he said into his cell phone. "Or an attack. Don't know which, only that there's blood." He gave the address and our location in a calm and authoritative voice. "We'll wait outside."

After he hung up, I said, "Maybe we should look inside his apartment. He could be in the bedroom." Even if Ethan wasn't dead, he was likely hurt.

Or someone was.

"No. Leave it to the police."

This time I didn't argue.

The patrolmen tromped in first. I hung around in the hallway, staying out of the way while straining to hear what they were saying inside the apartment. From what I could tell, they hadn't found Ridge or anyone else in the other rooms.

"Ms. Lightfoot?"

I turned to find that Detective Quinn had entered the building from the other end. Sneaky. He didn't look too happy with me, either.

"What are you doing here?"

My thumb ran over the dragonflies embossed on my amulet, and I cleared my throat. "I came here to talk to Ethan Ridge."

He considered me for a long moment. But instead of yelling at me, he asked, "Why?"

"Because you wouldn't listen to what I had to say on the phone. I found out that he and Mavis Templeton's nephew had a history. Possibly an unsavory one. Ridge was in jail for assault and fraud."

Irritation flitted across his face before he tamped it down. "We are aware of that, Ms. Lightfoot."

"Of course. But did you know Ethan's pulling some of the same tricks he was before he was convicted? At least I think he might be. And he's doing it with the help of Albert Hill."

Quinn was silent for a moment, then looked around at the gathering tenants. He beckoned to me. "Come with me."

I followed him out to a nondescript gray Chevy. He opened the door, and I got in. Was he arresting me? But he only started the engine, turned the air conditioner on full blast and twisted in his seat to look at me.

"Okay. I'm sorry I didn't listen. Tell me what you found out."

"Ethan Ridge and Albert Hill arranged a cremation for the husband of a Honeybee customer. A Mrs. Standish."

"So?"

"So she paid Albert directly, and he paid the mortuary. Or the crematorium. I'm not sure how it worked."

"And?"

"Well, Ethan does have a history of selling burial plots that don't exist."

He made a note. "I'll talk to Mrs. Standish and see if there was anything hinky about what they did."

I waved my hand dismissively. "She thinks they walk on water. The point is they knew each other."

Quinn sat back and regarded me. In the light of the setting sun I saw the dark half-moons under his gray eyes, took in the slumped shoulders and day-old stubble. This guy was in dire need of one of Lucy's seven-layer bars.

"You do realize that might not mean a thing," he said. "People know each other in Savannah. Hill will inherit the Peachtree Arms, and now Ridge will work for him. I know Mrs. Standish, and I knew her husband, Harry. I went to his service, the one you say the nephew arranged. And I've met Albert Hill before, as well as his aunt."

I protested. "Even if everything they did was on the up-and-up, it still proves that Albert Hill and Ethan Ridge were friends and/or business partners at least a year ago. Add in that Ethan had a history of violence, wanted to get away from the crappy job Mrs. Templeton had blackmailed him into, and Albert Hill gets a pile of money now that his aunt is dead. At the very least you've got somebody to investigate other than Benjamin Eagel."

Detective Quinn put down the pen he'd used to make notes. He met my eyes straight on. "This is good information. Don't worry—I'll follow up on it."

"Ethan could have killed her," I went on. "Albert could have known, or they could have been in on it together, and now Albert has cleaned up a loose end."

He raised his palm. "Hold on. Leave the speculation to us, okay? Your part in this investigation is finished now. Over. Understand?"

The muscles in my jaw flexed. "I only want you to realize that my uncle didn't kill Mrs. Templeton."

"We'll look into this other business of fraud. See what Mr. Hill has to say. But frankly, I doubt that what you found here today has anything to do with the murder. Ridge had a number of low-life associates, any of whom he might have angered. Either way, we'll find out what happened."

Alarm bells went off in my head. I could tell, whether from the angle of his head or the tone in his voice or something entirely woo-woo, that he still considered Ben his primary murder suspect. *Mr.* Hill, indeed. Albert might not be his aunt, but he still had the respect of the powers that be.

"It's that darn witness, isn't it?" I asked. "What happened when you talked to Frank Pullman?"

"How did you know I—" He sighed. "I don't want to know. But you're right. He does fit the description the witness gave."

"See!"

"But unlike your uncle, he has an alibi. He was with his sister's family over in Pooler, as well as two of their neighbors, from eight a.m. until six p.m. the day Mavis Templeton was killed. He simply couldn't have done it."

"But . . ." I trailed off. Rubbing my eyes with my fingertips, I muttered, "The man your witness saw probably didn't have anything to do with the murder. I mean, she didn't actually see him kill her."

"That's possible." He didn't sound convinced. "I think we're done here, aren't we?"

"I guess so." I opened the car door and got out. And perhaps I closed it with a little too much enthusiasm; it did sound awfully loud in the falling twilight. I turned and looked at Quinn through the windshield.

But I was already off his radar. He was speaking into his phone, not even bothering to look out at me.

Fine. I had resources, after all. Resources Detective Quinn would only scoff at.

Until I brought him the truth on a plate.

Back inside the Peachtree Arms a policeman was closing the door to the manager's unit. A babble of voices drifted out from James Sparr's apartment across the hall, and I peeked inside the partially open door to find Declan talking with half a dozen tenants.

His chin rose when he saw me, and his eyes smiled. I pushed the door farther open.

Mrs. Perkins perched on a wingback chair, her walker beside her, listening intently to the others. When she saw me, she twiddled her fingers in my direction. "Hello, dear. Did you hear?" The voices died down as the group took in the newcomer.

I glanced over at James, who was holding court from his recliner. "May I come in?"

He gestured me forward with a languid wave. "Knock yourself out."

The living room felt cramped with that many people in it. Three older ladies sat on a maroon velvet sofa so worn in places that it looked as though pink skin were showing through. Another man stood next to the doorway leading into the kitchen, and Declan leaned against the incongruously elaborate fireplace mantel.

Sitting on the ottoman next to Mrs. Perkins, I took her hand and said, "You mean about Ethan being missing?"

"Oh, yes. And all that blood! I looked inside after the nice police lady came to find out if I'd heard any kind of ruckus."

The others erupted again with their own stories of police questioning. Under the circumstances it was quite the convivial atmosphere. There were even cheese crackers and a bowl of green grapes on the coffee table. As I listened to the tenants one after another disappointedly relate that they hadn't heard a darn thing but wished they had, a short, round woman came in with a bag of chips for the coffee table and cracked open a plastic container. The smell of onion dip added to the festive climate.

Despite tragedy and the neglected property, the Peachtree Arms was a community. These people knew their neighbors and cared about them. Watching them interact, I felt my attitude about the place shift slightly.

I stood. Declan took a step toward me. The tenants stopped talking and looked at me.

"Did anyone see or hear anything that could help the police find out what happened to Ethan?"

Everyone shook their heads. Except, I noticed, James Sparr.

I turned to him. "Mr. Sparr? Were you in here earlier today?"

"Sure was."

Declan and I exchanged looks.

"Were you here when we knocked earlier?" he asked.

"Sure was."

Cocking my head to one side, I asked, "Why didn't you open the door?"

"Didn't know it was you."

I turned and looked at the door behind me. It didn't have a peephole. I turned back. "You heard something across the hall, didn't you?"

He nodded. "'Bout an hour before you got here I did."

Everyone went still. He'd been waiting to spring this.

"And you've already told the police about it?"

He smiled. "Soon as they asked me I did."

Declan got to the point. "What did you hear?"

"Quite the commotion, it was. Bunch of yelling and then a big crash. Door opened then and someone ran off down the hallway."

There was a general intake of breath at that.

"Just one person ran away?" I asked.

"Sounded like that. I kept my door shut, though. Don't have any interest in getting involved in Mr. Ridge's affairs."

Just then I heard a voice in the hallway and held my finger to my lips.

"You've searched the whole place?" Detective Quinn asked. "Top to bottom?"

"Yessir," came the reply. "Found some blood on the stairs, but other than the mess inside, nothing else."

In James' living room we all looked at each other, perfectly quiet and straining to hear.

"Is his car here?" Quinn asked.

"Right in his spot."

"And you've talked with all the tenants."

"Still working on the top two floors."

Quinn sighed. "All right. Check with all the hospitals regarding suspicious wounds and let me know what you find out."

"Yessir." Their voices began to fade as they walked away.

I peered around the doorjamb to see the retreating backs of Quinn and the uniformed man. I waited until the uniform opened the door to the stairwell, then grabbed Declan's hand.

"We'd better get going. I don't think the good detective is ready for another encounter with yours truly so soon." I waved back at the Peachtree Arms tenants. "'Bye, everyone."

"Good-bye, dear," called Mrs. Perkins, echoed by the others.

We made it to Declan's truck without incident. On the drive home I said, "Somebody hurt Ethan, and now he's gone but his car is still there. Did they make him go with them?"

He shrugged and flicked on his turn signal. "He may have hurt someone else, you know."

"Do you think Albert had anything to do with it? Because Detective Quinn thinks the whole thing might be fallout from the company Ethan keeps and nothing at all to do with Mrs. Templeton's murder."

"I don't know," he said.

"But what do you *think*?" I found myself almost bouncing in the seat.

"I think no one can answer those questions except Ridge himself."

That gave me pause. "So we have to find him."

"Good luck with that," Declan said. "He may not even be alive."

Chapter 21

After Declan dropped me at home, Mungo and I read up on location spells. For the most part they looked pretty simple. Which was good, because for my very first solitary spell I wanted something easy peasy. There was a common one that looked doable, safe, and didn't call for any crazy ingredients.

Still, I needed four blue candles.

I checked the time. A little after ten. Probably too late to drop in on Margie. Besides, borrowing a cup of sugar from a neighbor was one thing; borrowing candles for a location spell was something else. A quick run to the twenty-four-hour market netted me a box of short tapers. More blue-green than blue, they were still the color of water, so I hoped they'd work. I would have preferred votive candles because I didn't have holders for the tapers, but all the smaller candles in the store's limited selection were heavily scented and stank to high heaven. The tapers smelled like plain old paraffin.

I lit one of them and allowed the wax to dribble into a small puddle on a paper plate. Then I stuck an unlit taper in the middle and let it cool. The melted wax held the candle upright quite nicely. I repeated the make-shift candleholders on three more plates and set them at the four compass points on my living room floor.

The spell also called for jasmine incense, which I didn't have. But rooting around in my aromatherapy satchel netted a tiny bottle of jasmine essential oil. Lucy had added clove oil to the candles in Mimsey's scrying spell, so I carefully dribbled a little onto each candle-wick and let it drip down the sides of the candle. The volatile concentrated oil infused the whole house with heady floral tones.

I looked at Mungo. "How am I doing?"

Yip!

The final thing I needed was natural water. Perhaps bottled spring water would have been fine, but I had a stream running through my backyard and that seemed a great deal more natural than water encased in plastic. I grabbed one of the wine goblets Declan had brought the night before and opened the French doors. Mungo followed me outside and to the back corner of the lot. The scent of new-mown grass filled the darkness. Cica-das buzzed, and bright moonlight echoed off the stream water. I remembered that Bianca practiced moon magic. I looked up. The moon was slightly larger than half full, but I didn't know if it was waxing or waning. Oh, wait. Mimsey had said she'd charged her shew stone by the full moon, so it must be waning.

I had to start paying more attention to that kind of stuff.

"Am I supposed to say something when I get the wa-ter?" I asked Mungo, leaning down toward the stream.

"Katie? Is that you?" My neighbor's voice came drifting over the fence.

Startled, I dropped the goblet.

Moments later Margie leaned her elbows on the three-and-a-half-foot fence that divided our yards and peered down at me. "Who are you talking to?"

Mungo barked.

Forcing a laugh, I said, "Just the dog."

I could feel him glaring at me in the darkness.

"What are you doing out here?" I asked.

"Me? Oh! Well, um . . ." She licked her lips. Leaned forward conspiratorially. "I'm sneaking a little treat." She held up a length of Twinkie so bright yellow it glowed in the moonlight.

"A . . . Really? Why do you have to sneak it?"

"Redding thinks they're bad for me, throws a fit when he sees me eating one. He won't let the kids touch them. I think all the preservatives are what keep me going some days."

"Margie?" A man's voice came from her house. "Where did you run off to?"

"Oh, my Lord, he's going to wake the kids if he doesn't pipe down. See you later!" And she was gone.

"That was close," I whispered to Mungo.

The grass had cushioned the goblet when it fell, so it hadn't broken. I set the intention of using the water in a location spell in my mind, scooped some up from the stream and hurried back inside before Margie returned to finish her illicit junk food.

In my living room, I checked to make sure the window shutters were tightly closed and doused the floor lamp. I was a little nervous, but not because I had any

reservations about the spell itself. I had reservations
about me. Lucy had told me I needed to learn how to
manage my power, learn how to harness magic. I was
aware that doing a spell alone without really understanding the mechanics might be risky.

But it was a simple spell. For a good cause. And I
didn't have time to wait. Someone, probably Ethan
Ridge, had lost a *lot* of blood. Waiting until I could get
help from my witch nannies might do more harm than
good.

In order for the spell to do any good, I needed to cast
it *now*.

I lit the four candles and settled cross-legged in the
middle of them, facing west. Mungo snuggled into my
lap. Deeply breathing in the scent of the jasmine oil, I
imagined my roiling thoughts calming to the smooth
sheen of undisturbed water. When I felt ready, I looked
down into the wineglass and swirled the water clockwise with two fingers of my right hand. I put my hand
back in my lap, and my furry familiar licked away the
water droplets.

"Let the water show me the location of Ethan Ridge.
Let the water show me where he is."

I took a deep breath and let it out slowly.

"Let the water show me the location of Ethan Ridge.
Let the water show me where he is."

Four times I repeated the incantation, peering into
the water and waiting for an indication of where the
apartment manager might be. For a vision, a feeling
about a location, a nice big intuitive hit.

Anything.

But there was nothing.

I tried for more than half an hour and came up with exactly diddly-squat on the divination front.

Of course, Cookie had said she wasn't any good at scrying. But they'd also said I was a catalyst. Did that mean I couldn't do magic myself, could only help others? Heavy disappointment settled over my shoulders at the thought.

Suddenly I had an image of myself, sitting in the middle of four burning candles with a dog in my lap, muttering at a glass of water to find a missing man. Embarrassment and shame crowded out my disappointment at failing.

What was I thinking? I'd swallowed the whole witch thing hook, line and sinker. Poor Katie was a lonely little girl with a big imagination who made up stories that made her seem special. And then she'd grown up into poor dumped-by-her-fiancé Katie who grabbed on to a gigantic piece of nonsense that made her seem special and feel like she finally belonged.

I'd been so careful not to rebound to a man after my engagement failed. But that boomerang energy had to go someplace, and only now did I realize how primed I'd been for Lucy to convince me of my magical heritage.

Hedgewitch. Oh, brother.

Disgusted, I blew out the candles, threw them in the garbage, and dumped the water down the sink.

At my feet, Mungo whined.

It hit me: I'd skipped supper, and he'd had only a snack of boiled chicken.

"There's kibble in your bowl," I said.

A tiny growl emanated from his throat.

"Okay, okay." I opened the refrigerator door and took out the leftover bourbon-pulled pork Steve had brought. I dumped some in Mungo's bowl, made myself a small sandwich, and grabbed one of Lucy's seven-layer bars. Then I put it back. She'd probably drugged them to give me more evidence that magic was real. Whatever she'd put in them had knocked me out, and I couldn't afford to oversleep again tomorrow.

Next to me on the bed, Mungo turned over on his back and went to sleep, pork fumes on his breath. Could have been worse, but it would have been nice if he was as willing to brush his teeth before bed as he was to eat people food.

I didn't want to think about how much I had liked the idea of being a witch or how pathetic that made me feel. Magic was hooey. I had to face the harsh reality that there was nothing I could do to influence the world around me.

Wait a minute. So waving a magic wand couldn't change the world. That didn't mean I had to give up the belief I'd held my whole life—that fate was what you made it. That people control their own destiny. And that even if they can't always control the things that happen to them, they get to decide their own reactions.

I could still help Uncle Ben and keep the Honeybee afloat. I just had to figure out how.

Mungo wiggled against me, as if he was scratching his back. He didn't bother to wake up, though, so maybe it was a dream. I stroked his wee head with my fingertips.

"Familiar, indeed. What a bunch of gobbledygook."

He was instantly on his feet, and I snatched my hand back in alarm. But he just stood there on the bed, blinking at me in the waning moonlight. It was too dark to really read his eyes, but I had a distinct feeling of disapproval.

Stop making up stuff like that, Katie. He's just a dog.

"It's okay," I said. "Go back to sleep."

He didn't lie down right away, but after a few more moments of staring at me like I was a piece of bacon, he did. Still didn't take his eyes off me, though. I closed mine and tried to ignore him.

The events of the day sifted through my waning consciousness. The joy of working in the Honeybee kitchen. All the enthusiastic customers at the bakery. Mrs. Standish's elaborate views and expansive gestures. The almost audible click as I'd put together the connection between Ethan Ridge and Albert Hill. Declan's disapproval on the phone, contrasted with his warm greeting when he came to pick me up. The way he looked at me when he didn't think I was paying attention.

The smell of blood and whiskey in Ethan's apartment.

The half-packed boxes sitting among the wreckage of a struggle.

Well, he'd said he was going to leave now that Mrs. Templeton couldn't blackmail him into staying. I thought about what he'd said. That she'd threatened him with exposure. Would that really be enough? Given what she did to Frank Pullman for leaving some sawdust on her floor, I could see that maybe it would be. But perhaps she used something more than an old prison sentence against him. Something a bit more specific. A bit more recent and possibly unknown by the authorities.

Real blackmail, with real stakes. Maybe she knew Ethan was back to his old ways with a new twist, taking advantage of grieving widows like Mrs. Standish. And if he was doing it with her nephew's help, the likelihood that Mrs. Templeton would learn of it was high.

That would give Ethan even more of a motive to kill her.

But then someone had gone after Ethan. Was it really Albert Hill? I found that hard to imagine, though I couldn't put my finger on why. He was mean and, though not fit, certainly physically capable of assaulting another man. He was greedy to the point of being unbalanced. His wore his ego like a bright yellow rain slicker—nothing subtle about it at all.

Ah. That was it. Albert might be a sociopath as Bianca and I had speculated, but he felt emotion. He was, in fact, a coward. I'd met him only once and seen him two other times, but it was evident even in the brief encounters. Insecurity lurked behind that glaring ego, and fear behind the meanness.

Still, cowards can be dangerous. Scared dogs bite just as often as aggressive ones; their own fear serves as enough provocation whether there's an actual threat or not. Albert could have incited Ethan to kill Mrs. Templeton and then been afraid Ethan would turn on him.

Or not. Whatever had happened to the apartment manager might not have had anything to do with the murder. As Detective Quinn had pointed out, he had enough low-life friends to account for an assault. For that matter, we didn't even know for sure whether Ethan had been attacked or had attacked someone else. Anything was possible at this point.

Would Ethan have opened his door to someone he thought of as a threat? Had he even known who waited in the hallway, since the doors didn't have peepholes? Maybe he didn't know to be wary of whoever had knocked. After all, the guy wasn't exactly the brightest bear.

Those boxes, half full, made me feel kind of sorry for the guy. He was so close to getting out, to leaving and making a new life. Maybe not a better life, but a new one, where he could at least make decisions about whether or not it would be better.

A NEW START.

My eyes flew open.

Those boxes seemed to be everywhere. Frank Pullman had them in his pickup. Ethan had them in his apartment. But so what? It was a popular moving company in town. Lots of people probably got boxes from there. Big deal.

I glanced down. Mungo still stared at me from the darkness.

"Will you stop it? You're starting to give me the heebie-jeebies."

He blinked, once, very slowly.

"Fine." I squeezed my eyes shut again.

And the image of the storage company logo came back, bright blue and insistent. However, this time it was emblazoned on the boxes I'd seen when Cookie and I had exited the laundry room at the Peachtree Arms.

The boxes in the wire-enclosed spaces in the basement reserved for apartment dwellers.

I snapped awake. Ethan's door had been open when Declan and I arrived. After we found that he was gone, I'd assumed that the door had been left open. But before that, I'd figured he was in the basement laundry room or someplace in the building, planning to return shortly.

He was in that basement. I knew it.

I could see it.

Abruptly, I sat up in bed. Mungo let out a sharp bark, ran once around the perimeter of the bed, and returned to his position by my side, panting. I tried not to be aware that he ran widdershins, or to wonder whether that was significant.

The impression of Ethan Ridge in the apartment storage area grew stronger as the seconds passed. I shook my head. It was my overly vivid imagination. Had to be. Besides, the police had searched the whole building.

Hadn't they?

But what if they hadn't gone into the locked storage spaces? What if he was hiding down there?

I reached for the phone to call Detective Quinn. Paused. He probably wouldn't be working this late. I could leave a message, but that would mean morning before he got it, and even then he might not pay it any mind. I wasn't exactly on his list of favorite people right now.

I could call 911 and report a crime in the apartment

building's basement so the police would have to respond. Could I do it in such a way that they wouldn't find out it was me? If they found Ridge, would it matter if they found out?

Hmm. Yes. And Quinn was already mad enough at me.

Ben was already upset with me about poking my nose into things, too. And he didn't even know about what Declan and I had found at the Peachtree Arms earlier that evening.

Cursing my shortsightedness, I swung my feet to the floor and stood. Even if the spell had worked, I hadn't thought ahead to what I'd do with my newfound knowledge. In my defense, I'd never dreamed Ridge would still be on the apartment property. I'd reckoned on finding him in another state or at a girlfriend's house, wounded or maybe sleeping off a bender.

If the spell had worked.

Had it? Was that why I had this strong feeling about where Ridge was? Or had it been simple deduction sparked by the twilight of approaching sleep?

It didn't matter. Not right now. I needed to get over there and find out if I was right. It was late. Mrs. Templeton had rented largely to the elderly, so most people would be asleep by now. And if the back door was open, I could access the basement storage area from the parking lot without going through the rest of the building. A quick run inside would tell me if I was right or not.

I half hoped I wasn't.

I dressed in jeans and a dark tank top without turning on the lights, put on my running shoes and grabbed my tote. Mungo waited by the front door.

"You are not going with me," I said.

Ar rarr arr.

"No, you're not. I'll be fine."

He lay down in front of the door.

I sighed. Considered taking him with me anyway. But what if he ran off? What if he made a noise and gave me away? I couldn't risk it.

"Mungo, honey. Please. I'll be right back."

He jumped up, ran to the sofa and launched himself onto it. Stretching toward the coffee table trunk, he sniffed the yellow roses that sat in the middle. Whined.

"You want me to do another spell? But—"

He shook all over. Sniffed the blossoms again. Whined.

Why was I playing along with all this? Imagining the little dog was my familiar. That he could communicate with me. Wasn't I over . . .

Then I got it. "Steve?"

Yip.

I hadn't thought of asking him to come with me. Truth be told, I had carefully avoided the idea. Besides, he was mad at me. But for what? I hadn't done anything. Declan was the one who'd showed up unannounced. As had Steve. How dare he be angry about something like that?

The memory of his lips brushing mine rocketed from my brain southward. "Okay, I guess it can't hurt to call him."

Mungo sat back and beamed doggy approval at me.

I dug out the card he'd given me and punched in the numbers on my cell phone. He answered after one ring.

"Katie-girl!"

I sighed. At least he wasn't mad at me. "Did I wake you?"

"Hardly. I'm out playing pool with some friends." The clacking of enameled balls in the background punctuated his statement.

Mental palm smack. It was Saturday night. "Friends" no doubt included a female companion. It hadn't even occurred to me that I could be interrupting a date.

"Oh. Of course. I wasn't thinking."

"You want to join us? We're in the basement of Churchill's Pub. You know where it is? On Bay?"

"Um, thanks, but no."

He paused. "Katie? Why are you calling me?"

"I, er . . ."

"Tell me."

Deep breath. "I was kind of hoping you'd go over to Mavis Templeton's apartment house with me."

"When?"

"Now."

A pause. "What?"

My laugh was strained. "What a good little reporter you are, with your four w's."

He didn't respond. The sound of the pool game receded and then faded altogether as he moved away from it.

"I'm sorry," I said. "That came out a little more sarcastic than necessary. Don't worry about it."

"How?" he said.

"What?"

"How do you want to go? Shall we meet there? Or I could swing by and pick you up."

Oh, dear. Better for him not to come here. Margie

might still be up with the teething baby and wonder what the heck was going on.

"Meet me at the convenience store at the corner of Forty-fourth and Habersham," I said, remembering where Cookie and I had stopped to get something to drink after she'd used her Voice.

Had that really happened?

"I can be there in fifteen minutes," he said.

"Are you sure you want to do this?"

"Oh, yeah. You've appealed to my good little reporter, after all. I want to know exactly what you're up to. See you soon."

I ended the call and turned to Mungo. "That's a nice contrast to having every other male in my life question what I'm doing. Are you happy now?"

He rolled over on the sofa and kicked his stubby legs in the air. I shut the door on a teensy canine snore and hurried out to the Bug.

Chapter 22

Steve's black Land Rover was already idling at the edge of the convenience store parking lot when I arrived. I pulled the Bug in next to it and got out. The temperature had dropped. I hugged my bare arms and regretted not wearing long sleeves. The halogen lights overhead hummed against the night, drawing a swarm of flying insects.

He walked around to where I stood and stopped just inside my personal space. Nudging boundaries out of habit, perhaps, and not the intentional disregard of my comfort level he seemed so fond of. Or maybe he really didn't get the whole idea of boundaries.

Either way, my blood hummed beneath my skin. I took a step away. His hair was tied back, and he wore a silky green T-shirt over khaki shorts. The white light of the parking lot gave everything a strange glow.

"What's the plan, Agent Lightfoot?" Steve's voice was low.

"Oh, please. I only want to take a quick look inside the back door. It's probably nothing."

"What makes you think it's something?"

"I cast a—" My hand clamped over my mouth. What was wrong with me?

His eyes narrowed, catlike, and he practically purred. "Cast a what?"

Darn it. "Cast a location spell."

"And what were you trying to find, Katie-girl?" He was inside my space again, his breath teasing my skin.

"Ethan Ridge," I said.

He jerked back. "What on God's green earth for?"

"De— I came here earlier today to talk to him after I found out he might have had some shady dealings with Mrs. Templeton's nephew. But I didn't get a chance to ask him anything because all I found was a messy apartment—with a bunch of blood in it and no Mr. Ridge. Then the police showed up, but they didn't find him, either. His apartment looked like there'd at least been a fight, maybe worse."

Steve's eyes widened.

"I figured it would be a good idea to find out where he was sooner rather than later, especially if he's hurt. So I, you know, did the spell thing." My hands waved in the air as if that would dispel my awkwardness.

"What did you use for the scrying? A mirror?"

I shook my head and mumbled. "Just water in a goblet."

He laughed. "And it worked? You saw him on the surface? You are something else, you know that?"

"No. It didn't work at all. That whole spell business is a bunch of hogwash."

Frown lines creased the smooth skin of his forehead. "Oh, really. Then why are we here?"

"Because I got to thinking about the packing boxes in Ethan's apartment. About how I'd seen them in the basement of his building when I'd been there before. And I wondered, well, I kind of saw, no, not really saw, but had the notion, the feeling, if you will, that he might be down there. Where I saw the other boxes, I mean."

Steve's nostrils flared a tiny bit, but he managed not to laugh at me. "Sounds like maybe your spell worked after all. It doesn't happen the same way for everyone, you know."

I shrugged and looked away.

"Let's go take a look." His fingers clasped my elbow, and we walked the half block to the apartment building in silence. The cool, humid air brushed my cheek, tempering the heat in my face. Was I blushing because I felt silly for admitting to the spell work? Or because I sounded so goofy trying to explain why I'd dragged Steve away from his night out with friends? Or maybe it was a combination of fear, anticipation and his hand on my arm.

He headed for the front entrance, but I pulled him toward the back door. The moon, so bright earlier, had set, and the night had turned pitch-black. I added not bringing a flashlight to my growing list of regrets. A square of light flared, weak but targeted. It emanated from Steve's hand in a blue haze, and for a moment I thought he had manifested it. Then I saw he was holding his cell phone open.

Stop it, Katie!

It was enough light to help us find the doorknob. Which then wouldn't turn. Someone had locked it.

Mrs. Perkins had specifically said it was unlocked *during the day*. The news about their apartment manager would have spread among the tenants, and one of them might have locked the door, knowing he wasn't around to do it. Or the police might have done it.

So why couldn't I shake the idea that Ethan Ridge had locked it himself?

"Let's try the other door," Steve said.

I nodded and led the way back around to the front of the building.

That door was locked, too.

Disgusted, I leaned back against the dirty siding and crossed my arms.

Steve peered through the dingy glass, but I didn't see how he could make out anything in the dim light of the bulb down at the other end of the hallway. He rattled the metal handle. Muttered something under his breath. He sounded a lot like Lucy when she added "extra" ingredients to my recipes.

A *snick* sounded, and out of the corner of my eye, I saw the door ease open. Openmouthed, I whirled to find Steve standing in the entrance with a big grin on his face.

A tall figure moved behind him, and my heart went *thumpa* for a completely different reason than it usually did when Mr. Dawes was in the vicinity.

James Sparr loomed into view. "Well, now, for someone who says she don't want to rent an apartment, you sure do show up here an awful lot, miss. What can I do for you this fine evening?"

I cleared my throat. "When I was here earlier today—"

"Yes, indeed, with that young man you showed up with the first time."

I felt Steve's eyes slide to me.

"Uh, yes. Anyway, I left through the back door, downstairs, you know? And I think I dropped something."

James didn't ask what I'd dropped. "Well, you know where you want to look, then." He motioned us in. "Go on ahead. But if you leave through the back, make sure that door locks behind you, all right?"

"Of course. Thank you."

"Mmmm-hmmmm." He wagged his head. "That sure was a lot of fuss this afternoon." He trudged to his own door and stepped inside. "Mr. Ridge disappears pretty regular. Don't know if he'll be back this time, though." He raised one hand. "Good night."

When we were alone in the hallway, I turned on Steve. "What did you whisper out there?"

"Just a little incantation, Katie-girl. A quickie, you might say."

I echoed his tone. "To unlock the door? But ha-ha, it didn't exactly work, did it?"

"The door's unlocked, isn't it? And we're inside. Magic doesn't always work the way you think it will. Or think it should. That's why it's a good idea to be careful what you wish for."

"I wish you'd stop calling me Katie-girl, that's what I wish," I mumbled.

"Done. But only because I see it truly irritates you. I'm getting to like you way too much to irritate you on purpose. I'm sure I'll manage just fine by accident."

"Oh, come on." I grabbed his hand and pulled him down the hall to the stairs.

The heavy door creaked open, then closed behind us with a final *chunk*. Steve followed me down the metal steps, taking in the rattletrap washers and dryers, moisture-streaked cinder-block walls, and the scents of laundry detergent and mildew. We went out the other door and down the basement hallway toward the back door. As we neared the storage area, the weak light glinted off the metal of the enclosures. We paused to examine the contents through the chain link. Caged belongings stacked to the ceiling in two spaces, evidence of their owners' hopes and ambitions of moving to another abode soon. I wished their owners luck in that. The exercise bike in another offered good intentions gone awry. The rubber raft looked uniformly unseaworthy, and my guess was the owner held on to it out of stubborn sentimentality more than any true belief that he—or she, I supposed—would be fishing again soon.

At the end, right by the back door, were the piles of boxes with the NEW START logo on them. In the pale light, they looked the same as they had before. Pillars of flattened cardboard leaned over a tumble of empty boxes in the center. A hodgepodge of sizes tipped into the pile, looking as if they'd been tossed in from the gate to deal with later. I hooked my fingers in the fence and craned my neck to peer into all the spaces visible from that angle.

Nothing.

I hoisted myself up and jammed the toes of my shoes into the chain link, straining to get a slightly better view. As my head neared the ceiling a faint miasma teased my nose.

Whiskey. And blood.

"Katie! Get down!"

The pile of boxes in front of me exploded as Steve grabbed the back of my tank top and pulled me backward. Arms pinwheeling, I landed hard and we both went down, letting out twin "oomphs" when we hit the floor.

A jagged knife jammed through the diamond-shaped space in the fence where my abdomen had been pressed a moment ago. The shaking hand holding it belonged to Ethan Ridge. He glared at me through red-rimmed eyes. Dried blood on his neck flaked onto his streaked T-shirt. We remained like that, a frozen tableau with Steve and me on the floor and Ridge looming above us on the other side of the gate, for what seemed like a long time but was probably only a few seconds.

Then Ridge's other hand moved, reaching for the chain that held the gate shut. The padlock dangled from one end, open. His fingers curled around the links, and he began pulling the chain through the vertical bar.

He was letting himself out.

Himself and his big, fat knife.

I scrambled to my feet, a move that unfortunately involved waving my legs in the air much like Mungo before rolling to one side and launching upright. I heard Steve behind me, and hoped he possessed more grace than I did.

What was I thinking? Of course he did.

Ridge responded by yanking on the chain and the knife at the same time. Both were giving him trouble, though, and as I watched, ready to sprint, a red trickle bloomed on the side of his neck. Our eyes locked. He didn't seem to recognize me. Or maybe the fear that emanated from him like a freakish halo overrode everything else.

His eyes rolled back, and he sank to his knees. Shaking his head as if to clear it produced a low moan. The blood from the wound in his neck flowed more freely. His right hand released the knife, which hung on the storage unit fence like wicked fruit. The chain wound around the fingers of his other hand as his head lolled back, and he slumped to the floor.

Or mostly to the floor. The chain held him partially suspended. It bent his neck to the side. Steve pulled at my arm, but I pushed him away.

"We have to help him. He'll die if we don't!"

He looked at Ridge, and his hand fell away from me. "Call 911."

But I was already on it, my hand trembling so much the phone knocked gently against my jawbone as I waited. When the dispatcher picked up I told her to send an ambulance, where we were, and that the police had an interest in Ethan Ridge. She tried to keep me on the line, but I could see Steve was having difficulty getting inside the enclosure, so I instructed her to send the ambulance around to the back door and ended the call.

I hurried to Steve as he extricated the other end of the chain from the gate, keeping a firm hold on it so Ridge wouldn't drop to the concrete below. Together we dragged the chain-link barrier open, the metal screeching against the floor so loud it made my teeth hurt. I slipped in through the opening and helped lower the wounded man gently to a prone position.

Steve gave the gate another yank, winced at the noise, and joined me inside the storage space.

"Press on his neck," he said, ripping open the T-shirt to expose Ridge's tan chest. "He has a knife wound."

I did, feeling a weak pulse beneath my fingers. "He's been down here since early this evening. If the blade had hit his jugular he'd be dead by now."

"That's his carotid," he corrected. "Could just be a nick, or maybe it missed it altogether, but either way this guy has lost a lot of blood." His face was inches from mine, and he snagged my gaze and held it. "He's fading quickly, Katie."

"Can't we help him?" I couldn't keep the desperation out of my voice.

He hesitated, then gave a small nod. "Maybe. Healing isn't my strong suit, but I'll try."

Healing? With magic? I stubbornly tamped down the hope that flared behind the thought. But if there was any chance . . .

"What can I do?" I asked.

Still looking at me, Steve put his left hand on the dying man's chest and closed the fingers of his other hand around my wrist. His hand was hot against my skin, and I had to fight the temptation to pull away. "Let me draw on your power."

"Um. Okay." Sounded easy enough.

Finally breaking eye contact, Steve bowed his head.

I didn't know what healing protocol was, so I closed my eyes and concentrated on Steve's hand, mentally sending power flowing into him through the contact of our skin. I had no idea if I was doing it right. In fact, I still didn't know if I believed in the whole witch—

"Stop it. You have to be wholehearted, or you might as well not do it at all."

Stunned, I opened my eyes and stared at the back of his head.

He didn't look up, just squeezed my wrist. *"Katie. If you want to save this man's life, you have to believe."*

I closed my eyes and tried again, pouring everything I had into the link between us. Banishing all doubt. Determined not to let Ethan Ridge die. Wanting to be useful, to help him. Crackles of energy moved between us. Steve's hand grew hotter and hotter on my arm. I began to imagine the faint smell of burning hair.

Still, I didn't stop.

Power thrummed through me. It pulsated in time with my heart. Throbbed behind my eyelids. Sweat trickled down my forehead and threaded down my back. Panting, I opened my eyes. Steve's were squeezed tight now. Moisture dotted his upper lip. The hand on Ethan's chest shook.

Sparks flickered at the edges of my vision. Colors took on new dimensions as if they glowed internally.

And everywhere solid surfaces seemed to teem with movement. I blinked, but it didn't stop. I became aware of the dragonfly amulet against my chest, chilled and getting colder by the second while everything else blazed.

Beside me, Steve gasped and let go of my arm, breaking the link between us with a jolt. We fell back on the floor on each side of Ethan and stared wide-eyed at each other.

After a few beats, I examined my wrist, expecting a burn or a bruise. The skin was perfectly smooth and unscathed. Looking up, I saw Steve wipe a trembling hand over his face.

"What are you?" he whispered.

"I think," I answered slowly, "I think I really might be a witch after all."

He wheezed out a laugh. "I've never experienced anything like that before," he said, taking another shaky breath.

A loud banging on the back door made my heart buck. "Oops," I said. "I should have unlocked the door."

"Then they might have walked in on something we wouldn't have wanted them to see," he said. He rose and staggered out to the hallway. "Be right there!" he called, but stopped to look back at me through the diamond-shaped wire. "You half scare me, you know."

But I was concentrating on Ridge. "He doesn't look as pale." And he seemed to breathe a little easier, too.

Steve opened the door to flashing lights and a phalanx of first responders. He greeted a patrolman by name and they moved to one side, murmuring together. Paramedics hurried past and pulled the gate open as far as it would go, then entered the enclosure, where I still knelt beside the apartment manager. Two men carried large duffels, and two others brought in a collapsible gurney.

I scrambled backward to allow them access. "His neck is bleeding. He's lost a lot of blood."

Strong arms hoisted me to my feet and pulled me into the hallway. "Let them do their job."

I twisted away even as I recognized the voice. I turned to face Declan. "What are you doing here?"

"*My* job. Katie, more to the point, how did you end up in this godforsaken hole in the middle of the night with a wounded animal?" He frowned down at me. Concern and frustration warred on his face.

"He's not an animal. He's a human being. And he didn't stab himself, either. Maybe you should worry more about who did this than about an unconscious man who can't even defend himself to you."

Wrinkles creased his forehead under the dark curls, and his eyes flashed blue. "You seem to be doing a pretty good job of defending him, though. Is there something I don't know?"

"No, only . . . he . . . he almost died, right there in front of me. I don't think we'd have been friends in real life or anything—in fact I'm sure we wouldn't have—but anyone who almost dies while you're fighting to keep him alive gets to have me on his side."

"Oh, honey." He pulled me toward him and wrapped his arms around me. "Such a tender heart."

I gave him a gentle shove. "Bah."

"Hang on." He went in and talked to one of the uniforms, returning with a handful of damp hand wipes. I accepted them with gratitude, and suppressing a shudder, began scrubbing off Ridge's blood.

"The team has things under control. Let me see if I can get away to take you home."

"No need." Steve stood beside us. "She came with me, and I'll make sure she gets home."

Declan looked between us. "She came with you, did she? Well, that figures."

"Why does that figure, Declan McCarthy?" My fists had found their way to my hips, and I matched them glare for glare. "Listen, I know you two have problems, but you both live in this town. Can't you sit down and talk it out?" I wanted to go on, smooth the waters between these two new men that had barreled into my life in the last week, but the other uniformed personnel in the room were watching us and listening as hard as they could. My bet was that most of them, at least the firemen, knew the story between them already, but it wasn't my place to talk about it in front of them.

"No," Steve said. "There is no talking it out. Now, are you ready to go?"

"Not so fast." Detective Quinn approached, wearing a tuxedo and a black tie. His thick gray hair had been tamed and brushed back from his forehead. Despite his fancy duds, exhaustion pinched the skin around his eyes and mouth. "I want to talk to you."

My heart sank. I glanced at Declan. He barely shook his head. There would be no help from that quarter. Oh, well. Might as well buck up and get it over with.

"Sure, Detective. Where would you like to talk?"

"Come outside. And Dawes?" He pointed a finger. "You're next."

I was happy enough to escape the bedlam inside the basement. There seemed to be an awful lot of people for one little emergency. Well, not little. But still. Half of them were standing around watching the others work on Ridge, who was still unconscious. I could only hope he would live through the night. They unfolded the gurney, lifted him onto it, and wheeled him out right behind Quinn and me.

He led me away from the fray. The lights on the ambulance were still painting the night in flashing swaths, but the other vehicles had doused theirs. In the rhythmic illumination, I watched the detective as he adjusted the cummerbund of his tuxedo and loosened his tie.

"Must have been attending quite the fancy do," I said. "Sorry to drag you away."

His eyes narrowed. "Why did you come back here?"

"I kept thinking about the moving boxes in Ethan's apartment, you know? He'd mentioned that he wasn't going to stay on as manager here, so he must have been packing to move out. And then I remembered seeing the boxes down in the basement, in that storage area."

Quinn waited a few beats. When I didn't add anything, he said, "That's it? You and your boyfriend came over here because of moving boxes?"

"It was just a hunch," I said, obsessively rubbing at my fingers with the towelettes. "And he's not my boyfriend."

A paramedic climbed into the back of the ambulance and closed the doors. The vehicle roared off, taking its flashing lights with it. Detective Quinn and I were left in darkness relieved only by the weak light that spilled from the open door.

Which was fine. I didn't need him trying to read my expression right then. I wasn't lying, exactly. Just not sharing everything.

See, Detective, I cast a location spell, and then called my sexy witch friend, and he got us inside, and we found a dying man and saved his life.

The waves of power I'd felt as Steve healed Ethan still lapped in my veins, and I hugged my bare arms again. "It was a long shot, of course. I didn't really expect to find him. After all, your people searched the apartment building, right? Do you know if they checked the basement?"

"Of course. They discovered blood on the stairs. He may have left and come back."

"Perhaps," I allowed. But neither of us believed that. Though I couldn't really blame the police for not searching inside locked storage spaces. I didn't know much about warrants, but it seemed like they would have needed one. Or more.

"Tell me about that knife," he said.

A frisson of remembered fear ran through me. "I climbed the fence to see inside better. He was hiding under a bunch of empty boxes, and ran at me with the knife." I swallowed. "He would have stabbed me right through the fence if Steve hadn't pulled me down in time."

Quinn passed a hand over his face.

I held up my palm. "I know, I know. You told me things could get dangerous. But would you have followed up if I'd called you? Would you have believed my hunch?"

He hesitated. Then, "I don't know. Maybe. After all, you're the one who discovered he was missing in the first place."

"Oh. Well, I thought you were still mad at me for interfering. At least I brought someone with me. And if we hadn't found him, Ethan could have been dead by morning."

His head inclined. "I'm not even going to try to argue with you. But please, do me a favor, okay?"

Hmm. "What?"

"Call me next time. I'll listen."

I grinned. "Deal."

"I need to go talk to your newspaper guy now."

"Would you tell him—and Declan McCarthy—that I'll see myself home without their help?"

He glanced toward the doorway. "Are you sure?"

I nodded.

"Is your car here in the lot?"

"No. It's down at the convenience store on the corner."

He called to an officer, waved him over. "Walk Ms. Lightfoot to her car."

"Thank you," I said, almost regretting my message to the two men waiting for me inside. But I felt raw and vulnerable after that intense contact with Steve, and I simply couldn't bear them squabbling over me right then.

Chapter 23

I doused my headlights before pulling into the drive-way a little before three a.m. so they wouldn't wake the Coopersmiths. I closed the driver's-side door as quietly as possible and practically tiptoed up the walk to my front door. Mungo greeted me on the other side with a wiggle and a bark.

"Hey, boy. You're a pretty clever pup, you know that?"

I closed the door and went to turn on the floor lamp by the couch. Sitting down, I patted the purple fabric beside me. Mungo jumped up, and I looked into his soft brown eyes.

"I'm sorry for what I said earlier. About you being just a dog."

He grinned.

"Forgive me?"

Yip!

"Thanks." I kissed him on the head. "Let me take a shower, and then I'll tell you about what Steve and I did tonight!"

I didn't need any magic seven-layer bar to go to sleep, but I set my alarm anyway. When it went off an hour later, I awoke feeling fully rested. Mungo bounced up, ready to go. He snuggled up to my neck and licked my cheek.

"Stop it."

More licking.

I pushed him aside.

He came right back.

Pretty soon, I was giggling in the darkness. Flipping on the light, I said, "Okay, okay. I'm up. Are you happy?"

He signaled his delight by furiously wagging his tail.

"You ready to come to the Honeybee today?" Well, of course he was. And so was I, in a ridiculously good mood and energized to jump into the day's baking. Today's special would be cornmeal-maple donuts.

Yum. That's all there was to say to that.

Before I left the house I called Candler Hospital. The woman who answered the phone confirmed that Ethan had been admitted and treated. I expected him to be in the ICU, but she informed me that he was in a regular room. Not just alive, but doing well, then.

Nice to know. I thought about calling Steve to tell him, but that would have to wait. Most people had the good sense to be asleep at this time of day.

Driving through the dark and deserted morning streets of Savannah, I promised myself a run that afternoon. I'd fed my running jones most afternoons when I lived in Akron. When I'd left that job, my runs had moved to the early hours of the morning, since those were no longer spent in the kitchen. But now that I was at work in the mornings again, I needed to get back to my old afternoon routine. If I didn't run, sometimes things got a little nuts.

Though I had to admit, this morning I felt great after downing a cup of coffee. I'd grab a bite at the Honeybee when I got there. I reveled in the calm I felt, very much like the endorphin high after a really fabulous run.

I remembered Steve's fiery hand on my arm the night before. The current of power, of energy, from me to him—and then, I felt sure, to the life force of Ethan Ridge. I could sense Steve's power, but I knew how much I'd contributed.

A *lot*.

I should be exhausted, giving all that away. But I wasn't. I felt like Goldilocks in Baby Bear's chair—just right.

I'd always had too much energy. Maybe giving it away, using it, was actually good for me.

No wonder I'd run so much over the years. Not to anything or from anything, only to expend excess energy. No matter how much I said I loved it, I'd really run out of desperation, to tone down the mania that thrummed constantly under my skin.

The lights were already on in the Honeybee kitchen. Surprised, I locked the alley door behind me and called out, "Lucy?"

Mungo popped his head out of my tote bag as my aunt bustled around the corner from the storeroom. "Good morning, Katie. Oh!" She stopped, pressed her fingertips over her lips, eyes dancing. "What have you

been up to, dear?" Her tone suggested something las-
civious at best.

I raised my eyebrows.

"My, yes. You had a wonderful evening, didn't
you?"

I sighed and put Mungo down. He ran into the office, and I saw him take up his station on his favorite
chair as I tied a plum-colored chef's apron over my
bakery uniform of skirt and T-shirt.

"I wouldn't call it wonderful."

Her knowing smile vanished, replaced by surprise.
"Oh, dear. No wonder Honeybee woke me early today
and urged me down here. I think you'd better tell me
about it."

So I did, sparing nothing. I told her about my feeble
attempt at a spell and what I had interpreted as failure.
I even told her I'd decided the whole idea of being a
witch was stupid and pathetic.

"I'm sorry, Lucy."

But she shook her head. "That's okay, honey. You've
had a lot of new things thrown at you lately. I don't
blame you for resisting. But I can see you've changed
your mind again. Something happened?"

So as I mixed lemon-nutmeg shortbread dough and
she sliced honey-anise biscotti and laid them out on
cookie sheets to bake, I told her the rest: remembering
the moving boxes, imagining Ethan Ridge in the basement, getting Steve to come with me, and witnessing
his spell casting on the door lock.

"Steve Dawes is a witch?" she asked with obvious
delight. "That's wonderful! I had no idea. I wonder if
the other ladies know that."

"He told me Mimsey does," I said. "And Cookie suspects. He's figured out what kind of 'book club' you have, too."

"It wouldn't be hard to figure out if he knows about Mimsey." Lucy began loading sourdough loaves into the preheated oven. "Go on."

She wasn't surprised when I told her Ethan was exactly where I thought he'd be. Of course, she hadn't doubted my witchiness in the first place. But she stopped working, and worry creased her forehead as I related the whole trying-to-stab-me-before-he-passed-out thing.

Then I told her about saving Ethan's life, doing my best to describe how it felt to have all that power flowing through me, the strange colors, and the burning smell. "It was almost as if I could see the atoms moving within things. The whole experience convinced me once and for all that there's real power, real magic in this world, and I'm part of it."

"Amazing," she breathed. "And you're okay?"

"I feel great."

"That's unusual after such a large working."

"I wondered. Have you ever healed someone like that?" I was hoping to compare notes.

"Heavens, no. You're far more powerful than I am, Katie."

"I don't see how. What about when Mimsey did her scrying spell—didn't she draw power from the rest of the spellbook club to augment her casting?"

"She did, but nothing like what you describe. But that day was also different from when we've all worked together before. You remember that loud sound? And how sure Mimsey was about what she'd learned? Usually what she senses is a bit more iffy than that. A bit more open to interpretation."

I began grating cheese for another batch of cheddar-sage scones. They'd practically flown out the door the day before.

Lucy said, "We're pretty sure you're a catalyst. That you stimulate the power of others. Spice it up."

I stopped grating. "I remember when you said that. So being a catalyst is a good thing?"

"Of course." But there was something in her eyes.

"But . . ."

"Well, you have to learn how to control it. So you don't augment the wrong kind of magic."

"Black magic, you mean?" The thought terrified me.

She nodded. "You need to start studying right away. Can you come over for dinner tonight?"

"It sounds like I'd better."

Eight people were waiting on the sidewalk outside when we opened the Honeybee at seven, an auspicious beginning to the second day of business. Lucy propped the door open to allow the heady aroma of freshly baked goods to spill out onto Broughton Street, and soon we were doing a brisk business. Ben joined us at eight, taking over the register so Lucy could concentrate on making coffee drinks, and I restocked the biscotti and scones in between constructing more orange-and-chocolate sandwich cookies and frying up another batch of cornmeal-maple donuts.

The rush settled a little after ten. Six tables were still occupied by customers sipping from half-empty cups. I checked in with the group of students hanging out in the reading area and made the rounds of the tables to collect crumb-dusted plates. I was putting them in the dishwasher when loud voices out front drew my attention. I pushed the rack in and closed the door, then rounded the corner of the refrigerator to find that none other than Albert Hill had decided to grace us with his presence.

Again.

His eyes widened when he saw me. He raised a long, bony finger and sighted down it like it was the barrel of a gun. "How dare you!" he shouted. Spittle sprayed with every word.

I forced myself to stand my ground.

Ben moved from behind the register, raising his palms like a crossing guard. "Now, hold on. What's this all about?"

An elderly woman came in, took one look at the tableau, turned around and went right back outside.

Great.

Ben dropped his hands and parted his lips as if he wanted to call her back.

Albert didn't even notice. His finger shook with rage, and his already flushed face deepened to crimson. "That . . . that *girl*. She sicced the police on me. I've been down at the barracks all morning, answering questions and accounting for my whereabouts." He took a step forward.

So did I, despite quaking in my sensible shoes.

"How dare you," he repeated. "Telling them I killed my aunt when you know very well it was *him*." His accusing finger moved to my uncle and wavered inches from his nose.

"I never said that—," I began.

"Take your hand out of my face." Ben's voice was flat and low.

I heard an intake of breath behind me. Lucy had come out of the office, but I kept my eyes glued to Albert and Ben. Conversations had fallen silent. Everyone was watching the two men. Violence hovered in the air.

After a long moment, Albert's hand dropped to his side. Lucy pushed past me to stand in front of Ben. "Perhaps you'd like a fresh cornmeal donut?" Whether it was brave or simply rash, I admired her guts.

I moved to her side as Albert sputtered, "No! I don't want a *donut*, you stupid little woman."

Ben's eyes glittered behind the lenses of his glasses. Lucy put her hand on his chest. He covered it with his own, but his gaze never left the man who had just insulted his wife.

My uncle was about to blow, and however much Mrs. Templeton's nephew deserved it, I couldn't think of anything that could make an already bad situation even worse.

"Mr. Hill, I never told the police you killed your aunt." I leaned toward him, doing my best to ignore his weird, wormlike lips. "If they questioned you, it wasn't because I told them to." Hmm. Not quite as soothing as I'd intended.

"You told them I paid her apartment manager to kill her!"

"Oh, for Pete's sake," I said. Which wasn't exactly denying the accusation. I tried to remember exactly what I had told Detective Quinn. "If you have a problem with the police, or with Ethan Ridge, you should take it up with them."

If he hadn't already, at least in Ethan's case.

"You know he's in the hospital, right?"

"Of course I know," he said. "They think I attacked him, too."

"Did you?" The words slipped out and hung in the air.

The flush drained from his face, leaving his complexion mottled and doughy. "I am filing another lawsuit, Miss Lightfoot. Oh, yes, Detective Quinn let your name slip when he tried to get me to say something incriminating. I am going to sue you for defamation of character. For libel, slander and anything else I can think of."

"That's ridiculous," I scoffed. Fear arrowed through me. "I'd have to libel you in print."

The finger came up again, and he shook it at me just like his aunt had. Her manicure had been much better, though. "We'll just see about that." And he turned and stomped out to the sidewalk.

"Kind of a weak exit," I observed, trying to lighten the mood. One look at Lucy and Ben told me I'd failed. Two customers hurriedly packed up their laptops and left. I sank into a chair and covered my face with my hands.

Ben squeezed my shoulder. "You didn't tell me any of this."

"I'm sorry. It happened last night and I haven't had a chance to talk to you today. Lucy knew because she came in early to help get the baking done."

"You didn't tell me, either, Luce."

She patted his arm. "It has been kind of hard to talk, dear."

"Katie, you shouldn't be mixed up in this thing."

Lucy said, "None of us should be mixed up in it."

I looked up at both of them. "But we are, and there's nothing we can do to stop it except find the truth."

Whispers erupted from the reading area as the students reacted to what they'd just witnessed.

"See?" said a scantily clad girl with long blond hair and an upturned nose. "I told you more weird stuff would happen in this place."

I exchanged glances with my aunt and uncle. "And we'd better find that truth pretty darn soon, too."

That afternoon I packed up half a dozen cornmeal-maple donuts to take to the hospital. Ethan Ridge might want a treat even if his buddy Albert hadn't.

Before I left, I called Steve. He picked up on the third ring. "Why'd you leave without even saying good-bye last night?" he demanded.

"Hello to you, too."

"Well?"

I sighed. "Because I needed to get home and . . . No, the truth is I hate seeing how much you and Declan despise each other. I hate it even more when I end up in the middle of it."

He was quiet for a few moments. When he spoke again his voice had lowered. "You know, what we did last night was very . . . intimate."

I paused. "Um, yeah. I know." Even Lucy had thought

I'd been involved in something untoward when I walked in the Honeybee that morning.

"And you didn't even say good-bye."

"I'm sorry."

"And furthermore, you don't know the story between Declan and me," he said.

"Actually, I do."

The silence stretched out, then snapped.

"Steve?"

"Maybe you think you do, but that's only one side of things."

"That's possible," I replied. "Is this really a conversation you want to have on the phone, though?"

"No. It's not."

"Then do you want to come to the hospital with me this afternoon? I'm going to drop in on Ethan and see if he can shed any light on what happened. I called early this morning, and it sounds like he's doing quite well after our little, er, intervention last night."

He muttered, "Wish we'd stopped sooner, then."

"Steve! That's a terrible thing to say."

"Only because it took so much out of us. I don't know how you got up and went to work so early."

Ah. No wonder he'd sounded tired and cranky. Apparently working magic had the opposite effect on him than on me.

"So do you want to come?"

"Can't. I'm on deadline. But let me know what he says."

"Will do."

Leaving Mungo to supervise things from his perch

in the bakery office, I drove to Candler Hospital, on Reynolds Street in Midtown, and parked. Inside, I inquired about what room Ethan Ridge was in, found the elevator, and rode up to the third floor. I stopped at the nurses' station and asked the scrubs-clad woman on duty if it was all right to bring food to the patient in room 303, offering her a culinary bribe for good measure. She said it was fine, and waved toward an open door just down the hall.

Ethan leaned against the pillows, staring at the television blaring down from the ceiling mount at the end of the bed. The other bed was unoccupied. His neck was swathed in white bandages beneath several days' growth of beard. His scraggly hair spread in a dark halo on the white pillowcase. The tough-guy swagger had been swallowed up by a generic hospital gown and the acrid scent of disinfectant.

I knocked lightly and stepped into the room. Ethan slightly turned his head to look at me and winced. I moved into his direct line of sight to lessen his discomfort.

"Whaddaya want?" Despite the greeting, most of his bravado had vanished.

"You remember me, then. Good. But you should be nicer to the person who saved your life," I said. "Besides, I brought donuts."

He frowned. "Where's your friend?"

"You mean the man who also saved your life?"

He was silent, and I realized he'd meant Cookie, not Steve.

"Ethan, don't you remember? Last night, in the basement?"

"Remember what?" Still trying for cocky, but not quite getting there.

I scooted the vinyl visitor's chair closer. It squeaked as I settled into it. "Well, for one thing, you tried to stab me."

Ethan's swallow was audible. "Last coupla days are kind of a blur."

"It didn't really seem like you wanted to hurt me." He had been pretty out of it. "Did you?"

"Did I what?"

I sighed. "Want to hurt me."

He shrugged. "I don't even remember, okay? So I'm sorry. What else do you want?" He'd turned sullen. "You gonna press charges, too?" Eyes skittering away.

"Who's doing that?"

His lips pressed together as if he was determined to keep the answer from escaping.

"Someone you scammed when their loved one died? Maybe someone who bought a nonexistent grave plot from you? Or is Albert Hill threatening to sue you?"

Ethan's eyes widened, then narrowed. "How could you—" His mouth clamped shut.

But I could see his fear and desperation, and without thinking, I patted him on the hand. He jerked away. But when his eyes met mine again, there was a little more openness. A little more relief. Magic didn't have anything to do with it; Ethan wanted to be able to trust someone.

"I really tried to stab you?"

"Well, you ran at me with a knife."

"Jeez. I really am sorry."

"Hmm."

"What kind of donuts?" he asked.

"Cornmeal and maple."

"Sounds weird."

"Suit yourself." I took one out of the bag and bit into it. Other than the testing nibble I'd had after the first batch, it was the first one I'd allowed myself. I let my pleasure show on my face.

"I guess I'll try one." He held out a hand.

I smiled and put a napkin-wrapped donut into it.

He sniffed it. "Smells all right." Took a bite. "Pretty good. Sure beats the food in here."

A high compliment indeed. "The police sure asked me a lot of questions," I said.

Ethan swallowed. "Me, too. Didn't seem to matter that I was in the hospital, either. That detective wasn't nice at all."

"Did you tell them what happened?"

He shrugged. "What I remembered. Like I said, it was all a blur."

"But you must know who attacked you."

He looked away again.

"Is there any chance they might try again? Because if that could happen you have to tell someone."

"He wouldn't . . ." Ethan's voice trailed off as he considered the possibilities. Again his eyes met mine, and he swallowed convulsively. I handed him the glass of water by the bed, and he took a sip.

"You didn't tell the police everything, then."

"Don't like cops," he muttered.

"Maybe you should tell me."

"What for?"

"Because you could have hurt me, and I'm not pressing charges. Because the police suspect the wrong man of killing Mrs. Templeton, and I think you know who really did it."

He licked his lips.

"Because I think you're scared, and you want to tell someone. Just in case."

The appeal to self-interest did the trick.

"See, there was this woman," he said. "At the apartments."

A woman. Great. The attack on Ethan didn't have anything to do with Mrs. Templeton's murder. It was all about a babe. I struggled to hide my disappointment.

"Her name's Gwen. She didn't live there, but she got hurt there. The elevator fell, and she was in it."

My interest quickened, remembering the story Mrs. Perkins had told Cookie and me in the Peachtree Arms laundry room.

"She broke her neck, see. Paralyzed her. Arms and legs both."

I nodded encouragement, afraid to speak and at the same time thinking how suddenly a life can be changed forever.

"I sort of knew her, because she came to visit her folks every Sunday for supper. Gwen was nice that way. And sometimes she brought her fiancé. He seemed nice enough, too, though kind of highfalutin."

Ethan paused for a bite of donut. "I heard that after the accident she broke up with him. Said she couldn't saddle him with a cripple for the rest of his life. He didn't take it too well, insisted he wanted to take care of her. But she refused to see him anymore."

"That's sad." I could hear the distraction in my voice, however much I meant the words. Where was this going?

"So when I heard someone had broken the Templeton lady's neck, I thought of him. A neck for a neck, you know? Poetic justice."

I stared. "What's his name?"

There was a long pause as Ethan worked something out in his mind. Then he seemed to make a decision, because he gave a little nod. Ran his tongue over his lips.

"Name's Jenkins."

Chapter 24

Seeing my expression, Ethan asked, "Do you know him?"

I nodded, speechless. Jack Jenkins. President of the DBA. Unable to attend the brunch because an employee had called in sick. Mavis Templeton's tenant. And a man full of loathing for the building that had nearly killed the woman he loved.

Or not so much for the building. For the highly negligent owner of the building.

"Ethan, what did you do when you made the connection between Gwen's accident and Mrs. Templeton's murder?" I dreaded the answer, having a good idea what it was.

"I called him and told him I knew it was him that killed the old woman, and that he needed to give me some money to keep quiet." Now that he'd started telling the story, he seemed compelled to finish it, despite how it made him look. Compelled entirely by his own need to get it off his chest.

"What did he say?" I asked.

"Denied it, of course. Called me crazy. I told him I'd give him another day to think about it and give him a call back. You know, let him get used to the idea."

"Oh, Ethan."

"I thought I could get a stake so I could move and start a new life someplace else. Someplace where no one knows me, where I could be anyone I wanted."

He sounded so hopeful, relating his dreams of a new life. It sounded familiar, actually. But one thing I knew even though I was a few years younger than Ridge: No matter where you go, there you are.

I took another bite of donut. "But he knew who you were and came after you rather than paying up."

"But I didn't tell him who I was when I called. I'm not stupid, you know." Sullen.

"Maybe he had caller ID," I said, my tone wry.

Ethan looked smug. "I called from the pay phone at the convenience store."

Hmm. "Did you happen to mention his fiancée?"

The look on his face told me he had.

"Then he probably figured out it was you."

His face fell. "Yeah, maybe. 'Cuz he showed up at my place yesterday, and he was really mad."

"You let him in?"

"I thought it was James from across the hall."

I grimaced. No peepholes.

"I told him it wasn't me who called, but he didn't believe me. He went kinda crazy, started yelling at me and waving some old knife around. He sliced me pretty good, too. But I managed to get to my buck knife, and all of a sudden he wasn't so brave. Ran off like a scared girl."

I let the chauvinism pass. "And you didn't call anyone?"

He shrugged.

"Ethan, you almost died!"

"I feel pretty good, so it couldn't have been that bad."

Thanks to Steve and me. But I couldn't exactly explain that, could I?

"He kept going on and on about how I didn't have any right to talk about Gwen. He was really mad."

"Were you hiding from him in the basement?"

"Naw. I'd already quit the job at the Peachtree and was packing up to leave. I thought with Jenkins on the warpath it would be a good idea to get the rest of my stuff together and hightail it out of there. I guess I must've passed out or something for a few minutes downstairs."

"More like a few hours. And you didn't tell Detective Quinn anything about Jack Jenkins?"

Ethan looked at me like I'd suggested he eat a live mouse. "Are you nuts?"

"Are you? Why wouldn't you turn in a man who tried to kill you?"

"You mean a man I tried to blackmail? Jeez, you think that might be a parole violation?"

"He killed a helpless old woman and almost killed you, but you're not going to tell the police because you might get into trouble for blackmailing him?"

"I don't want to go back to jail," he whined.

"No wonder Mrs. Templeton could keep you in a job you hated. Your own fear did the job for her."

"I'm not a coward!"

I stood and looked down at him. "Prove it."

We glared at each other for a long moment.

This time he didn't look away. "Okay. I'll tell that detective. But only if you don't tell them I asked Jenkins for money."

"Deal," I said.

Detective Quinn answered his phone on the second ring. He said he was nearby and would be right over. Ethan and I waited for his arrival, sharing the donuts while he watched a basketball game on television and I watched him. No way was I going to leave until he had told the authorities everything he knew.

A calm settled over me. Finally, it looked like Uncle Ben was off the hook. Once the police had arrested Jack Jenkins, Albert Hill would have to give up any notion of a civil suit. Even if he was crazy enough to try suing me for defamation of character, he wouldn't win. I could concentrate on the everyday business of supplying Honeybee customers with the best baked goods around, study witchcraft, and stop the nonsense of a murder investigation.

"Mr. Ridge, you have something you want to add to your statement?" Detective Quinn said from the doorway.

Ethan jumped at the words, and if he hadn't been hooked up to the IVs he might have rabbited right then. But there was no place to go, so he just sat in his hospital bed and looked terrified. I had to feel for a guy who was so scared all the time.

"Go ahead," I said as gently as I could.

"Perhaps you'd better wait in the hall," Quinn said.

"Uh-uh. No way. She stays," Ethan insisted.

I raised an eyebrow at Quinn, and he relented. "All right."

Voice shaking, the apartment manager related the tale he'd told me, leaving out his feeble attempt to blackmail the killer. Instead, he said he confronted Jenkins because he was trying to get a confession from him that he'd killed Mrs. Templeton. Puzzlement descended on Quinn's face at that, but he let it go, scribbling notes and asking questions to clarify what Ethan was telling him.

When he was done, Quinn asked, "Why didn't you tell me about Mr. Jenkins this morning?"

"I was, uh, I was afraid I'd get in trouble for not telling someone I thought he was the murderer."

Weak.

"But then Katie here convinced me I could still be in danger, you know? So I thought you'd better know about him after all."

"And what about Albert Hill? Are you associated with him in any way?"

Ethan blinked rapidly. "What do you mean?"

"I understand you and he were kind enough to help a woman named Mrs. Standish when her husband died."

"I, uh, that was just Albert."

"Sounds very much like the kind of 'help' you used to provide before you assaulted one of your marks and ended up in prison."

Ethan started to shake his head and winced. His hand went to the dressing on his neck. "No, no. I didn't do anything wrong. Albert was the one who helped that lady. I only met her once. If he did anything he wasn't supposed to, I didn't help."

"Is that what Albert will say when I ask him?"

"How should I know what he'll say? We're not best buddies or anything. We have a beer once in a while is all. But I will tell one thing." Ethan leaned forward conspiratorially. Quinn and I echoed the motion. "Albert Hill has been stealing from his aunt for years and years. If Jack Jenkins hadn't killed her, someday Albert would have."

Leaving the rest of the donuts with Ethan, I walked out with Quinn. Outside, he turned to me and said, "I guess I ought to thank you."

I ducked my head.

"This information is huge. Really. We'll pick up Jenkins next, get to the bottom of it," he said. "And take a closer look at how much access Hill had to his aunt's finances, too."

"Neither of them matches the description your witness gave. Are you willing to give up on her story yet?"

Quinn shrugged. "Jenkins attacked Ridge with a knife. Something provoked that—fear, guilt, I don't know. Why did Ridge really contact Jenkins again? His story struck me as a little thin."

I quirked an eyebrow.

"Blackmail?" he guessed.

"He doesn't want to get in trouble."

Quinn looked skyward. "What a piece of work. I hope he knows how lucky he is that you found him."

"Maybe it's better if he doesn't."

*　　*　　*

I called Steve on the way to the Honeybee. When he heard what Ethan had told me, he whistled quietly.

"Now, Jenkins is one guy I'd never have suspected."

"Me, too. Quinn, three. It's a good thing we saved Ethan Ridge, or we might never have known the truth."

"And your uncle might have actually ended up in jail."

"I'm still trying not to think about that."

"What are you doing tonight?"

"Sorry. I have supper plans with my aunt and uncle."

"I wasn't asking you out."

"Oh."

"Because tonight my plans include takeout and sleep. Lots of both. But don't worry—I'm not giving up. Good night, Katie-girl."

"I thought you weren't going to call me that anymore."

But he'd already hung up.

I got to the Honeybee just as Lucy and Ben were locking up. In the office, Lucy transferred Mungo into my arms. "Since you're coming over tonight, I thought I'd bring him home. But now that you're here . . ."

"Hi, sweetie." I nuzzled his neck, then looked up. "Don't go yet. I have to tell you my good news. Ben!"

My uncle came into the office. "You don't have to yell, honey."

"You're off the hook." I couldn't keep the broad grin off my face.

My aunt and uncle looked at each other. Mungo wiggled.

"I know you were upset about all the questions I was asking, but it paid off. Today we—and by 'we' I mean Detective Quinn and me—found out who killed Mrs. Templeton."

"Who?" Lucy breathed.

"Jack Jenkins."

Ben jerked back in surprise. "Why would Jack kill her?"

My words tumbling over each other, I related everything Ethan had told me and then Detective Quinn. Lucy's eyes searched my face as I spoke, and Ben's expression was sober as he listened.

"I'd bet anything he ducked away from his shop that morning, came over to kill her and went back with no one the wiser," I concluded.

"And no one saw him?" Ben said.

"Remember, most of the DBA members had already left by the time Mrs. Templeton tried to stiff us. The ones who hadn't were still in the bakery. And it's possible someone else did see him, but didn't realize what he'd done. It wouldn't have taken very long to break her neck."

Lucy's hand flew to her own neck at my words. "That poor man."

Ben gave her a hug. "You're right. It's a sad business."

She came over and kissed me on the cheek. "You did a really good job, Katie. Thank you for helping Ben. We'll see you in a little while?"

"As soon as I get the sourdough going, I'll be right behind you."

As I slid the loaves into the refrigerator to slow-rise,

I thought about what Ben had said. It was indeed a sad business, and I felt bad for Jack Jenkins. It would be bad enough if someone you loved were injured the way his fiancée had been, and even worse for her to refuse to see you because she didn't want to be a burden.

But I was still glad we'd discovered the truth.

Potted herbs and flowers crammed the front entryway at my aunt and uncle's town house in Ardsley Park. The neighborhood echoed Lucy's abundant roof garden where I'd spent so much time when I stayed with them before buying my carriage house. The scent of sautéing garlic and onions wafted out to the front step as I knocked on the front door. Mungo sniffed the air enthusiastically.

Lucy called for us to come in, and I opened the door into the living room. Vaulted ceilings rose above, making the space feel larger than it was. Skylights and lots of big windows gave their home a light, airy feeling. Hanging ferns reached out toward the light, and ivy crept up the brick wall behind the fireplace. Rugs with geometric patterns set off the rich, cherrywood floors, and white-upholstered furniture clustered in casual seating areas that welcomed all who entered.

My aunt's orange tabby walked languidly out of the kitchen to greet us.

"Hello, Honeybee." I looked at her with a new attitude now that I knew she was Lucy's familiar.

The cat slowly squinted her eyes in greeting.

I sneezed. Familiar or not, I was still allergic to her.

Mungo bounced up and down in my tote bag.

"Okay, okay." I lifted him out and put him on the

floor. "Honeybee, this is Mungo the Magnificent. Mungo, meet Miss Honeybee."

The terrier wagged his tail and trotted to the cat. She touched her nose to his for a long moment, then ducked her head and rubbed it against his chin. Together they turned and went into the solarium.

I sneezed again, sighed, and followed the sounds of pots and pans into the kitchen. Lucy stood stirring something in a big cast-iron Dutch oven on the stove. Ben sat at the kitchen table, thumbing through the newspaper. The aromas of cooking tomatoes, basil, oregano and onion joined the pungent garlic.

"Supper will be ready soon. We're having pasta."

"With your homemade sauce? Yum."

She smiled and wiped her hands on a towel. "That can simmer for a bit. I want to show you something."

Curious, I followed my aunt to her workroom. Dried lavender, mint and sage hung from a rack on the ceiling. Their fragrances teased my nose, along with that of the pasta sauce. A table ran along one wall, covered with Mason jars full of dried herbs, a mortar and pestle and a digital scale.

"Most of this wasn't here the last time I visited," I said. Not that I'd spent much time in this room, but I'd had the impression it was more of a sewing room than anything.

"I . . . tidied it up before. But now there's no need to hide anything from you. Including this." She opened a door at the other end of the room that I didn't remember being there.

I approached and looked inside. A table took up most of the space. A black-and-white batik scarf covered with depictions of Celtic knots was draped over the surface. Red, blue, yellow and black candles were placed at each corner, and in the middle sat a blue glass bowl, a pentagram-shaped brooch, a feather and a letter opener.

"This is your altar?"

Lucy nodded. "Yes. I meditate, make offerings and sometimes cast here." She closed the door. "And it's mine. Totally private."

I thought of my little house. "Not much chance of that for me if I have anyone over. I don't even have a proper closet."

She held up a finger. "You don't have to keep an altar all the time. You can make anything an altar when you need it—a cloth on the kitchen table, a rug on the floor. But I have something for you."

Now I followed her back through the living room to the solarium. Mungo and Honeybee looked up from where they were sitting together on a chaise lounge.

"Getting to know each other?" Lucy asked.

They touched noses again.

"Good. Katie, come over here." She indicated a desk in the corner.

I complied.

"This secretary desk is for you." It was made of oak, buffed to a rich patina. The front of it opened on hinges to reveal a writing surface and a series of compartments, letter slots and wee drawers. "This was my first altar, when I didn't have much space and wanted a little privacy." And when she flipped up the fold-down writing surface again, I could see how perfectly it would work for that purpose.

"You can put it up in the loft."

Wrapping my arms around her, I said, "Thank you."

Yip!

Honeybee gave Mungo a reproachful look.

"Oh, darlin', you are welcome as can be. There's one more thing, though." She pushed on the side of the secretary and released a hidden panel.

"Cool!"

Smiling, she drew out a red leather book with silver leaves embossed on the cover. "This is your grimoire."

"My . . . ?"

"Think of it as a recipe book. Only the recipes are for spells instead of cookies and brownies. As you learn and develop spells, you need to keep track of them. I've added two basic spells, one for banishing fatigue and another for getting rid of aphids, to get you started. But remember: Your personal spellbook is something to keep very private."

I took the book from her, admiring the Italian leather and running my fingertips over the smooth paper. "Thank you. Again."

"Ben will bring the secretary over in the Thunderbird this week. You should take the grimoire tonight, though. Make notes in it and record your spell work as you learn the Craft."

Hugging her again, I said, "I can't think of a better teacher than you."

She blinked away tears and took my hand. We returned to the kitchen, to Uncle Ben and the burbling sauce on the stove.

Chapter 25

The next morning Ben unlocked the front door to let in a few customers I was already coming to think of as our regulars. Detective Quinn followed them in.

"Peter!" Ben held out his hand with a smile, and Quinn shook it.

"Can I interest you in a cranberry-walnut turnover, Detective?" I asked as Ben slipped behind the register and started taking orders. "You must work twenty-four-seven."

"I do when I'm on a case. Any chance I could get you to call me Peter, too?" he asked.

I smiled. "Well, to tell you the truth, I think of you more often as Quinn."

"I like that better anyway . . . Katie?"

I nodded. "Of course. The turnover?"

His expression sobered. "I'm afraid I'm not here to socialize. May I talk to you in the kitchen? Ben, come on back when you can."

"Of course."

I led him to a spot by the industrial mixer. It provided a view of the front so Ben would still be able to see customer comings and goings when he left the register. Plus, I didn't want Quinn to find Mungo napping in the office.

"He shouldn't be long," I said.

But Quinn didn't wait for Ben. "We went to pick up Jack Jenkins late yesterday afternoon, but he wasn't home. His neighbors say he hasn't been there for a couple days. The mail's piling up, and his car's gone. His brother on Tybee Island hasn't heard from him, and his parents, who live in Baton Rouge, claim the same thing."

Oh, brother. Were we going to have to cast another location spell? Slumping against the wall, I folded my arms over my chest.

"So we did some more checking yesterday, but no luck. This morning I stopped by his store and ran into a guy who says he's worked at Johnny Reb's for two years. He's been off for a week—Jenkins gave him a paid vacation right *after* Mavis Templeton's murder—and he just got back from Myrtle Beach. Turns out he was working the morning of the DBA brunch."

"And Jack said the reason he couldn't come to the brunch was because his employee didn't show up," Ben said as he joined us.

"So that blows away his alibi," I said. "That's even better than the idea that he snuck away for fifteen minutes to kill Mrs. Templeton."

Quinn nodded and continued. "The guy at Johnny Reb's also said a lot of things were missing."

"He raided his own store?" Ben asked.

"Mostly little stuff, valuable and easy to dispose of. We're checking his bank accounts now."

"Well, that's it." I threw up my hands. "He's long gone, I suppose."

Quinn shook his head. "I'm far more worried that he might still be in the Savannah area."

"Why?" Ben asked.

"Because one of the neighbors we talked to reported hearing an argument shortly before he left. She couldn't tell me much about who Jenkins was fighting with— only that it was a man. And she couldn't hear specifically what the problem was, but one name came up two different times."

I leaned forward. "What name?"

"Katie Lightfoot."

"What?" I croaked.

Ben put his arm around my shoulder and pulled me to his side. "Why her?"

Quinn shook his head. "We don't know. Only that it's possible that you're in danger." He held his palms up. "On the other hand, it might be nothing. Just be careful, all right?"

Stunned, I nodded.

Having felt the power Steve drew from me in order to save Ethan Ridge's life, I no longer questioned whether I possessed a gift for magic. But untrained and unpracticed, I had no idea what I could really do. Had the locating spell I'd cast on my living room floor really worked like Steve had said? Was that how divination worked for me? Or was I like Cookie, who couldn't divine to save her life? If the latter, finding Ethan had been plain old deduction.

Or was that really magic, too? From what I could tell, the definition was pretty fluid.

At any rate, I couldn't afford another miss. We needed to find Jack Jenkins—to ensure that a killer was brought to justice, to get Ben off the hook once and for all, and so I could stop looking over my shoulder and jumping at every loud noise. If Ethan Ridge's injuries were any indication, the guy was unhinged and dangerous.

It was nearly four thirty in the afternoon. I'd mixed the sourdough sponge, scrubbed counters, appliances and the floor, planned the next morning's baking and checked the inventory in the storeroom. I took off my sexy-maid apron, hung it on one of the hooks that marched along the back wall and went to stand in the office doorway.

"Lucy, how quickly can you get the ladies over here?"

"It depends. What do you have in mind?" She folded her arms and leaned one hip against the desk.

"I'd like to try another location spell. The one Mimsey did to find possible suspects in Mrs. Templeton's death worked pretty well. Now we have a very specific person to find. Do you think she could do it again?"

She reached for the phone, eyes sparkling. "Let's find out."

I would have laughed if we hadn't been talking about tracking down a murderer.

All four of the spellbook club members showed up within an hour. We closed the blinds tightly and locked the door. Lucy turned on the overhead lights, and we all settled into the reading area.

Mimsey, wearing royal blue augmented by a splashy yellow scarf, shoes and chunky necklace, listened carefully to what I wanted to do. When I finished, she shook her head.

"I don't think we should do a location spell. For one thing, they can be kind of iffy. And he's probably on the move, so even if we do find him he could slip away."

Jaida shrugged out of her suit jacket. "We'd also have to convince the police to follow up on knowledge we shouldn't have and can't prove."

I grimaced. "Yeah, that is a problem. Detective Quinn was already suspicious of my hunch that Ethan Ridge was in the Peachtree Arms storage unit."

Bianca rolled her eyes. "If his men had properly searched the premises they would have found that apartment manager without your help."

"I chose not to bring that up," I said.

Cookie grinned. "We should do an attraction spell. I'm good at those."

Now Jaida looked at the ceiling. "I bet you are."

Cookie laughed. Her miniskirt showed off coltish legs, and she'd tied her hair into a ponytail high on her head.

Mimsey and Lucy exchanged glances. "You want to bring Jenkins here?" Lucy asked.

I shook my head. "That doesn't seem very safe."

"Don't be ridiculous. We're *witches*, Katie. We can protect ourselves, certainly long enough for the authorities to come and take him away," Cookie said.

"I don't know," Lucy said. "That's not the kind of magic we usually—"

"Just because we don't *usually* doesn't mean we *can't*. Jaida, what do you think?"

A slow smile lit her face, and she sat forward. "I think we should do a justice spell. That way we don't have to deal with Jenkins directly or explain anything to the police. The spell will simply see that justice is done."

We all looked at each other.

"Well, why didn't we do that in the first place?" I asked. It sure would have saved some time—and trouble.

Bianca's forehead wrinkled in concern. "Because justice isn't a human concern. Casting for it is like playing goddess, and that's arrogant. And dangerous."

Cookie piped up. "Also, we didn't know who we were dealing with, so there was no focus for our intention. There is so much injustice in the world. A general spell for justice right after the murder would have been swallowed up without a trace."

I looked at Mimsey. "You told me there was no magic cure-all to solve crime."

She inclined her head. "There isn't. Or for justice. But Cookie's right that we have a specific target in Jack Jenkins. I think it's worth a try."

"We don't know what will happen, though. There are too many kinds," Bianca argued. "What type do you want? Ethical? Spiritual? Legal? Are we the ones who decide what's 'just'? Jaida, are you willing to take on the karmic responsibility if it backfires? Because I don't know that I am."

I nodded. "For all we know, Jenkins' killing Mrs.

Templeton after all the grief she brought the world—not to mention the fact that she might have been practicing black magic—could be considered by some to be justice."

Cookie murmured her agreement, but Lucy and Mimsey frowned.

Jaida considered me. "Do you want to let him go?"

"No. Of course not. I don't think killing is ever justified."

"What about self-defense?" Cookie asked.

My gaze lit on *Self-Defense for Pacifists*, which had found its way to the table in front of the bookshelf again. I wondered which of our customers was reading it. "Maybe. Or in defense of another. But there are other ways to defend yourself besides killing." I gestured at the book for emphasis.

"We'll have to be careful—and very specific in our intentions," Jaida said. "We should cast explicitly for legal justice, quickly rendered. I've done it before."

"You have?" I asked, surprised.

Her lips curved up. "I'm a lawyer."

"And did it work?"

"The jury brought in the right verdict."

I thought for a moment, then made a decision. "Okay, what do we need to do?"

"I need to get my tarot cards. Lucy, we'll need white candles."

My aunt nodded. "We don't have any here right now, but I can pop home and pick some up."

"Don't bother." Mimsey stood. "I have some at the shop, and that's closer. Jaida, I assume you'll be using the Justice card?"

"Naturally."

"What flowers supplement Justice?"

"Verbena, I believe. And hyacinth. Do you have any in supply?"

"We have both. White again, for protection?"

"Yes. And purple if you have some."

Mimsey nodded. "Perfect." She turned to Bianca. "It should be fine, honey. Jaida is experienced at tarot magic, and she's cast this spell before—with success."

"What else do you need?" Cookie asked.

"Let's see." Jaida ticked items off on her fingers. "Tissue paper. Matches. A cauldron."

"I'll run to the stationery store," Cookie said.

Bianca picked up her shoulder bag. "I guess I'm in, too, then. But first I need to go home, check on Colette, and arrange for the babysitter to stay later. While I'm there, I'll pick up my cauldron."

"Excellent. Oh, and Katie, you've already got a scale here, don't you?" Jaida asked.

"Of course."

"Well, it's about to become a scale of justice."

Lucy snapped her fingers. "I bet you need a picture of our illustrious DBA president, don't you?"

"You mean you have one?" Jaida asked.

"Not yet. But I remember there was one in the *Morning News* about a month ago. While everyone is gathering supplies, why don't Katie and I run over there and get a copy?"

"I was planning to simply write his name of a piece of paper, but a picture would be much better," Jaida said. "Do you mind?"

My aunt looked at me, and I joined the others on

their feet. "I don't mind. But if it was only a month ago we probably don't need to go to the newspaper office. There should be a copy of the article online, and we can print the picture out here." I stopped and considered. "On the other hand, if we go to the *Morning News*, Steve Dawes might be there. He might be able to help."

Cookie grinned triumphantly. "I told you he's a witch!"

Bianca and Jaida looked confused.

Mimsey and Lucy shook their heads in unison. "I don't think so," my aunt said. "This isn't a good time to introduce yet another element into our workings."

"You mean besides me?" I said.

She nodded.

"All right, everyone," Jaida said. "Let's meet back here in an hour."

As Lucy and I went into our office, I heard Jaida ask Mimsey, "Since when is that columnist a sorcerer?"

Mungo jumped onto Lucy's lap as we waited for the computer to get going.

"Is Jaida planning to boil up a justice potion?" I asked.

He and Lucy cocked their heads to one side like comical bookends.

"I don't think so," she said. "I'm the only one of us who brews very much, and generally I do that at home, in my own kitchen. It's a vital skill for a hedgewitch—even herbal tea is a potion, you know. Especially if you add intention to it with a little ritual or incantation."

I typed *Savannah Morning News* into the search engine. "Is that on the course syllabus for Witchcraft 101?"

She laughed. "Indeed it is."

"Seriously, you have a real witch's cauldron?"

"Sometimes I even cook pasta sauce in it."

I turned and stared at her. "Holy cow! You mean last night?"

"Don't worry." She patted my knee. "That was plain old pasta sauce. Though I think all cooking is a kind of magic."

"It's starting to sound like everything is," I muttered. "So if Jaida isn't going to brew, why does she need a cauldron?"

"To burn in. You'll see."

As I pulled up the newspaper's archive, I remembered the scent of burning juniper berries in the Honeybee right after I'd met the spellbook club ladies for the first time.

I plugged the name *Jack Jenkins* into the newspaper archive's search function—and there was the proprietor of Johnny Reb's, looking out at us from the screen.

"Oh. My. God."

"What is it?" Lucy asked.

"He has a beard and glasses!"

She peered at the picture. "Well, no wonder that witness thought the man she saw looked like your uncle."

I buried my head in my hands. "If only I'd known, maybe I'd have figured it out sooner."

"What are you talking about?"

"I've never seen him with a beard. By the time I went to Johnny Reb's the day after Mrs. Templeton was killed, he'd shaved, had his hair cut shorter, and wasn't wearing glasses. I did see him wearing glasses later, but I never made the connection."

"You couldn't have known."

I sighed and printed out the picture.

I should have known.

Chapter 26

It was almost seven o'clock when we started. Jaida had changed into olive-drab capris and a light cotton blouse, while Bianca returned dressed in a flowing white linen skirt and tunic.

"I thought it would be inappropriate to wear my robe," she said.

Uh-huh.

My stomach was growling, but Lucy insisted we wait until after casting the spell to eat anything substantial. Then she passed around cups of ginger tea.

"This will ground us and add a little oomph to our magic," she explained to me.

We pushed two of the smaller tables together and cleared the other tables and chairs from that area. Jaida folded the picture I'd printed three times and put it on the table, along with the purple and white flowers Mimsey had brought. The cloying fragrance of hyacinth surrounded us, completely overwhelming the spicy smells I associated with the Honeybee.

Then Jaida unwrapped a brand-new deck of tarot

cards. "This is a classic Rider-Waite deck. It was created by Arthur Edward Waite and Pamela Colman Smith in 1910, and published by William Rider and Son."

"Why isn't it called the Waite-Smith deck, or the Rider-Smith-Waite deck?"

One side of her mouth quirked up ruefully. "Why do you think?"

"Because Smith was a woman?"

"That would be my guess."

I made a face. "So why a new deck? I thought people who read tarot cards used the same deck over and over."

"You're right," she said. "But I'm not reading these. You'll see why I'm using a new deck when we do the spell."

My curiosity felt like an itch, and I found myself holding my breath as she flipped through the deck, extracted two cards and put them on the table. Leaning forward to take a look, I saw the first was the Justice card. It depicted a king on a throne with a sword in one hand and a set of old-fashioned scales in the other. The other card was the Ace of Swords, and it showed only a hand holding a sword with a crown on top of it.

For someone who didn't like knives, I sure seemed to be running into a lot of things with blades lately.

"What's this for?" I asked, pointing to the second card.

"I've added the Ace of Swords to the spell because it represents truth," Jaida said.

Lucy brought in my smallest kitchen scale and set it on the table, too. Mimsey began arranging the white candles at compass points around us.

"Tell me more," I said.

"Well, the white candles emphasize protection—rather than aggression. So do the white flowers. The purple flowers represent the spirit. See, we're seeking not only legal justice but also the highest spiritual good of all."

Bianca smiled at that. "I like the way you think. Here's the cauldron." She set a silver bowl in the middle of the table. It was about ten inches across, and embossed with interlinked pentagrams.

"That's gorgeous," I said.

She smiled. "Thank you. I had it made."

Of course she did.

"But I only use it to burn—which is what I assumed you want to do, Jaida?"

"That's right. Are we ready? Cookie, do you have the tissue?"

Cookie held up a piece of white tissue paper.

Jaida said, "We need an envelope."

Cookie quickly folded and creased the paper into a small bag.

"Okay. Mimsey, will you cast the circle?"

"Of course." We gathered around the table, Lucy on my right and Jaida on my left. Mimsey lit the candle in the east first and called upon the support of the Archangel Raphael.

"That's different than when you cast the circle before," I whispered to Lucy. She shushed me, and Jaida shook her head at me.

Oops. I pressed my lips together, determined to shut up, watch and learn.

Next, Mimsey moved to the southern candle and

called upon Michael as she lit it. Then on to Gabriel, and finally Uriel, the archangel of the north. She returned to the eastern candle before joining us. Then she added a call to Above, Below and Within.

Talk about thorough. Now *that* was a circle.

Jaida nodded to Mimsey. Then she took three deep breaths, letting each one out very slowly. She placed the two tarot cards on the scale and added the folded picture of Jack Jenkins, weighing them in precise fractions of grams. When she was satisfied, she removed them and zeroed the scale out again. Then she began gently stripping petals from the flowers and sprinkling them onto the scale. Some fell off, but she ignored them and continued adding flower petals until they equaled the weight of the cards and picture.

She held out her hand for Cookie's tissue bag. With great care she transferred the hyacinth and verbena petals to the bag. She handed it to me and reached for the cards. When I saw her tear them into pieces, along with Jack Jenkins' picture, I knew why she hadn't used her own tarot deck.

The pieces of paper went in with the flowers. She stirred them three times with a fingertip. She folded the top of the bag down, sealing it lightly, and into Bianca's silver cauldron it went. Jaida opened the wooden kitchen matches and took one out. Holding it against the box, ready to strike, she intoned,

"Justice turns.
Truth burns.
For highest good,
As it should.
This man—"

A crash interrupted her incantation, startling us all. The sound came again, and glass tinkled onto the Honeybee floor. Wide-eyed in the candlelight, we stared as a hand reached in through the broken door and unlocked the handle.

"We call upon the Archangels to protect us. We call upon you, Raphael, Michael, Gabriel and Uriel. Help us now in our time of need," Mimsey whispered.

The others joined her as the door opened, and Jack Jenkins entered the Honeybee.

"We call upon the Archangels to protect us. We call upon you, Raphael, Michael, Gabriel and Uriel. Help us now in our time of need," the ladies chanted, low but desperate.

Jenkins squinted in the relative darkness. "What the . . . Now, what are y'all up to?"

Jaida lit the match and tossed it on the tissue bag. Flames flickered up from the paper cards, and smoke curled around the flower petals. The smell made my eyes water. Then the cards and picture flared, fully illuminating the circle and all the women within it.

Jenkins' eyes widened behind his silver-framed glasses as he took in the tableau. "You!" he screamed. "You're the ones who did this to me!" Terror had stripped away all remnants of his Southern gentility. He pointed at me with a trembling hand and took a step forward. "He was right. It was you!"

"Who was right?" I asked, doing my best to keep my voice calm even though I was shaking all over.

"You sent the police after me." He advanced, and I saw something flash in his hand. "And now you're cooking up another curse. Witches! Evil witches!"

"Now, Mr. Jenkins, you stop that," I said. "No one

would ever have suspected you if you hadn't gone after Ethan Ridge."

His nostrils flared. "I had to. He would have told them about me. He said he was going to. "

"My point is that he *did* tell them about you—about why he thought you killed Mrs. Templeton, about how you came after him with a knife." I softened my voice. "About Gwendolyn."

"Don't you dare say her name!" Jenkins yelled.

I held up my hand. "Okay, okay. I'm sorry. But if you hurt anyone else it's only going to get you into more trouble. Leave these ladies alone." I moved to the edge of the circle, away from the others.

His eyes never wavered from mine. He took two more lurching steps toward me.

The spellbook club started their appeal to the archangels again. I could feel the rhythm of the words in the air, throbbing with power. The fire in the cauldron died down. From the corner of my eye I saw wisps of smoke curling up from it. Jaida nudged the contents with her fingertip, still chanting with the others, and the flames flared brightly one last time.

The brief flash revealed the knife in his hand. Not just any knife. It was the bowie knife I'd found in the trunk. The one I'd returned to him in good faith.

"Is that the knife you stabbed Ethan with?" I asked. "My knife?"

He didn't answer, but staggered forward, brandishing it. I took another step, only to find Mimsey beside me. She blew out the eastern candle.

Opening the circle for me.

I stepped outside.

"Put that down!" Cookie's Voice shouted.

Inside the circle, Jaida dropped the matches and Mimsey dropped the hyacinth stalk she was holding. As one they turned to glare at Cookie. Outside the circle, Jenkins sneered at me and waved the bowie. I backed away from him, toward the reading area. Backing into a corner, but that left the others a chance to get away and call the police.

Now that he was closer, I could see the knife was still worn and pitted, the edge dull.

"Is that what you used on Ethan Ridge?" I asked. "You almost killed him. But then he said you ran away like a coward."

Jenkins lunged.

I danced back. "Why are you here?"

"Albert told me."

"Told you what?"

"You made the apartment manager tell the police about Gwen."

A shiver ran down my back. "Albert knows you killed his aunt?"

Jenkins shook his finger at me, almost like he was drunk. But I didn't think he was. I wondered if he'd slept since going on the run.

"Oh, he knew. He knew better than anyone."

My heart sank. "How, Mr. Jenkins?" I held my hands out to my side. "Jack? How did Albert know?"

"He came up with the idea. Good ol' Albert. He understood, you see. Always stopping by and talking about Gwen." Jenkins waved the knife in the air. "He *knew* what his aunt was like. He realized what she was capable of."

"And he was willing to let my husband go to jail for something he didn't do," Lucy said.

Mimsey drew a sharp breath.

I glanced toward them. Why weren't they running away?

"We call upon the Archangels to protect us. We call upon you, Raphael, Michael, Gabriel and Uriel. Help us now in our time of need." Their voices rose, and together they advanced on Jenkins, trapping him between us.

No, no, no! He was already frightened and dangerous. Leaving him nowhere to go would only make things worse.

Jenkins swung the old knife toward them. Then toward me. Then back toward them.

I looked down and saw the *Self-Defense for Pacifists* book. What had it said? Stomp on his instep? Kick him in the family jewels?

Too far away for any of that.

He turned and started toward the spellbook club.

I scooped up the heavy volume, ran five steps and brought it down on Jack Jenkins' head as hard as I could.

He dropped like a bag of rocks, hitting the corner of a table as he went down. The lit candle on the table bounced into the air. Quick as a snake, Cookie grabbed it, but the table it had been on crashed into the two we'd pushed together as an altar. One scooted along the floor with a piercing screech, and the other overturned. The scale smashed against the display case, fracturing the glass into a spiderweb. Ash and flower petals erupted into the air as the silver cauldron slid along the floor and banged into the wall.

Two candles remained burning, undisturbed.

"What can we tie him up with?" Mimsey asked in an urgent tone.

I racked my brain. It wasn't like we had a length of rope conveniently at hand. Wait: "My apron strings!"

The women gave me blank looks, and then Lucy grinned. "Of course!" She hurried into the kitchen and returned with several of my funky aprons. I grabbed the pastel paisley and began wrapping Jenkins' ankles together.

He moaned.

Cookie picked up the sexy maid apron, but I waved at her. "Too flimsy. Try the striped chef's apron; it's tough." She nodded and got to tying.

By the time Jack Jenkins regained consciousness we had him all wrapped up like a present for Detective Quinn. While we waited for the authorities to arrive, Lucy got out the broom and began sweeping up ash. Bianca put the scale back in the kitchen and tucked her cauldron away, while Mimsey took care of spilled candle wax and Jaida rearranged tables.

"I'm going to tell them about you. All of you," Jenkins croaked from his prone position on the floor.

"What about us?" With an effort I kept my tone light. The other ladies exchanged worried glances.

"That you're witches. That you're evil."

"Bah. That's ridiculous."

"I saw."

"You saw nothing unusual," I Said. Voice and all. I could feel everyone's eyes turn toward me.

Kneeling beside him, I murmured, "We were seeking justice. Thanks for obliging us."

He looked up at me and blinked slowly. "I don't understand. I was the one seeking justice. And I got it."

"By killing Mrs. Templeton?"

He hesitated. Then defiance crossed his features, and he nodded.

"Did it really help?"

Looking away, he gave the slightest shake of his head. "I thought it would. She deserved to die, you know."

"I don't know. You may be right. But by taking that on yourself, you've ruined your life."

A weariness so extreme I could hardly bear to witness it settled into his face. "My life was already ruined."

Chapter 27

"Something smells funny," Detective Quinn said.

He wasn't being metaphorical. The big fan over the stove in the kitchen had removed most of the smell of burning flowers and tarot cards, but not all of it.

"We had a little incident in the kitchen," I said.

His eyes cut to where Mimsey was scraping the last of the candle wax off the floor. "Not just the kitchen, it seems."

I changed the subject. "Is Jack Jenkins talking?"

"Doesn't seem to be holding anything back at all. I feel bad for the poor guy, knowing what happened to his fiancée. He needs help. I've suggested a psych evaluation."

I stared at him.

"What? A cop can't have a little compassion?"

"I prefer that they do, actually." Maybe the spell had worked after all. Maybe the highest good included therapy for Jack Jenkins. I hoped so.

"Listen, can I make you a sandwich or something?" I asked.

"Why?"

"Because your stomach's growling. Have you eaten today?"

A quizzical look, then Quinn said, "I guess I haven't."

"Come on in the kitchen, then."

As he followed, I shot a glance into the office, but clever Mungo had made himself scarce.

I sliced sourdough and added mayonnaise, bacon, cheddar, fresh tomato and a layer of fresh basil leaves. "Sorry to be such a pain while you were investigating the murder."

He took a bite and nodded. Swallowed. "You were. But that's okay."

"Friends?"

"Sure."

"What'll happen to Albert Hill?"

"We're arresting him for conspiracy in Mrs. Templeton's murder. He knew all along who had killed his aunt. Given what Jack Jenkins told us and his apparent willingness to testify against him, Hill should go to jail. We've also found ample evidence that he embezzled funds from his aunt, and will likely find more as the investigation continues on that front."

I poured him a tall glass of iced tea.

Quinn took a swig. "You know, I wonder if Jenkins would have murdered Mrs. Templeton if Albert hadn't incited him. That may come up in court, too. He took advantage of a man unbalanced by grief. I think Albert was afraid his aunt would find out about the embezzlement and needed someone to take care of her for him."

"And I thought the inheritance would be his motive," I said.

"That, too. But what goes around, comes around, they say."

Threefold, apparently.

"I just can't believe that Albert fooled me so easily," Mrs. Standish said and took an enormous bite of homemade chocolate marshmallow.

"He fooled a lot of people," Ben said.

It was late afternoon a week later, and Mrs. Standish had come into the bakery with two custom cake orders for Lucy. While she was at it, she loaded up on enough baked goods to feed an army. After paying, she wedged herself into a chair and appeared ready to chat.

Fine by me. Most of the prep for the next day was done, and my feet hurt. Other than a couple making goo-goo eyes at each other at the far end of the Honeybee, we were alone.

"Do you know he charged me almost three times what a cremation like that should have cost?" Mrs. Standish said. "At least that lab test showed it really is Harry in the urn. I don't know what I would have done if it hadn't been him up on the mantel all this time. "

Lucy came around the counter and joined us. "Three times? That's terrible."

"My husband would have had a fit. He was always very good with money, you know."

We all nodded as if we did know.

"I felt as though I needed to make it up to Harry, somehow."

"Do you think you can get the money back from

Albert?" I didn't think so; Albert Hill had a lot of charges hanging over his head, and it was unlikely he'd be able to inherit Mrs. Templeton's estate.

"Oh, I've done better than that." She took another bite and chewed contentedly.

Ben raised his eyebrows. "Really?"

Mrs. Standish swallowed and took a swig of her mochachino. "I bought that apartment building for next to nothing."

"The Peachtree Arms?" I said.

"I'm beginning renovations immediately."

"How is that getting back at him?"

"It's not, really. But I'm getting my money back, and helping the people who live there. Otherwise they'd be left high and dry, waiting to see if Albert would be allowed to inherit the property after his trial."

She waggled her eyebrows at me. In her mannish face the gesture really did make her look a little like Groucho. "So I made a very good deal. A *very* good deal. See, with the help of some tricky probate lawyers and brokers I know, Albert released all claim of future ownership by donating the Peachtree Arms to my favorite charity, Paw Prints. It's a no-kill shelter. And then I bought it from them, and we all benefit. I've always wanted to be a real estate mogul, you know!"

Lucy laughed. "Good for you. And good for the shelter."

I tipped my head to one side. "How did you manage to convince Albert that would be in his best interest?"

"Well, now, I found out how he likes to sue people. So I threatened to sue him for what he did when Harry died. For a *lot* of money. Sure enough, he doesn't like the idea of being on the wrong end of a lawsuit, not with everything else he's looking at."

Ben shook his head at the irony, a smile on his face. "Doesn't that just figure?"

"Is Ethan Ridge going to stay on as your apartment manager?"

She shook her head. "I let him go. We don't need that kind of riffraff running the Peachtree Arms. I think I'll change the name, too. Make it something snazzy."

"Do you have a new manager yet?"

"Indeed, I do. It's a little lady I think you might know. I've seen her in here before. She's called Cookie?"

My jaw slackened.

Lucy looked at me. "Didn't I tell you about how Cookie gets just the right job at just the right time?"

"She can't start quite yet, so there is a very nice gentleman named James who's taking care of everything over there for the time being. Now I just need someone to help with the renovation. I don't suppose you know anyone with connections in the construction industry? Someone who can handle restoring all the old wainscoting in the hallways? And some of those apartments have lovely woodwork inside, too. "

I remembered the elaborate mantel above James Sparr's fireplace and smiled. "In fact, I do know someone who might be able to help. His name is Frank Pullman."

Ice cubes popped in my glass of sweet tea. I swiped the sweating surface across my forehead and settled back in the patio chair. A pile of bright red coals had burned down in the hibachi Declan had brought me. Soon they'd be ready to sear the thick tenderloin steak sitting on the counter in the kitchen. I'd rubbed it with ground sage, oregano, cumin, chili powder and turmeric. A salad of baby greens chilled in the fridge, waiting to be dressed with a simple balsamic and olive oil vinaigrette. A foil packet contained baby new potatoes, sliced garlic and sprigs of rosemary.

I examined my fingernails. My hands needed a good scrub before supper. I'd been gardening for three hours, teasing out weeds, working more compost into the area Declan had rototilled for me and planting a dozen organic herb plants I'd picked up at the nursery on the way home from the Honeybee. I'd even tried my hand at the aphid-banishing spell Lucy had included in my mostly blank grimoire. The roses on the side of the house had seemed to appreciate it.

The leather-bound book sat tucked into the secretary desk, visible up in the loft from the living room like any normal desk. But inside it I was gradually outfitting my altar. First I'd spread out a white lace shawl my grandmother had knitted. I reckoned she'd added a little extra something to her stitches, but even if it didn't have magic woven into it, it was special to me. I'd added a small blown-glass bowl from the flea market as a chalice after Lucy showed me how to purify it. And just because I liked them, three smooth rocks I'd gathered by the shores of Wingfoot Lake sat in the middle.

It was a start, at least.

The spellbook club had divided training duties, so that I was working with someone different each day. And the more I learned about magic and worked with it, the better I slept in that gorgeous bed Lucy and Ben had given me.

And that was a start, too.

Mungo approached the hibachi and sniffed.

"Nope. Haven't put anything on yet. You hungry?"

Yip!

"Declan mentioned coming over," I said.

He wagged his tail.

"But I said not tonight. Had to tell Steve the same thing."

Mungo cocked his head at me.

"Tonight it's just you and me, buddy. Right after I make a phone call."

I got up and went inside. Washed my hands in the kitchen sink and refilled my sweet tea. Back out on the patio, I entered the familiar numbers in my cell phone. As it rang on the other end, seven dragonflies glided in from the edge of the yard and took up station on the iron table.

"Hello?"

"Hi, Mama."

"Katie!"

"I think we need to talk."

Recipes

Peanut Butter Swirl Brownies

¾ cup chunky peanut butter
4 tablespoons butter, melted
½ cup confectioners' sugar
½ teaspoon vanilla extract
¾ cup cocoa powder
½ teaspoon baking soda
⅔ cup vegetable oil
½ cup boiling water
2 cups sugar
2 eggs
1⅓ cups all-purpose flour
1 teaspoon vanilla
¼ teaspoon salt

Preheat oven to 350 degrees. Oil and flour a 9x13" baking pan.

Mix together the peanut butter, butter, confectioners' sugar and vanilla extract. Set aside.

Combine cocoa powder and baking soda in a medium bowl. Add ⅓ cup of the vegetable oil and mix together thoroughly. Add boiling water and stir until mixture thickens. Add the rest of the vegetable oil, eggs and sugar and stir until smooth. Mix in flour, vanilla and salt until thoroughly blended. Pour brownie batter into the prepared baking pan.

Drizzle peanut butter mixture over brownie batter. Using a knife, cut through the topping and batter to create a marbled effect.

Bake for 35–40 minutes, or until brownies are set in the middle and peanut-butter-swirl topping begins to puff slightly. Allow to cool in pan before cutting.

Cheddar-Sage Scones

2¼ cups all-purpose flour
1 tablespoon baking powder
½ teaspoon salt
1 teaspoon dried sage
6 tablespoons butter, cut into 1-inch pieces and chilled in
    the freezer for fifteen minutes
⅔ cup sharp cheddar cheese, grated
1 egg
½ cup milk

Preheat oven to 400 degrees.

Set aside ¼ cup flour in a small bowl. In a medium bowl combine 2 cups flour, baking powder, salt and sage. Add chilled butter and cut into flour by rubbing with your fingers or a using a pastry blender until the consistency of rough cornmeal.

Add the grated cheddar to the ¼ cup flour and toss to coat. Shake to remove excess flour and add to pastry mixture, tossing with your hands to evenly distribute the cheese.

Whisk together the egg and milk. Add to flour mixture, stirring lightly with a fork until ingredients are moistened and just hold together.

Transfer to a lightly floured surface and knead twenty times. Add more flour to the surface if needed. Pat into an 8-inch circle, slightly higher in the center than on the edges. Using a very sharp knife, cut eight equal wedges. Place scones on a baking sheet lined with parchment paper, slightly apart from one another. Bake for 12–14 minutes, until golden brown.

ABOUT THE AUTHOR

Bailey Cates believes magic is all around us if we only look for it. She's held a variety of positions ranging from driver's license examiner to soap maker, which fulfills her mother's warning that she'd never have a "regular" job if she insisted on studying philosophy, English and history in college. She traveled the world as a localization program manager, but now sticks closer to home, where she writes two mystery series, tends to a dozen garden beds, bakes up a storm and plays the occasional round of golf. Bailey resides in Colorado with her guy and an orange cat that looks an awful lot like the one in her Magical Bakery Mysteries.

CONNECT ONLINE:

baileycates.com

Also Available
from
Sarah Zettel

A Taste of the Nightlife
A Vampire Chef Mystery

Charlotte Caine isn't called "the Vampire Chef" because she's a member of New York's undead community—she just cooks for them. Her restaurant, Nightlife, is poised to take the top slot in the world of "haute noir" cuisine.

But when a drunk customer causes a scene, a glowing review from the city's top food critic doesn't seem likely—especially when that customer winds up dead on Nightlife's doorstep. Now, with her brother under suspicion for the murder, Charlotte has to re-open her restaurant and clear her brother's name—before they both become dinner.

Available wherever books are sold or at
penguin.com

OM0065

Sofie Kelly

Curiosity Thrilled the Cat
A Magical Cats Mystery

When librarian Kathleen Paulson moved to
Mayville Heights, Minnesota, she had no idea that
two strays would nuzzle their way into her life.
Owen is a tabby with a catnip addiction and
Hercules is a stocky tuxedo cat who shares
Kathleen's fondness for Barry Manilow. But beyond
all the fur and purrs, there's something more to
these felines.

When murder interrupts Mayville's Music Festival,
Kathleen finds herself the prime suspect. More
stunning is her realization that Owen and Hercules
are magical—and she's relying on their skills to solve
a purr-fect murder.

**Available wherever books are sold or at
penguin.com**

OM0043